The Princess Who Forgot She Was Beautiful

Harry Ferguson Chronicles, Book 1

By

William David Ellis

William David Ellis/Altar Stone Publishing Company
Ben Wheeler, Texas/USA 75754
https://williamdavidellisauthor.com

Publisher's Note: This is a work of fiction. Names, characters, places, and incidents are a product of the author's imagination. Locales and public names are sometimes used for atmospheric purposes. Any resemblance to actual people, living or dead, or to businesses, companies, events, institutions, or locales is completely coincidental.

Book Layout © 2017 BookDesignTemplates.com
Cover by BRoseDesignZ

The Princess Who Forgot She Was Beautiful/ William David Ellis. – 1st ed.
ISBN 978-1-7338850-1-0

Acknowledgments

I want to pay special tribute to all my editors. First, my wife, Deanna, who tediously works to correct my grammar and punctuation so that others can edit my content. She is the inspiration for some of my characters and has a tendency toward genius in spite of her husband's ways. We survived another one, Honey, only 9999k more words to go!

Also, thanks to Amanda Huffer, who is great at finding incongruities and making suggestions to clarify the story. Finally, thanks to Carisa Wells, who looks for places in the story where I need more showing and less telling. By the way, she is also a great author, and her books can be found on her Facebook page: www.facebook.com/Author.CLWELLS/

Dedication

To all those who never gave up, who loved and lost, laughed, and learned to love again.

If your heart is right, your head will get there eventually.

Contents

Chapter One

The old man sat down slowly, listening to his joints crack as he eased into his chair. He wasn't sure he should be doing this. He had never been very good at speaking to children, but his daughter, the city librarian, had insisted, begging him to come and tell stories to the children gathered at the library for summer vacation. Mothers thanked him, grateful for the small break it gave them to shop, catch up on chores, or just take a nap. His daughter was excited the kids were doing something besides sitting in front of a video screen. Only the old man was struggling, unsure of what he would tell them. Should he try to tell a story? He had some storybooks he could read, but they didn't appeal to him much more than the pack of noisy, restless ankle biters that confronted him. Yet he didn't know many stories. Actually, he only really knew one, and that one was so outrageously unbelievable he did not want to tell it. As he creaked into his rocking chair and faced the squirming horde of children, he didn't know where to begin. So he took a deep breath and began with a question.

"Well now, my dears..." he began. His tone of voice changed, and he slipped into the magical mode he automatically moved into when addressing a group of people. He moved closer to them and bent down slowly, studying them until he had captured every gaze. Then, speaking in a slow, deep voice, he asked, "Do you know a story about dragons?"

He was immediately answered with a chorus of loud replies, some excited, others frowning and revealing their exposure to a virtual world where everything existed. One obnoxious little child, with a tight smile, started to mock the old man but was stunned to silence when he rumbled in a stern commanding voice, "No, I mean a *real* dragon." The group fell instantly quiet.

"My momma said there is no such thing as real dragons," touted a little tot with dark braids.

She said this in such a tentative way that the old man immediately responded, "And she is right, little one. There are no more dragons now. But there were. This story only has one dragon in it, and it's really not about the dragon."

"So, what is it about?" the same little girl asked.

The old man smiled and said, "It is about a princess who forgot she was beautiful."

"Really? How did she do that?" a curly-haired darling with wide brown eyes asked.

"Was she hurt?" a pigtailed little freckle-faced cutie wanted to know.

"Did she get hit on the head?" a rambunctious little boy laughed, then stopped for a moment to hear the answer.

"Well, let me tell you about her," the old man said, leaning forward in the old rocker. "Once upon a time, there was a princess who forgot she was beautiful, so she didn't act like she was beautiful. Townsfolk always lavished her with compliments, telling her she was a beautiful young woman, who, at sixteen, *should know how beautiful she was* and should act accordingly. But she could not believe them. She was the princess, so of course they would say such things, so instead, she acted poorly. She spat on her maids, said bad words, got into fights, laughed at inappropriate times, and generally made a nuisance of herself. And that was just the beginning of her troubles... but I am getting ahead of myself. Now, where was I?"

"She was spitting and acting mean," answered the big-eyed little girl on the front row, her gap-toothed smile beaming.

"Oh yes, she was a mess and headed for bigger messes... until she met the boy who had forgotten how to be brave. But I'm still getting ahead of myself, and that's not in the best tradition of stories, is it? Now, where was I? Yes, the princess had forgotten she was beautiful. How could such a thing happen, you might ask?"

"Are you sure she wasn't dropped on her head?" a busy little boy with blue teeth from sucking a lollipop asked. "My sister was a cheerleader, and her squad threw her into the air and then dropped her. She couldn't remember anything for a whole day!"

The old man shook his head, looked down his reading glasses, and frowned. "Everyone knows that princesses are always beautiful. But she had forgotten because the people she loved never told her. They rarely spoke to her. You see, her parents were so busy running the kingdom and doing royal things that they didn't talk to her much. When they did, it was always: How are your grades? Are you minding your manners? And such as that. She didn't remember sitting on her father's lap or at her mother's knee. She didn't remember being told she was *so pretty* by an adoring father or having her hair combed by a preening mother. She had never even ever, *ever* been told a goodnight story, so quite naturally, she forgot she was beautiful.

"Now many unscrupulous young men tried to tell her she was pretty, but they often stammered out such things as 'I like me and want *you*,' or 'I would look good with you,' and other things not suited for this story. Their words came out garbled but true. The princess's *fiery* godfather had given her a gift, a simple jeweled ornament. It was a discern-ornament. It would make anyone who spoke to her have to say what they meant, even if they didn't mean to say it.

"So, no one told her she was beautiful until one day when the princess was strolling through the town market visiting at all the little shops and vendors. The market vendors were selling everything from chickens to toys that made bubbles when, all of a sudden, the princess heard a loud clamor, then a clatter, then squealing and screaming and more clamor!"

"Excuse me… excuse me," the little girl on the front row interrupted, raising her hand and demanding to be seen. "*Excuse me*!"

"Yes?" The old man peered over his glasses, stopped the story, and stared at her. "What is it…?"

"What's a clamor? I never heard of it before."

The old man looked at her, stroked his chin, and wiped the itch off his mustache. Then, forcing a frown in front of the smile that hid in his eyes, he said, "Clamor means bellow or bawl or a holler. It can mean an uproar, commotion, or racket… understand?"

"No, sir," she said quietly.

A little boy in the back stood up quickly to laugh at the young girl and accidentally knocked over a small bookcase. Books went flying, children went sprawling, and finally when the commotion had settled down, and the librarian and the old man had gotten everybody's attention back, the old man rubbed his temple and sighed, "Young lady, *that* was a clamor."

She looked up at him and smiled brightly, showing the gap in her baby teeth, and said, "Oh." Then like a royal princess addressing a court jester, she said, "Carry on, please."

Caught off guard by her imperial ways, the old man laughed aloud, "I'm trying," then began again. "The commotion in the market was so great the crowd merged like a muddled river. The townsfolk ran, walked, and stumbled in the direction of the noise. When the princess was finally pushed and shoved to the center of the racket, she heard the loud squeals of a full-grown piney woods rooter."

Several small heads tilted like a puppy convention, and the old man stopped and asked, "You mean you don't know what a piney woods rooter is?"

The snaggle-toothed spokeswoman addressed him so shyly he almost laughed. "No, sir, we don't."

"It's the dragon, isn't it?" the little boy who had knocked down the bookshelf yelled. "It's a dragon. I know."

The old man looked at him and said, "Of course not! If it were a dragon, the market would have been engulfed in flames! It was an escaped boar hog. A huge, five-hundred-pound big, bristle-back, sharp-tusked, angry pig! It seems a local farmer had wanted to sell the animal and brought him to market in a most unusual fashion. The hog was so big its pen would not fit in the back of the farmer's wagon. So, ingenious fellow that the farmer was, he kept the pig in its pen but carved out some places for the animal's feet to fit through, and then walked the squealing pig inside his mobile cage to market." The old man squealed, "*SQWEEEE, EEESQWEEEEEE!*" and the children laughed and laughed, tried to mimic him, and asked him to teach them how to make that sound. Of course, they upset a few chairs in the process, and finally, once again, settled down, and the old man continued the story.

"But the pig was so big, and the pen so flimsy, that when the piney woods rooter got to market and smelled the roasting pork and frying bacon, he panicked, began to buck, rammed the boards that held him, and broke out of his fragile pen! Squealing and snorting, the pig ripped through the market, upsetting tables with his great tusks. He knocked people down and smashed through fruit stands. Finally, the pig's deep-set beady little eyes sighted a poor young man. The pig grunted fiercely, lowered its head, and charged the boy, who tore down the street running for all he was worth, but still, the pig trapped the boy against a vendor's fruit table. With a great twist of its head, the pig dug its snout into the young man's pants and nipped. The boy screamed and twisted away, leaving a large portion of his pants behind. The pig jerked up, the rear of the boy's pants hanging from its mouth, and looked for its prey. Tossing its great dome about, he caught sight of the young man burrowing under a fruit table and shoved again, forcing his big, slobbery pants-full mouth under the table. The pig's squeals and the boy's cries ended suddenly.

"The young man, tired, angered, embarrassed, and unwilling to be humiliated anymore, reached up and grabbed the big pig by his nose..." The old man halted in mid-sentence, compelled by the confused faces of his audience. "You see, the boy had been brought up on a farm and knew how to get a large hog's attention by pinching it on the nose and climbing on its back. With one arm still wrapped around the beast's snout, and two fingers in its nose, he pushed the hog's great head out from under the table and proceeded to jump on its back."

"Yuck! That is nasty." The little girl on the front row frowned, then turned to see a studious young man seated next to her with his fingers in his own nose trying to figure out the proper hog-taming technique. The little girl gagged and leaped away from her companion, shrieking, "Boogers!"

The old man chuckled, shook his head, ignored the turmoil, and continued his narrative.

"The young man did just that and began riding the hog back through the market to the farmer. The gallant hero, caught up in the moment, concentrated on getting the hog safely back to the farmer. He'd forgotten the appalling state of his britches, which were gaping wide open from the tear of the hog's tusks. The market vendors, appreciative of the young man's efforts, applauded. In response, the unthinking lad, reveling in the attention of the crowd, bowed, proudly revealing his battered bottom to the unmerciful mob, which erupted in laughter. Suddenly aware of his deplorable condition, he reached behind him and without looking, seized the closest person to him and shouted, 'Shield me!'

"The princess, who had been walking up to the young man at just that moment, obeyed. When the young man bowed, she was the closest person to him and wound up being nabbed for the duty of backside covering. The crowd roared in laughter at the young man's discomfort. He still had not noticed who he had grabbed to shield his backside. He was facing the crowd, carefully walking backwards, causing the princess to walk backwards with him.

"Together they'd nearly cleared the central market, moving like a pair of crabs cautiously retreating from a net, when one of the market vendors recognized the princess and gasped, 'Your Majesty!' The young woman quickly tried to hush the man, but it was too late. The whole crowd took up the cry. The backpedaling pig warrior stopped, turned red as a beet, closed his eyes, and gently shook his head in unbelief. He couldn't bring himself to look at the princess behind him.

"The princess grimaced at his discomfort, embarrassed for him. He had been holding her tightly to him to cover his ripped pants and bare backside. Suddenly the young man realized the awkward and presumptuous way that he was holding the princess. Jerking his hands away like she was a hot coal, he brought his hands around to cover himself and, glowing bright red, turned to face her.

Chapter Two

"The princess winced. She attempted to say something comforting, but being tongue-tied, she only managed an awkward 'Hi.' She closed her eyes in extreme discomfort and embarrassment as the young man clenched his teeth and answered, 'Hi,' back. Finally, the young man's courage broke. He could bear his shame no longer and took off running. He tripped over a pile of spilt vegetables on his way out, jumped up, and ran as fast and as far from the laughing crowd as he could.

"The princess, however, wasn't laughing. She was very, very quiet. One person in the crowd caught her look and immediately grew still. Another stopped to see why his friend had become quiet and saw the same cold stare from the princess. He gulped and also grew still, silenced by the princess's chilling gaze. Soon, a chain reaction of stillness fell upon the whole group. One by one they slinked away until the princess was left standing alone in the street. She didn't notice. She walked slowly away, dazed. She should have been angry because she was the one the young man had grabbed to cover himself, but she was not. She was angry because the people had mocked the young man. He had single-handedly pulled down a five-hundred-pound, sharp-tusked, wild animal that could have torn someone to pieces, and the crowd, whose fortunes, and possibly even lives, he had saved, only laughed at him. That made her mad! She also realized she didn't know the young man. His bravery should be rewarded. So, she made up her mind, right on the spot, she would arrange a reward for him.

"The princess hurried home to organize her friends and servants into a search committee to find out who the young man was and what the proper recognition and reward should be for his valiant efforts in the marketplace. Meanwhile, the young man who, by the way, was named Harry…" A chorus of hoots and snickers interrupted the old man. He looked around and saw the children trying not to laugh. "And just *what* is so funny?"

"His name!" The clamorous boy at the back of the group smirked, his lip beginning to curl. "His name is hairy, like he had hair growing all over him."

"Oh, my friend…" the old man said in a very low tone that sounded almost like a growl, "he was not a ridiculous-looking figure… not at all… and his name… his name means leader… leader of an army. It was a very strong name and an honor to wear it. Names mean things. His problem was not that he had an overabundance of hair, but only that he was very shy and extremely uncomfortable when speaking to people he did not know. So, quite naturally, at least for the time in which he lived, people thought he was cowardly and did not even think to consider he had just brought down a full-grown pig, which made him a hero. They didn't even consider it. They just laughed at him because Harry had a terrible habit of turning red or stuttering and stammering when he talked to someone, and sometimes he would be so overcome with embarrassment, he would just drop what he was doing and run away and hide. But the princess was determined to find him and reward him. And, if the truth be known…" the old man bent over and whispered, "I think she liked him."

The little girls on the front row giggled and blushed as he whispered that. He quickly continued, "Now where was I... yes, yes... meanwhile Harry was troubled."

"Excuse me... excuse me..." the little girl with the gap-toothed smile interrupted.

"Yes?" the old man answered.

"Did the prince have a last name? Or did people just call him Harry?"

"Why of course he had a last name... and a first, and one in between. Now, where was I? Yes, yes... Harry was troubled."

"Excuse me... excuse me," the snaggle-toothed little naglet continued. "What was it?"

"What was what?" the old man asked innocently, teasing the young lady.

"You know what. What was his last name?" she fumed, exasperated.

"Oh... well, to be honest, I forgot."

"What!" she cried. "You don't remember his last name?"

"No, I don't," the old man lied, crossing his fingers behind his back.

"Well... well..." she puffed, hands on her little hips and head cocked to one side. "You have to... you have to give him one!" And with that she sat down, satisfied that the matter was as simple as that and had been cleared up.

"No, I don't," the old man responded calmly.

"Yes, you do," she answered firmly. "He has to have a last name."

"Why?"

"Why? Because he has to. Everyone has a last name. It's part of their family."

"Well, in that case, since I don't know what it was, you give him one."

"I can't give him a last name! You're the one making up the story! You have to do it!"

"What makes you think I am making up this story?"

"Well, aren't you?" she asked, confused.

"No, I am not. It is true. It really happened, and that is why I can't just make up a last name for Harry."

"Humph," she said. Her eyes frowned and her eyebrows crowned the top of her forehead. "I guess I will give him a last name."

"Really?" The old man bit his lip to keep from laughing but was unable to keep the twinkle from his eyes. "And what are you going to call him?"

"I am going to call him… Harry the Brave."

"Okay. Now that we have that settled, may I continue?"

"Yes, carry on."

The old man hid his amusement behind a cough, but not before the little nagahina had cocked a fierce eyebrow in his direction. He hurriedly continued, "Now, where was I? Oh yes, Harry, still burdened by the incident in the market, felt as though he had besmirched the honor of the princess by grabbing her and roughly handling her, even though he had not meant to be rude or crude. He had brought her into his humiliation and was thoroughly ashamed."

"Excuse me… excuse me," the little snaggle-toothed girl started to say.

The old man shushed her and tried to continue. "So," he started, "Harry determined in his heart to find a way to honor the princess."

But the little girl was persistent with her interruption. "Excuse me… excuse me!" the nagahina continued impatiently.

"He thought and thought and then decided…" the old man pushed on, attempting to ignore the disruption.

"*Hey*! I have a question!" she shouted.

"So?" the old man answered. Then looking around the class, he asked, "Is there anyone else with a question?" The whole class was getting disturbed with the little girl's interruptions and was not happy with her. "Sorry," he said, sending her the sternest look he could muster. When the other kids giggled, he knew he'd failed. "You have met your quota for questions, and since no one else is asking, I shall continue." Her lips quivered, and a little tear began to trickle down her cheek. He sighed and said, "Okay... Okay... don't cry. What is it you want to know?"

As quick as lightning her countenance changed to a gap-toothed radiance, and the old man knew he had been played. "All I wanted to know was what besmirched means?"

The old man drew in a long breath and let it out very slowly, trying not to surrender to her grin, and craftily answered, "It means sullied." When he looked at her, she cocked another eyebrow and it made him laugh.

"The young man did not want to dishonor the princess by exposing her to his embarrassing situation. It never occurred to him that she might feel honored and even wish to reward him for his bravery. And it certainly never entered his mind that she might have found him attractive. He only thought that she must have been as embarrassed as he was. So, Harry was thinking of ways to honor her, and she was thinking of ways to reward him, and that is when tragedy struck.

"The land that the princess lived in was a beautiful land surrounded by mountains that acted as natural barriers to the kingdom's enemies. There were narrow passes that led to other lands, and they were easily guarded, that is until the land became so prosperous and the people so wealthy that no one thought anything bad could happen. So eventually the narrow passes were left unguarded, and the land was left open to anyone or anything that wanted to attack it. And that is where the dragon entered. Where he came from, or how he came to be, no one knows. The dragon's name was Romlott Hus. A vile creature choosing to weaken its prey before devouring them, it would drive the people it had chosen for destruction mad, using their own weaknesses against them. Then, finally having bound them into terrible habits, would swoop down and carry them off, feasting on them like fattened cows. The people of the kingdom believed the stories about the evil serpent were lies—it didn't really destroy people and devour their souls. So, the dragon ate and ate and grew and grew until one day about the same time as Harry the Brave had fought the pig, it came for the princess."

The room had grown quiet as the dragon was described, and the look on the children's faces was solemn. Then, as the old man finished the last sentence, the peevish youngster with the tight, mean smile said, "This is a silly story, and I'm not going to listen to it anymore."

"You don't have to be afraid," the little girl on the front row answered. "It's just a story."

"Is it?" the old man asked under his breath.

"Yes, of course it is," answered the little girl. "It's just a story."

"Then what about it troubles some of you?" the old man continued. "If I were to say oranges and sailboats, no one would be alarmed, but when I say dragons, and people lying to themselves, and being fattened for destruction, it bothers you."

The little girl sat down and even the peevish young boy looked thoughtful, got quiet, and continued to listen.

"Hold on a minute," the thoughtful snaggle-toothed little girl said. "Why did the dragon choose the princess?"

"Oh, that is simple, my dear: the dragon wanted to destroy the country and knew the best way to destroy a people was to steal their heart. The princess was greatly loved by her people, and even though she didn't realize her beauty, everyone else did. When she would laugh, people would think the sun was shining, even on a dreary, cold day. Wherever she went, she could say just the right word to just the right person and give them the strength to carry on. The heart of the country beat within her, and she didn't even know it."

"Oh," the little snaggle-tooth said quietly and scooted back into her chair.

"Now, as I was saying, the dragon stole the princess, flew back to his mountain cave, and chained her to a pile of rocks. She cried her heart out because she feared no one would ever find her, and if they did, she would probably be dead before they could rescue her, and then something even worse happened."

Chapter Three

The old man's voice carried the imaginations of the children away with a scary tone that clouded their tender hearts.

"I want to go home!" the peevish boy said. "I am tired of this, and I need to watch TV or play Nintendo."

His friends all tried to shush him, and some of them said, "You can't leave. Your mom's not here, and you're just scared."

The old man, seeing the storm rising, said, "Hold on a minute... Hold on. The children are right, son. Your mother is not here."

The peevish little boy's face shriveled like a prune, and just as he was about to wail and cause ignorant adults to come running, bringing their leech-like lawyers with them, the old man looked squarely at the boy and said, "Could you help me?"

The shriveled little face swelled with curiosity, and he said as intelligently as possible, "Huh?"

"I need a page turner."

"What?" the child asked. "You aren't reading, you're telling us the story."

"Are you sure?" the old man asked. "Come see. Come up here, sit with me, and look at what I am looking at."

The little boy, a bit confused but calmed and looking a little like a trick was about to be played on him, came forward. Before he could get to the front, he looked squarely in the old man's eye and saw him wink. Then he knew there was a game being played, and he was one of the principal players. He could trick the other kids into thinking he was special and not afraid if he turned the pages of the imaginary book.

"So," the old man began again, "I will tell you when to turn the page, okay?"

The boy nodded his head. "Okay."

"Now, where was I?"

The young page turner gently elbowed the old man, leaned down, and whispered in a barnyard whisper that every child in the room heard, "Something worse happened."

"Yes, it did indeed," the old man straightened up and continued. "The king gathered his greatest knights and sent them bravely into battle against Romlott Hus, the dragon. They marched off courageously only to be attacked, devoured, or badly burnt by the dragon, who only laughed at their feeble attempts to slay him, roaring his defiance from the highest hill in the land. After a few days and scary nights, when the dragon's shadow could be seen flying against the moon's bright light, the whole land wept in despair. All the brave soldiers were gone, yet the princess was still captive… or dead. No one knew.

"People began to load up their belongings in carts and wagons and flee down the country roads to get as far away as they could from Romlott Hus. Occasionally, the dragon would attack a convoy of refugees, but for the most part, he let them depart in peace.

"In the middle of all this, Harry the Brave was greatly troubled. He paced the floor of his humble cottage. He read the newspapers, and he prayed. It hurt him greatly that the princess had been carried off. He thought about it day and night, but there was nothing he could do. Until one night, as he lay down to sleep, he began to dream a dark and fitful dream. In it, he was walking down a dark trail. Barely able to see, he often tripped or stumbled over uneven places. Yet in the dream he also saw, way off in the distance, the light of a campfire. Cautiously approaching the fire, he saw the princess shivering in its glow, trying to keep warm. Her clothes were tattered, and her complexion darkened like she had been exposed to smoke and grime for a long time. Harry could see her cheeks, where tears left trails of white through the smudge on her face. He felt terrible and began to weep.

"The princess heard his crying and peered into the gloom that surrounded her. Finally, out of the corner of her eye, she saw him move. Then her eyes focused and she said, 'I see you, and… you look so familiar. Wait! You're the young man who pulled down the hog in the market! Can you see me? If you can, please come get me. I don't know how much longer the dragon will spare me. I don't know how much longer I can keep myself from changing.'

"Harry was confused, especially by the last words of the princess: 'keep myself from changing.' So he asked her, 'What do you mean keep yourself from changing?'

"'The dragon wants to change me into a dragon! He fights against my mind and invades my thoughts. It is so hard to remember who I am some days, and once I completely forget, I will change. So please, please help me!'

"'What can I do?' Harry cried. 'This is just a dream. I am not a warrior, and the king's greatest knights have failed. I want to help you so much, but how can I?'

"The princess said, 'Talk to me. Remind me of who I am. Sing to me. Visit me often. Don't forget me, and pray. Perhaps the Lord will send an angel to guide you.'

"Harry said, 'I can do that. I have been praying. You're in my thoughts every moment I'm awake, and every time I sleep. I will remember you, and who knows, perhaps I can visit you again in our dreams.'

"The princess smiled. Harry smiled back, and then she was gone. He awoke. It was morning, but he was not refreshed."

"Wow! What's he going to do?" the whole ankle-biting chorus echoed.

"Will he save her? Will an angel tell him what to do? What happens next?"

The old man answered, "Well, my voice is getting hoarse." He would never admit the story made him emotional. "Besides, it's about time for your mothers to come and pick you up, so perhaps we should stop until next week."

"No, no!" they roared. The room shook with the nos, and library workers scurried, as well as parents, to see what the ruckus was about. The old man tried to quiet everyone down, but the children were persistent and announced that if the old man didn't finish the story, they would ask for water all night long, not eat their vegetables, and whimper till their parents tore their hair out.

The old man scolded them and said those were not nice things to do. If they misbehaved that badly, he would never finish the story, which caused them to begin to sob and blubber. By that time, the parents had come to pick their children up and were curious to hear the story themselves.

Finally, the old man's daughter, Lizzy Ferguson, the head librarian, came up with a solution. "Let my dad take a break, get some dinner, and then, how about we all come back here to the library and let him finish the story. Say about six thirty? Will that work for everyone?"

Children looked at parents. Parents looked at children. The parents were so amazed that no child wanted to play video games or watch television, but actually begged to stay, that they agreed. All, that is, except for one parsimonious parent, who also made her child brush after every single meal, vacuum his room twice a day, wear starched shirts, and never allowed him to own a puppy.

The snaggle-toothed girl solved that problem by walking over to the stingy mother, saying, "If you don't let Thomas come back tonight, I am going to sneak into your house, track mud through it, drop your dental floss in the toilet, and put my kitty, who just had babies, in your attic!"

The well-meaning but inflexible mother's eyes grew wide and rolled back into her head, and she fainted. Once someone revived her with smelling salts, she agreed to the extortion and promised to bring Thomas, who was, by the way, the page turner to the after-dinner theater, which somehow the children's story time had been renamed.

Chapter Four

Finally, six thirty broke free of its afternoon doldrums. Anxious children and curious parents, and by now, older brothers and sisters and some cousins, crowded in to hear the story. They met in the spacious reading room of the library that held a makeshift stage equipped with curtains that had hung through one world war and two international conflicts. The fire marshal complained about a serious violation of local code but was losing ground to his granddaughter, who smiled and begged and wheedled her snaggle-toothed way through his concerns. She graciously assured her brow-beaten grandfather there was no danger unless the dragon, Romlott Hus, flew down from the sky and devoured them all. He was finally convinced that the volunteer fire department, stationed right across the street, was more than enough protection. And now, with imperial sovereignty, she sat on his lap on the front row of the completely filled reading room and prepared to listen to the old man finish the story.

Peeking through a slit in the stage curtains, the old man drew in a sharp breath and almost had a panic attack.

"I don't know if I can do this, Baby Girl," he whispered. "My hands are shaking. I have to use the restroom, and what if I have to go during the story? The whole place is full, and I just don't know if I can do this..."

His daughter, excited about the attention for the library, and knowing her father, said, "Dad, just tell the story to the children. You don't have to speak to the crowd; they will hear you fine. I'll put a wireless microphone on you. You call up the kids, and when they are settled in, continue the story. Got it? Can you do that? You don't have to look at the people, just the children. You don't have to raise your voice, just pretend it's all about the kids and be yourself."

"I don't have to stand on the stage?"

"Nope, just sit on the middle stairs and have the kids gather around you. If they squirm, scold them. If they ask questions, answer them, and take it from there. You are a master at this. You have told me stories all my life. Now you get to share that gift with others."

The old man took a deep breath, let it out, and sighed, "Okay, okay. I think I can do that."

"I know you can, Dad. Now let's go."

His daughter hooked him up, tested the mic, and led him to the center of the stage. People applauded, and the kids laughed and shouted. His daughter called all the children to the front, had them sit down along the stairs, and the old man began.

"Now, let's see, where was I?"

The idea of a rhetorical question used as an introduction was completely lost on the children. When they heard a question, they assumed it was intended to be answered. So a host of replies filled the air and caused the old man to say, "Now that is right... that is right. So, Harry woke up, and began pacing the floor back and forth worrying and wondering about his dream and the princess and how in the world he would ever rescue her.

"Finally..." the old man started to say when suddenly little-imperial-snaggle-toothed-now-enthroned-on-her-grandfather's-lap raised her hand and said, "Hey! Excuse me! Excuse me!" which caught the old man off guard and caused him to cock an eyebrow so high it touched his hairline. All of this was lost on the tooth-poor wonder, who continued with, "You didn't tell us the name of the princess!"

The old man looked at her and said, "You are right, I didn't. Now as I was saying, Harry was pacing and pacing until suddenly he stopped."

Not to be put off or surpassed, the little urchin interrupted again. "But she has to have a name. She just has to. People can't just go around calling her princess!"

"Why not?" the old man asked, pretending to be irritated.

"Because she does," the imperial highness stated with both hands on her hips, jumping down from her grandpa's lap and staring at the old man. The crowd was starting to snicker, but neither combatant seemed to notice as their focus was so intent on each other.

"So, what's her name?"

The old man got a sly look on his face and asked, "What's yours?"

The little girl looked at him suspiciously and said, "Sarah."

"Isn't that the most amazing coincidence," the old man replied. "That's the same name as the princess."

"Reaalllly?" her imperial majesty questioned, head tilting in disbelief.

"No, but that is what I am going to call her."

By this time the crowd was into it. People were howling and laughing at the impasse and listening for the next round to begin.

"What's her *real* name?" her riled-up highness demanded.

"Fine, her real name was Princess Arimathea Moni Caitlín Joline Bethany Mary Jane Stewart."

"No, it wasn't!"

"Yes, my dear, it really was. See, royal families with a lot of kindred to pacify tended to name their children for everyone in the family of any distinction, and that is why, by the way, most of her friends just called her Sarah. Are you happy now?"

As she crawled back into her chuckling grandfather's lap, the little girl grumbled, "For now."

The old man shook his head and started again. "Harry decided, finally, after a night of pacing and pondering, that he would just have to start out and see what happened. He had no one to go to for counsel, no armorer to grant him shield or sword, and no horse to ride into battle. All he had were the clothes on his back and the wits in his head. And with that he walked out of his house and headed toward the dark hills that hid the dragon's lair.

"The trip to the mountains was long and treacherous, especially now that Romlott Hus was guarding the way to his lair. He didn't get far before he got hot, and sweat began to stream down his face and body, soaking his clothes and skin. He stopped for a moment under a shade tree and took a drink from his water bag. He only intended to stop there a moment, but it was so hot, and he was already tired from his troubling dream and lack of rest, that he fell asleep. As soon as his sleep deepened, he began to dream and was soon dreaming the familiar dream of the princess seated at the flickering fire. As he approached her, she seemed to sense his presence.

"'I'm so glad you are back,' the princess said. 'I don't know how you are doing this, but I am so glad you are, even if you're a figment of my imagination…'"

Immediately several hands shot up. The old man, ready for them, said, "Figment means fabrication or hallucination." He smiled as he saw that many of the children didn't know what fabrication or hallucination meant either but were getting the idea.

One little boy elbowed another in the ribs, leaned over, and said, "That means you make it up."

The old man continued, not missing a beat, "'But right now, you are all that is holding me together. Can you hear me?'

"'Yes, I can, Princess. I am on a journey to find you. Is there anything you can tell me that might help me find you?' Harry asked patiently.

"'I don't know. I don't know where I am!'

"'Can you describe what you have seen or heard or even smelt, anything to give me a clue as to your location?'

"'Let me think. It's dark and musty, always dark. I must be in a cave. I am sure of it. I am underground surrounded by rock, and there is a stream here, but it stinks like marsh and something else, very nasty. I think maybe it's runoff from the city's sewer. I can't drink that filth and have to find water from other sources here in the cave.'

"'Hmmm,' Harry said. 'The city's sewer, that's a couple of miles north of here, and it runs toward the mountain valley and then out to the sea. I'm coming, Princess, hold on. I will come for you. Don't give up. Please don't give up.'

"'What's your name? When I pray, I want to call you by name.'

"'My name is Harry, Princess. Just plain old Harry.'

"'I will do my best, Harry. I'm just so tired, and the dragon's onslaught against my thoughts is relentless. The only time I get relief is when I am dreaming, like now. Be careful, Harry. So many have died. I can't forget the screams I heard as the dragon sprayed them with flame and devoured them.'

"Harry exhibited courage he didn't feel—and realized it wasn't what you felt that was courage, it was what you did in spite of what you felt. He also noticed he was slipping away and shouted as he began to fade, 'Don't give up,

Princess! No matter what, don't give up! I will come for you!'

"Then he was gone. He woke under the only shade tree for miles. He started to move but realized that the moment he walked out from under the tree's protective covering, he would be spotted, especially in this open field. So, he waited. He hated to wait because while he waited, he worried, and fretted, and battled fearful thoughts for the princess's safety. But not once, and he didn't even realize it, did he think of his own safety. He thought only of hers.

"Twilight finally fell, and Harry stepped out from the shade of the lone tree and began to slowly move through the sea of grass toward the city's sewer marsh. The largest city in the realm was Brookstone. It had built miles of tunnels that captured its waste and took it to the marshes. The people worked hard to keep the city clean, and the marsh acted as a natural deposit of waste, which, after a season, also became extremely fertile soil that farmers would collect to use in their fields and gardens.

"Early in the afternoon Harry reached the marshes. The weather had cooled, and he was glad that a breeze was blowing because the marsh stank terribly. The ground bubbled up a thick, slimy goo that gurgled, and even fizzed, releasing a noxious stench. When he first smelled it, Harry thought he was going to throw up. Barely able to hold on, he wondered how he was going to find a way through the marsh and into the dragon's lair. He searched all day before finally stopping to camp for the night. He had marsh water all over him, stank to high heaven, mosquitoes began to bite, and he was miserable. *Some hero I am,* he thought sadly. *How will I ever find the entrance to the cave? Am I even going to survive this night? The mosquitoes are carrying me off a little at a time, and I smell terrible. Oh gosh, this is awful!*

"At this point you would think something should happen. The hero is at his wits' end. He is helpless, despairing, miserable, weak, and lost. It's time for something great to happen, right?" the old man asked the little ones scattered in front of him. "What do you think? Is it time?"

"Oh no," a freckle-faced little boy answered. "He's got all night. It *is* time for a commercial though, and a bathroom break, and a pizza nuggets break. But no, I don't think Harry is going to get any help. He just has to man up and get through."

"Sadly, you're right, young man. There were no lights in the sky, no special help sent his way, just stench, stale bread, and mosquitoes all night long. Finally, Harry realized if he spread his blanket over his head, he could keep most of the mosquitoes off most of his flesh, so he did. The blanket was thin and was soon covered in stinky mud, but even that helped to keep the bugs off. Harry curled up against a log, covered himself with his muddy blanket, and fell mercifully asleep to the tune of a million frogs orchestrated against the night.

"In the middle of the night or early morning, Harry didn't know which, he was awakened by a terrible roar. The dragon burst forth from its lair, bellowed, and blew flames from its nostrils. Its horrendous scream pierced the night, and Harry felt as if the marsh itself trembled beneath its blast. The dragon flew right over the place where Harry lay covered with mud and marsh. Harry just knew that, at any moment, the dragon's piercing eyes would catch sight of him, and he almost yelled when the dragon flew so close that he felt the warmth of its body and smelled the odor of its rotted breath. But the dragon did not see Harry, nor did it smell him. Since he was covered with mud and muck, he was invisible to sight and scent. The dragon was not aware that a mighty warrior had watched his flight and also seen the rock formation he had flown out from. Harry had just found the way into the dragon's den, and the dragon was the one who showed him.

"Harry had gone to bed a miserable, cold, wet young man who had followed his heart into a filthy, stinking swamp. When he awoke, he was a soldier with a cold-hardened resolve to track the monster to its lair and kill it. Funny what a night of misery and fear can do for a person.

"As soon as it was light enough to see, Harry began to trudge through the marsh toward the hills on the other side. It took all morning, but finally, he began to reach higher ground. The rocks and the hills became steep. He wondered if he had misjudged the climb from the bottom of the wetlands. It had looked closer, but when he put feet to the trail, it seemed a thousand miles away. Sweat streamed down his cheeks and left small white trails through the marsh muck that covered his face. Once, a vulture even flew down to have a closer look at him thinking something that stunk that bad couldn't possibly be alive. But Harry was alive, and with every step toward the dragon's hidden entrance, his will grew stronger. He was on a mission, and nothing was going to stand in his way. Finally, during the hottest part of the day, he found the cleft in the rock where the dragon had squeezed through to go on its nightly patrol, and Harry entered the cave.

"The cave was dark. Only a sliver of sunlight penetrated its opening, and it wasn't long before even that had faded away. Harry had to light a small torch that barely lit the path a few feet in front of him. He worried that the light would draw the dragon's attention but pressed back his fear and bravely pushed ahead. Every few feet he would stop and listen as intently as he could. He was so quiet and attentive he could have heard a rat run across cotton, but only the drips of water seeping through limestone came to his ears, and so he carefully crept forward. He felt like he had been in the cave for hours, but it was probably only a few minutes. Sweat dripped down his forehead, burning his eyes. *A cave should be colder,* he thought, but then he realized this one was warmed by the dragon's breath. Harry's heart pounded so hard he could feel it beating in his chest. He thought, *If I don't do something about this quickly, my fear will consume me, and I will make a terrible mistake. What can I do?*

"A few feet farther down the hall, the tunnel divided, with a smaller passage leading away from the larger. Harry felt like he should walk down the smaller tunnel and perhaps hide for a moment to rest. He had been hiking all day and was exhausted. His fear had also drained him, and as he thought it through, he knew it must be past midnight and that the dragon might soon be marching down this tunnel to go on his nightly patrol. So, Harry turned down the smaller tunnel and pushed his weary body along the narrow path. After several yards, he came to an extremely narrow crevice that Harry could only navigate by turning sideways and sliding along with his chest squeezed tight against the rock.

"And there I am going to have to stop the story for the night. It has been a long day, and I can see your eyes are drooping," said the old man.

"No, no!" the children cried but not too strongly. Their parents and grandparents started clapping, and the idea caught on, and the little ones joined in. Finally, after he shooed them into their loved ones' arms and promised to continue the story on the next library story day, the children and their parents left.

The old man escorted his daughter, arm in arm, out of the library. She locked the doors behind them and continued walking her father to his old pickup truck that had seen more miles than most vehicles and had a terrible habit of backfiring. It didn't bother the old man much because it had a tendency to scare anyone who was too close and not prepared for the sudden noise, which pleased its driver way more than it should have.

As his daughter kissed him goodnight, she said, "Dad, I have had this question on my mind all day and, through the cascade of events, have forgotten to ask, but now that I have you all to myself, I can finally ask it."

"What is that, Roo?" Roo, the baby kangaroo from Winnie the Pooh books, was the pet name the old man had called her since she was the tiniest of tots.

She smiled at his favorite name for her and said, "What did you mean when you said the story wasn't made up, and that it was a true story?"

He looked at her for a moment and then said, "Every legend is founded in some form of fact. It may be embellished or parts added for color, but the best of legends are true, even though they may not be historically accurate."

"So, this is a myth with a moral," she responded matter-of-factly.

He looked at her, smiled, and asked, "Is it?"

She shook her head and punched his arm playfully. "Goodnight, Dad."

"Goodnight, Roo," he responded automatically and crawled into his old truck, turned the key, and started home. As he drove out of the library parking lot, he sighed and thought, *If only it were not true, honey. If only.*

Chapter Five

The next library day rolled around sooner than the old man wanted it to. The story had brought up memories so vivid he dreamed about them. He lived alone, so there was no one to wake him from groaning in the night or notice that his cheeks were hot with tears. His dogs knew and occasionally would be so disturbed that instead of lying at the foot of his bed, the female animal would jump into the bed and lick his salty face. This, of course, would wake him. He would shoo her off the bed and fall back asleep, only to return to the dream.

As he walked up the drive to the library, the old man noticed a lot more cars in the parking lot than usual. Then he remembered the kids' parents and grandparents had all wanted to hear the story and apparently had made a way to do so. He walked into the library, an old museum-like Victorian house remodeled to suit the literary needs of their small community, and noticed the crowd. He was starting to get nervous and had just about decided that he would just turn around and quietly leave when he heard the shrill young voice of his snaggle-toothed nemesis.

"There you are! I wondered when you were going to get here. We have been waiting on you. Come on, we need to get this show on the road!"

He looked at her grey-haired grandfather, the city fire marshal, who just grimaced and shrugged his shoulders. He had been captured by the little matriarch long ago and was no help in thwarting her plans. The little girl grabbed both old men by their extended hands and said, "Come on!" She then yelled at her friends, "He is here! Come on! Story time is about to begin!"

The old man's librarian daughter had corralled the children and had them temporarily subdued like puppies waiting on a snack. She couldn't hold them long, and the old man knew he had better get started, so he shuffled to the front of the room, sat down in the rocking chair, and quietly began to speak. He deliberately didn't yell for order but began by saying, "All right now, where did I end last?"

His page turner looked at him and said, "Don't you remember? Harry had crept into the dragon's lair and was squeezing down a narrow tunnel."

"Oh yes, then what happened?" the sly old man asked.

"Huh? I don't know."

"Well, yes, of course, but you might, so I thought I would ask."

Everyone had gotten quiet, listening intently to the conversation. Waiting for just that moment, the old man began. "When we last left off, Harry had slipped into the dragon's lair, found a side tunnel that got smaller and smaller, and had finally squeezed so far back into it he felt safe. He knew the dragon could not get to him. He also knew that there were enough twists and turns in the pathway that even if the dragon tried to spew flame down the tunnel, it would not reach him. What Harry did not realize, however, was that he was stuck."

"What?!" his audience erupted. "Stuck? What do you mean 'stuck'? How did he get stuck? He can't be stuck. How is he going to get out?"

The old man hid a sneaky grin beneath his sparkling eyes and said, "Yes, Harry was stuck. He had climbed so far back into the tunnel that he couldn't get out, nor could he go forward. So, he stayed there till he starved and died."

"No, no, no! That's not fair!" the angry chorus of children shrieked. Like a nest of irritated wasps, they rose up and shouted, some cried, and all had something to say about it. The old man started laughing, and the parents of the children, vainly trying to settle them, saw that something else was coming.

Finally, the old man barked a cough and said, "Oh my! I am so sorry. I got my stories confused." At that everyone in the room quieted instantly. Every eye was focused on him. He looked back at them, raised his eyebrows in response, and said, "I am sorry. It wasn't Harry that got stuck. But he did see someone in front of him who had gotten stuck. Harry pushed his way down the ever-narrowing tunnel, his small candle flickering against the cave walls, and then he stopped. Had he not been afraid of the dragon finding him, he would have screamed, but before he could shout, his good sense stopped the cry in his throat. He stood, mouth gaping because there before him was… Oh my! Look at the time. Story time is over."

Once again, the pathetic squalls of the mob of story-starved children broke against his ears. Sarah, his favorite little snaggle-toothed tyrant, jumped up with a mean look on her snout and walked up to the old man. She pointed at his watch and said, "The little hand is on ten, and the big hand is on six. That means you have plenty of time to go on with this story!"

The old man laughed. In spite of his cantankerous ways, she had caught him red-handed. The rest of the children chimed in and, finally waving them off, he said, "Okay, okay, I will go on with it. My eyes aren't what they used to be…"

The children went back to their places harrumphing and grumbling but victorious, so he continued.

"Harry gulped, swallowing hard. He knew he could not go back and really didn't want to go farther, so he just stood there." The old man waited, pausing for effect, watching the intent eyes of the children around him who somehow reminded him of a school of piranhas waiting to bite at the first sign of blood. Deliberately the old man waited watching his audience grow more and more impatient.

"Okay, what next?" someone said.

"What are you waiting on?" asked another little girl in the far corner who was usually too shy to breathe hard around her prancing teammates.

"I am waiting on my page turner to turn the page," the old man said good-naturedly. He looked at the little boy standing beside him, who sheepishly reached up and turned the imaginary page. "There now… Harry stood there facing a cobweb-covered skeleton of an armored knight.

"Harry thought the old knight must have been stuck for a very long time, since his body was a skeleton, which would have taken years. So, Harry gathered his courage, like children might gather their dish plates after a meal to help their parents clean up." The children started to frown, and the parents grinned, and the old man continued before the storm broke.

"Harry held his torch high and cast shadows down on the ancient figure of the old knight who had died hiding from the dragon. Then it occurred to Harry: How could that be true? The dragon had only been in the country for a few months, not near long enough for the knight's body to turn to a skeleton and be covered with dust. So how had the knight gotten into the cave? Why was the knight in the cave? Had the dragon been using the cave for a long, long time and only just now started raiding the countryside close to its cave? Harry did not know the answers to his questions, and he did not know what to do.

"*So,* he thought, *what did my father tell me to do when I don't know what to do? I am standing in a cave tunnel, and I can see by the light of this torch. There is a very old skeleton of a man dressed as a knight in armor, and that skeleton is blocking my way through the tunnel.* Suddenly his mind cleared, and he remembered what his father had said, 'When you come to a dead end, you have three choices: sit there—*I don't want to do that;* go back—*I can't do that;* or look very carefully at what you think is a dead end. You may discover the road doesn't stop, it just changes.'

"*Okay,* Harry continued, *I am going to look very closely at that old skeleton. It can't hurt me, and I may be able to squeeze around it or move it and keep going.* So, that is exactly what he did.

"He slowly moved toward the old knight's body. It was covered in cobwebs that melted as the torch touched them. He noticed the knight had a sword. He noticed the knight was covered from head to toe with armor. Harry also noticed that the cave kept going, and the knight had just been stuck in a very narrow part of the tunnel. As Harry looked closer, he grew braver. Sometimes, when we face our fears, they get smaller, and we get braver," the old man interjected as a teaching moment.

Three small, large-eyed children all raised their hands at once, and then the most impatient of them, a little red-headed boy with freckles and a blue tongue from sucking on a lollipop, blurted out, "But, but… that can't be true. In the movies, this is the point where the music gets scary and you can tell something bad is going to jump out and grab the person, and I run and hide behind my dad's chair."

"What do you mean it can't be true?" the old man asked.

"If you get closer to a scary thing, it can get you. And it gets bigger, not smaller!"

"Well, hang on a minute. That is not always the case," the old man countered. "Sometimes we are afraid of things we should not be afraid of, and when we look closely at them, we see there is nothing to be afraid of.

"But you are right..." the old man said, his voice growing quieter, "sometimes we should not be looking, we should be running. And the only way you can know is to get closer... and... closer." As the old man talked, his voice grew quieter and quieter, and the children leaned in, and then he couldn't help himself. He yelled, "*And then the monster grabs you!*" The whole crowd of the terror-sensitized-horror-movie-generation children screamed and jumped and yelled and griped and started crying.

The old man laughed and laughed until his little nemesis got in front of him and said sternly, "That was not funny! You are *mean!*" She shook her little finger at his nose with a look on her face that was destined to corral wayfaring men for decades to come.

The old man snickered, recognized she was right, and said, "You are right. I am sorry, but isn't that what you were expecting?" The rest of the children began to settle down as the old man started to cast his enchanting voice again. "Didn't all of you really sort of wish, or at least expect, something to reach out and grab Harry?"

The blue-tongued, red-haired boy grinned and said, "Yeah!" and then was joined by a chorus of nods and laughs and yeses and yeahs.

Only one stalwart child, the old man's page turner, begged to differ. "No," he yelled sternly. "I don't like to be scared. Not at all."

The old man looked at him, leaned in, and whispered, "But you are the page turner. Didn't you see that coming? It was right there in front of you. Didn't you read ahead?"

The little boy, delighted in being a part of a whisper, answered, "Not at first, but I do now!"

"Good," the old man said. "I knew you weren't frightened, so next time read ahead and listen carefully, and if a scary part is coming up, I will nudge you with my elbow, and you will be prepared. Is that okay?"

"Absolutely," the timid page turner of the invisible book said.

"Now let me get back to the story. Are you listening?" the old man asked the merry band of distracted white-sugar eaters.

"Harry got real close to the old skeleton. He inspected every part of it, saw that the ancient sword of the old knight had special letters and pictures etched on it… that means scratched," he quickly interjected without skipping a beat and was rewarded with a unanimous choir of "Oooohs." "And then Harry looked closer at the hands of the old skeleton. He noticed a ring on the right-hand ring finger of the old knight. It was covered in dust and dirt from countless years of lying in that dirty dark tunnel. He gingerly touched the ring, and then carefully, slowly tried to remove it from the old knight's finger, but as Harry lifted the ring, the whole finger bone came off with it!"

"Ew! Yuck!" The children groaned. Someone made a gagging noise.

The old man agreed, "Yes, that's exactly what Harry said too. He caught his breath, blew the dirt off, and gingerly took the finger bone out of the ring. Then he gently polished it on his shirt and held the torch close. Then his eyes got big, his mouth dropped open, and he gasped! And that is about all we have time for today, children!"

The old man's evil grin stopped at his lips, but the little snaggle-toothed girl, who had become his warden, scowled at him. She looked up at the wall clock and frowned. The old man was right. It was time to go. She had to leave, but she didn't have to like it, and she let him know it.

As the old man scooted the rocking chair he had been sitting in back to where it belonged, his daughter walked up to him and stood there with her hands on her hips, shaking her head. "Dad, you are *mean!*"

"If I am so mean, why are you trying so hard not to laugh?"

"Ha! Because I remember you being that way all my life, and you'll never change!" She kept shaking her head.

"Well, I thought I would just mix things up a little," he said while thinking, *Truth is, I don't know how to tell this next part to a bunch of kindergarteners, and I was stalling. I don't know how to tell it to anyone. I don't even know how it comes out. But I have started, and now I have to finish.*

She woke him from his thoughts, "You okay, Dad? You seemed to have left me there for a moment."

"Just thinking, Hon. I am not sure how this story ends, and really don't know where to take it from here."

"Well, seems to me that if you are the one making the story up, it can go where you take it, right?"

He looked at her, smiled an expected smile, and said, "Yep, I suppose you are right. So now I just have to work it out, don't I?"

"Always," she laughed. "Now come on and let me treat you to dinner."

"I am not in the mood for boiled water and corndogs, Roo."

"Dad! I'm not cooking. I am buying."

"So, Sam's pizza then?"

"How'd you guess?" she laughed.

"Last of the big spenders, baby!"

The old man's reputation for entertaining the children and those parents who could break away and come to story time was growing. After each story, the wild-eyed children would run home to their parents chattering about the latest episode in the story. They began to dress up like Harry, or the princess or the dragon, and act out their fantasies, then ask their parents to tell them stories. Ironically, many found themselves leaving the television off and turning their imaginations on.

The next library day, the old man pulled into the parking place for director and staff at the library like his daughter had instructed. He looked around fearfully, shook his head, placed his hand on the key, and almost drove back out of the parking lot. The place was full. The children had been talking. He would have left in a faltering heartbeat had he not seen the library window full of wide-eyed and expectant children searching for him. As soon as one saw him, the whole pack raced out the door, down the sidewalk, and clamored around him yelling and laughing, excited that he was back. The story was going to continue.

He had gotten used to being grabbed by his callused old hands and hauled into the library. As usual it was the notorious ringleader, the infamous snaggle-toothed champion of story time, Sarah, who held his hand and directed him to his seat. He was tempted to say: *Young madam, you are going to make a wonderful mother and horrible wife if you continue this type of behavior,* but restrained himself, just shook his head, and did what he was told.

He looked at Thomas, his invisible book page turner, made eye contact, and directed him to his place at his side. The young man had been waiting for the signal and quickly took his prestigious position. The old man looked around the room and waited. Two parents new to story time were busy chatting about the sale at the grocery store. His eyes lit on the ladies, and all the children turned to see what the delay was. A tornado-like "Shush!" burst forth from a multitude of directions aimed with laser-like precision at the chatty culprits. They caught on and quieted.

Before the old man could begin, Sarah proceeded to decree, "Hey, quiet on the set!" She looked around, saw all her subjects were ready, and then gave the old man a nod. "You may proceed."

"Yes, ma'am," he said, laughing and frowning at the same time. "Now, where was I, page turner?" He looked at his invisible page turner, Thomas, waiting on a reply.

"Uh, Harry was in the tunnel."

Another voice interrupted, "And he got stuck!"

"No, he didn't get stuck! He found a dusty old skeleton that got stuck!" another intolerant ankle biter corrected with the fervency of a stringent reverend explaining liturgy.

"I was getting there!" Thomas barked back.

"Oh yes," the old man interrupted the potential torrent. "Oh yes… Harry had found a ring and something about it had greatly surprised him."

"Hold it! Hold it!" Sarah interrupted.

The old man groaned, looked desperately around the room for her grandfather, the fire marshal who had suddenly and conveniently felt inclined to visit the restroom and was nowhere to be found. So he rolled his eyes, looked back at his nemesis, and said, "What is it? Do you want me to tell this story, or are you going to tell it?"

"Well, I talked to my grandmother about it, and she said…"

"Wait… You talked to your grandmother?"

"Yes."

The old man backpedaled. He was about to ask why she didn't talk to her mother when it dawned on him. She was with her grandfather and talked to her grandmother, therefore, no mom and no dad around. *So, I do not need to ask the question that was about to pop out of my mouth,* he thought, stopped in mid-syllable, and simply said, "Okay.

"What, my dear, did your grandmother say that is worth delaying the beginning of this part of the story a moment longer?!" The scowl in his voice dripped like perspiration off a bricklayer's brow.

Sarah, impervious to the glower, continued on her imperial way. "She wants to know what is going on with Princess Sarah."

"What do you mean 'going on'? She has been captured by the dragon, and Harry is trying to figure out how to rescue her. So, what else is there?"

"She wants to know where she is being kept: How she is feeling? Has the dragon hurt her? Is she sick? Is she losing hope? Has she dreamed anymore about Harry?"

"Wow!" the old man said, impressed. "You sure that was all your grandmother?"

The snaggle-toothed smile beamed, and her head nodded. "Some of it anyway."

The old man's eyebrows rose in wry salute, and he sighed, "This story has taken on a life of its own." And then he thought, *And why shouldn't it; I am living it out even now.*

"Okay, okay… we will leave Harry the Brave gasping and staring at the ring and go to the other side of the cavern and check in on Princess Sarah. Is that okay with everyone?" He didn't expect to be taking a vote, but the literalness of his audience and their assumption that he was actually asking them surprised him.

"No-no."

"Uh-uh."

"Yes."

"Nope."

"Ah…"

And then, "Hey! We are going to check on the princess," rang from the frowning tyrant of story time, and everyone settled down. "Now proceed, please," she said as she sat down in the child-sized chair on the front row.

"Princess Sarah," the old man continued, staring down at his beaming darling on the front row, "was huddled around a sad little fire in the back of the dragon's lair. She was chained to a large pole that gave her very little room to move around. The dragon would bring her bits of burnt meat occasionally, and she could only hope it was a cow or a sheep and not someone she knew."

"Oh, gross!"

"Yuck!"

"No way!" his crowd echoed, but he kept on speaking.

"She was always cold and shivering, and her clothes were tattered, captive now for months. Every time someone had tried to rescue her, whether it was an individual knight or a whole army of knights, they'd failed.

"And the dragon, who was quite the conversationalist, would come and tell her all about how he had destroyed them and burned them into tiny bits of broken ash. She hated the dragon's visits but had begun to hate her solitude even more." Seeing the questions pop up in the expressions of the children, the old man added, "Solitude means loneliness, okay?

"So, the princess had started listening to the dragon's lies because she had no one else to talk to and was all alone in the dark cave huddled around a small fire. What she didn't realize was every time she spoke with the dragon, its poison seeped a little deeper into her heart and her thoughts, and bit by bit, she was starting to think more like the dragon. The only time she felt different was when she slept and Harry visited her in her dreams. One of those nights, as she lay her head down on the hard rock that was her pillow, she prayed, 'Oh Lord, help me. Don't let my heart grow cold and my mind grow hard. Give me strength to resist the words of the dragon. But, Lord, help me quick because I am growing weak.'

"That night she dreamt. In that dream she was in her cave still chained to the pole, still huddled next to the sad little fire, when she heard her name, 'Princess Sarah! Princess Sarah!'

"She looked up, stood up, and there he was, the young man who had saved the market from the wild pig. 'You're here,' she said softly.

"'I think we are both in a dream, but I am as much here as I can be,' Harry answered.

"'Have you come to get me out?' she pleaded.

"'I am trying, Princess. I am in the caverns of the dragon. I don't know how to find you, but I am not going to give up.'

"She looked down at her feet and said, 'So many have tried before and they have all died.'

"Harry thought a moment, then answered, 'Princess, have any of them appeared to you in a dream?'

"She frowned and shook her head. 'No, none of them ever appeared to me in a dream, but you have. Surely that means something!' Hope blossomed in her heart.

"Harry kept staring at her, occasionally blinking. She looked back at him and asked, 'Harry, is there something wrong?'

"He shook his head, then said, 'Something is different about you.'

"'What do you mean? Am I acting differently, talking differently?'

"'No, you look different. Your face is leaner and harder. Your complexion is darker.' He paused a moment, sighed, and said, 'But this is a dream, and I can't expect a dream to get all the details right. I am looking at you through the lens of my own heart and I only met you once.'

"About that time Harry heard a terrible growl and roar. He moved toward the princess and held her behind him to protect her."

"It's the dragon, isn't it?" the red-haired boy asked fearfully.

"The dragon found them, didn't it?" another little girl in a pretty sundress asked.

The old man looked around the room, noticed that his favorite little nagahina was staring wide-eyed into space, brushed over the sight, and quickly responded, "Yes, the dragon had entered their dream, and he was raging against them.

"Harry bravely stood between the princess and the dragon. The dragon towered over him and screamed. Foul breath reeking of rotten food and dead things blasted them. Harry did not flinch. He only wished he had a sword or shield.

"'You cannot have her!' the dragon roared.

"Then it occurred to Harry he was in a dream, and he had as much power in that dream as he wanted to have. So, he railed back at the dragon…" The old man saw questions arise in his young audience and quickly switched to dictionary form, "To rail means to be angry in your response. Harry was mad at the dragon and let him know it. 'Neither can you, you old serpent. You are going to die if you don't leave her be!'

"The dragon answered by spewing flames. They burst around Harry. Suddenly he bolted upright, fully awake. He looked around. He was still in the tunnel, still huddled close to the old knight's skeleton, and still had no idea how, or even if, he could rescue the princess. Then he heard the faraway roar of a very angry dragon."

"But what about the ring?" several of the children asked. "Remember, Harry found a ring, and he was amazed, and then you switched over to the princess and her dream and..."

The old man grunted, scowling, then asked, "Whose story is this?"

Without hesitation the whole room echoed back, "Ours!"

A deep sigh surrendered from his lips. He was owned, and he could do nothing about it, so he pulled the switch and, rather than suffer derailment, simply altered the tracks, and said, "You are right." The room lit up with tooth-gapped smiles and sparkling eyes. "But my dears, who is *telling* the story? Hmm?"

The puppies quieted and looked a bit sheepish, all, of course, except the indomitable queen of story time, Sarah, who simply scowled. The old man looked at her a moment, saw schemes of mischief brewing, and wisely decided to move on before they matured.

"Yes, I know. The question you are all wondering is what happened with the ring? That is where we are. So, let's go back before Harry visits the princess in the dream. Remember, he had just discovered the ring and was stunned. As he cleaned the dirt off and studied the ring, he could not believe what he was seeing. He rubbed the ring, looked closely at it, shook his head, and then looked again. *He knew that ring,* or at least he had seen a ring an awful lot like it. It looked like the ring his father wore, which had been handed down through the generations to every first-born child of his family. The ring was old. It had patina— that is a stain from age; only old, old things have it, and usually only old metal things, okay?" His puppies nodded in chorus, and he continued, "The whole ring was shaped like a boar's head complete with tusks that protruded—that means stuck out a little bit, in this case like tiny bumps— except... one of those tusks was broken off. The tip was broken, and it had been that way for a while because the break was almost smooth."

His pet nagahina looked puzzled, rubbed her chin, and then, in spite of her best intentions, abruptly raised her hand and declared, "Harry tamed the boar hog. His family had wild hogs on its ring. Did everybody in his family for a long, long time know how to capture wild hogs?"

The old man looked at her and smirked, then hid the answer behind his eyes, and said, "I don't know," and tried to go on with the story.

"Hmmmph!" she grunted. "Something is going on here. I can feel it."

The old man stared down at her. She sat with one knee up where her elbow rested. Her fist ended under her chin, and she was leaning on it in a way that would have made a French sculptor proud. The old man listened, barely able to keep from snickering as she talked to herself, "Something *is* going on here."

The rest of the children were not privy to the interchange and were in danger of growing restless. With this threat looming, the old man quickly continued with the story.

"Harry looked at the ring carefully, then shrugged his shoulders and stuck it in his pocket. The ring was a mystery, but one he didn't have time to dwell on. He had to move forward, and that meant moving the old skeleton out of the way so he could continue moving down the tunnel. With as much respect as he could muster, Harry gently grasped the skeleton by its dusty chest piece and, with both hands, picked up on it. The skeleton broke in half."

"Ewww!"

"Gross!"

"Did the bones crack and tumble out?"

"Was it loud?"

"Did dust get in his eyes? I saw a movie once where dust from old things like that caused people to get sick."

"No, no. He was more embarrassed than frightened. He didn't know who the skeleton was, but he knew it must have been somebody great and ancient, who fought for good and apparently lost. So, when the skeleton fell apart, his first response was to apologize, but then he realized whoever the skeleton had been, they were no longer there and couldn't  hear him. So, he just picked up the rest of the bones and gently moved them out of his way. But as he did, he spied something shiny, something he had not seen during his first observations of the bones. The shiny object was round, similar to a coin but larger, and it had a blue tint to it. Etched on one side of the disc were three lines. Each line moved out at an angle with the center line being straight up and down. At the top of each line there was a small dot. So, three small dots and three lines. Can you see that in your imagination, or do I need to draw it and hand it around?"

"Draw it! Draw it!" the small mob of screeching children cried.

The old man smiled, stroked his chin, and said, "No."

"What?" they all bellowed. "What do you mean 'no'? Ah… come on, show us what it looks like! Pleeeeease?" they begged in shrill voices.

The old man stood firm. He had an objective in mind. "No, my dear ones, I won't show you. Instead, I want you to show me!" And with that, his perceptive daughter quickly handed out paper and crayons. The old man continued, "I will describe the disc to you again. You then must draw it and color it to the best of your ability. Most of your pictures will look very much alike, and that is fine. But listen close, then draw and color it, and we will see who sees the most and listens well. Now get to it." With that, a tornado of activity began with squeaks and squawks and bellows and whines commencing in their normal course. "Okay, now are you ready to listen while I describe it again?"

"Yes!" they echoed. There was, of course, the humbug or two who declined to play, but then the old man bribed them with more story and candy corn left over from last Halloween, and most fell in line, except Thomas, who wasn't allowed to eat candy corn. Sarah saw the poor boy's dilemma, walked over to him, and whispered something in his ear. His immediate smile threatened to break his freckled face, and he nodded fiercely.

Sarah walked back to her place at the small table, which was now full of intricate disc designs, and began to draw. The old man, having seen the whole affair, quietly walked over to the little sovereign and whispered, "Sarah… what did you just tell Thomas?"

She beamed in triumph and innocently cupped her hands around her mouth, bent over to the old man's ear, and in a barnyard whisper said, "I told him he didn't have to chew."

"What?!" the old man asked, puzzled.

She continued her virtuous pronouncement and again whispered, "I told him he didn't have to chew the candy corn. His mama insists that he has to chew all his food so many times, and that if it is in his mouth, and it is food, it must be chewed before it can be swallowed. So, I just told him not to chew and let it dissolve. If it's not chewed, it's not food; therefore, he is not eating it, right?" Her naïvely sweet expression reminded the old man of a baby cobra he had once seen devour a mouse. The serpent just figured that is what you did with mice. And apparently, Sarah thought, in her savant and shrewd manner, this is how you got around parents.

Amused, he shook his head, about to leave the little monarch to her own devices when he noticed what she had drawn. On the paper before him was a rendering of the small coin-like disc, only it was the side of the disc he *had not* described! His mouth gaped open as he looked at the little artist. At first, words wouldn't come; then he coughed, cleared his throat, and spat them out, "How did you know this?"

"What do you mean?"

The old man shuddered as his trembling hands snatched up the drawing and held it to the light. He blinked and looked back at Sarah, stunned.

"Sarah, this is a picture of *the other side of the coin*, and I haven't described it yet! But you drew it! How did you know what it looked like?"

The little girl looked back at the old man and meekly asked, "You didn't tell us what it looked like?"

"No, Honey, I did not," he bent down and spoke in a quiet voice, but not a whisper because he knew whispers attracted curious ears, while a normal, though quieter, conversation would just blend into the ordinary buzz of the room.

The little girl blinked and tilted her head in puppy fashion. "But I saw it as soon as you described it. You talked about the lines with the three dots, and then you talked about this side," she insisted, pointing toward her drawing.

"I am sorry, honey, but I did not. I really did not describe it, but here it is."

The old man looked closely. It featured a simple, child-scrawled drawing of a triangle inside a circle with a blue center. The old man almost expected to see the words *runā tikai patiesību*, or in English *speak only truth*, in the center of the circle. They were not there. He knew those words were on the flip side of the disc, but how did a six-year-old child know to draw the symbol?

After assessing the drawing, he moved around the room to see if other children had also drawn the back side of the disc. He carefully scanned their efforts and did not find any that remotely resembled what Sarah had drawn. He kept shaking his head, and his daughter, who had been overseeing the whole pictorial extravaganza, noticed his bewilderment and whispered, "Dad, I don't know what is going on, but I better move this forward." And then in a normal voice, "Okay, Dad, are you ready to look at what these young artists have drawn?"

The old man looked at his daughter, shook his head, and said, "No." He whispered, "I am not feeling well all of a sudden, Roo. Can you bail me out here?"

His daughter walked closer to him and placed a gentle hand on his arm. "Daddy, are you okay? Do you need to go to the hospital?"

Her question shook him from his trance and he said, "No, it's not like that, honey. It's just I don't feel well, and I need to go home and lie down. I'll call you later." With that, he left the building, got in his truck, and drove off.

Chapter Six

The old man screeched into his driveway, slammed on the brakes, and clambered out of his truck before the engine had quit sputtering. By the time the ancient machine backfired in protest, he was halfway to the front door. He jammed the key into the lock and stopped. *What am I doing? What can I do about it? What just happened? How did she see the back of the disc?* Those and a hundred other thoughts like them fought over the limited space in his soul. *And what do I do now?* His heart raced against his tired old chest, and he thought, *Well, whatever I do, I better sit on it, otherwise I'm liable to stroke out.*

He walked over to the threadbare couch, a holdover from a thrift store sale, and plopped down. He took several deep breaths trying to calm himself. It half worked. His mind kept racing, but his lungs decided to keep up with it.

So, what is going on here? His heart argued logic into a corner and held it there. *Truth is, I don't know.*

"Liar," he countered.

I am not lying, I just can't be. Not like this. He snorted, laughing at himself. "I'm talking to myself again. Old people do that. I guess that means I'm old. But what now?" The old man just sat there tossing and turning questions over and over in his mind, then finally slipped down into the soft couch and slept.

***

Back at the library

As the door closed behind the old man, most of the children at story time were busy with their drawings. The old man's daughter was a master of adaptation and had, with her father's sudden departure, been forced to move the children to another activity. Lizzy did not notice that Sarah, whose eyes had followed the old man out the door, had become very quiet and withdrawn.

Once the old man left, Sarah ran to the window that looked out onto the parking lot and watched as he climbed into his worn-out old truck and drove away. Sarah was about to move back to her place at the table when a movement outside caught her attention. Drawing closer to the dusty window, she placed her two small hands on the glass and stared wide-eyed. At the end of the parking lot, shadowed by trees, stood a tall man dressed in black, wearing a clerical collar. Sarah watched as this man's eyes followed the old man and watched him as he pulled out of the parking lot. Slowly, he turned toward her and sneered a cold smile that could not hide his cruel eyes. Sarah moved back as the man began to walk up the steps and into the library. She quickly took her place at the table and pretended to draw. She was afraid to look up but listened closely as the old man's daughter greeted the tall reverend.

"Good morning, Reverend Long. I suppose you have come to pick up your grandson, Thomas?"

"Yes, is he prepared? It is time, and he should be punctual."

"I am sure he is," the librarian responded. "Thomas, your grandfather is here. Are you ready to go?"

Thomas, the old man's invisible page turner, gulped, quickly chewed, and swallowed the candy corn he had been too impatient to let dissolve. Sarah, who had been seated across from Thomas, looked up just in time to see his face pale and his hands tremble. The young boy absently slid his hands down his side, quickly wiping the accumulated sweat off his palms, and turned to greet the stern form of his grandfather. He bowed his head, almost shrinking in size, as he turned to meet the towering cleric. He need not have bothered. The Right Most Reverend Laden Long was focused on Sarah.

"And just who is this little lamb, Thomas?" he asked as he leaned his dark, goateed face over the table.

"My name is Sarah, and I am not a lamb. I am a lioness. Would you like to see my picture?" Before the menacing cleric could answer, Sarah shoved her drawing of the disc in his face. "Do you like it?"

Reverend Laden Long's piercing grey eyes widened, and his thin lips instinctively began to snarl before he quickly covered the expression with stone-cold features. He continued to glare at the child's scribble, then down at her innocent face. He backed up and grabbed Thomas by his frail shoulders. The man's eyes narrowed, and his teeth gritted. He stared down at Sarah and whispered, "Very good, little girl. Such a nice picture. Such a shame it won't be finished." And with that he cast a hard glance at her and shoved his pale grandson forward.

Sarah, who had stood up, now collapsed back into her little chair and watched with sad eyes as they left the library. *Poor Thomas,* she thought and then turned back to coloring her picture.

***

Next library day

The old man hadn't wanted to get up. His eyes fluttered open at five thirty a.m. after sleep had eluded him most of the night. A sense of restless, dark dreams that wouldn't stay long enough to be remembered bothered him, and he wondered if that wasn't a good thing. He watched the clock as he sat in his kitchen drinking coffee, wondering if he should keep telling the story at story time. He didn't know what to say to his daughter. He even wondered if he was sane. Was life so tedious and boring? Had it become so tiresome and predictable that he had lost his mind? From all he had ever heard, some people never realized they were mentally ill, and one of the primary symptoms was that they thought their grand illusions were real. Perhaps that is what this was, and now, for the first time, he was getting a glimpse of the real world and starting to see his imagination had deceived him.

He had about decided this was true when he realized if it were true, and he had just imagined the story, little Sarah would not have known how to draw the symbol. This realization blew through his nicely arranged admission of delusion like a whirlwind through a junkyard. He had all the parts, and they had to have come from somewhere. They just didn't suddenly one day appear. So, what now? The clock on the wall continued to tick louder as the time drew closer. The quietness of the house haunted him, driving him forward step by step. The conclusion was coming; the story had to end, but how? He shrugged, took a deep breath, picked his keys off the table, and walked out the door.

As the old man pulled into his favored parking spot, he noticed that just like always, the lot was full and people were waiting. He looked at the large bay window expecting to see it lined with little faces and was not disappointed. His eyes softened as he climbed out of the truck and saw the children waving at him. He was half expecting them to run down the sidewalk and was a little surprised when they didn't. *I bet my daughter has them corralled today,* he thought as he opened the large, matching double doors into the foyer of the old house that was now a library. He heard the typical chaos of loud shouts and cries and laughter and chatter that marked this library as being alive with children, and not the sterile silence of stodgy, elderly women searching out genealogies. His eyes searched the room, glancing quickly around it, scouting. He was looking for his little nemesis, the psychic little princess, who had read his mind and blown it away with her amazing scribbles, when he saw his daughter's smiling face and lithe form walk toward him. He noticed she had started to get a few grey hairs, but on her, it was beautiful.

Looking him over, she asked, "Are you ready for story time, Dad?"

He smiled and replied, "As ready as I will ever be. Is everyone here?" What he really meant was: *Where is the holy terror that I've grown so fond of?*

"Everyone but Sarah," his daughter answered quickly, "but we can't wait on her. I am surprised though. Usually her grandfather brings her by early, and she is one of the first ones here. I am sure he would have called if something were wrong."

As soon as he heard Sarah wasn't there, the old man's heart sunk. He couldn't explain it, but it was like a dark cloud moved in and hovered close. As the seconds raced by, and he walked into the story room, foreboding hung heavy like a stale, thick blanket. A grey fog was circling, swirling; he didn't know how to deal with it. It was like grief but stealthy, an awareness of something being stolen, apprehension standing just far enough away to be felt, but not close enough to examine.

One of the children moved up front to sit where Sarah usually sat. The old man frowned but didn't say anything. He didn't have to because the red-haired boy with the persistently blue lips—didn't his mother ever feed that child anything but lollipops for breakfast? Good thing his father was a dentist—yelled, "Hey, that is Sarah's seat. You can't sit there!"

The wayfaring seat-snatcher was about to reply when he looked up and saw the front door open. Sarah's grandfather was walking through it holding her by the hand. A welcoming torrent of "Hey Sarah!" threatened to blow both her and her grandfather back out the door. Sarah smiled, then let go of her grandfather's hand and ran toward the old man. He was seated in his usual rocker and had bent forward to see who was walking through the front door. When his eyes lit on the little urchin, he sighed, and when she came running toward him, he caught her up in a big hug. He didn't understand why he was so relieved until she pressed her lips against his ear and said, "The dragon came for me, and then it got Thomas."

The old man carefully put her on the ground and looked down at her. His Adam's apple bobbed, and in a wavering voice he asked, "What? What did you say?"

Sarah looked around at all the children trying to settle back in, to her grandfather, and then back at the old man. "Oh nothing, I just had a bad night. A lot of bad dreams. I'm okay now, right, Grandpa?"

She looked up at the tired face of the grey-haired fire marshal. His back was military straight, but his shoulders stooped with the relentless burdens of time. A brief smile hurried across his face. His eyes had dark rings under them. Peering over the top of his Walmart readers, he put his finger on his nose and said, "I sure hope so, honey, because last night was a booger!" He leaned into the old man, who had risen to greet him, and took his hand. "She is okay now, but last night was scary. She screamed and cried and yelled. I couldn't make out the words. It seemed to go on for hours, so when she finally settled down, we let her sleep late. That is why we are coming in now rather than our usual time. Still, she insisted on being here today, said she had to hear the story. By the way, I am Kenneth Linscomb, Sarah's grandfather."

"Good to officially meet you, Kenneth. I am Hank Ferguson."

"You have quite a gift, old man. Now get these kids happy, and I'll treat you to lunch today. Deal?"

"Sounds good to me, sir. I will do my best." With that he turned back to the children, noticing that his rug-rat queen had taken her rightful place. He began to tell the story, but not before taking a hard look at Sarah's eyes, which were red and puffy, and her face swollen. It had been a bad night. He also noticed that his invisible book page turner was nowhere to be found.

That's disturbing, he thought as he shuffled into place and pretended to be opening the great invisible book. "Hey, has anyone seen Thomas? Or know where he is?"

The typical echo of voices replied, "No."

"Nope."

"No, sir."

"I haven't seen him."

"His mom didn't drop him off."

The old man looked at his daughter to see if she had heard any different but only got an I-don't-know-where-he-is shrug. So, not wanting to have to settle everyone down again, the old man looked at his favored little naglet and said, "Madam, would you like to assist me?"

Sarah smiled a weary smile and said, "No, sir, not today. I just want to sit here and re-coop-my-rate..."

"What?" The young woman seated by Sarah looked puzzled. "What do you mean 're-coop-my-rate'... is that two words or one?"

Sarah was grumpy and said, "Why four, of course. It's Re Coop My Rate. It means rest and feel better, right?"

The old man shook his head, amazed at the adaptable imagination of children, and asked another young crayon-gobbler to come and turn the invisible pages.

"Now where…" he tried to begin and was answered by a dozen shrill voices, each with a different version of where he had left off. "Hmmm," he growled in a low tone to get everyone's attention. "Maybe I should review things a bit…

"Harry is in a cave. He wants to rescue the princess, but the only way he can talk to her is through his dreams."

"People can't talk through dreams," one of the slightly older children declared to his younger sibling in a sarcastic I-know-better-than-that tone.

The old man was about to let it pass when the weary queen of story time rose to her duty and declared, "Oh yes they can! I did it all night. Now shut up and let the man talk!"

"It's okay. It's really okay… This is just a story." He looked at the scolded children and the sullen little scolder who silently mouthed back at him, *No, it's not!*

His eyes widened, and he knew he was going to have to have a talk with that young woman, but not yet. Now he had a story to tell. He continued on, pushing through, "Harry had discovered a ring that was shaped like a boar's head and a large coin-shaped disc. Both seemed to be very, very old. He stuffed them in his pocket, picked up his torch, and walked down the tunnel into the darkness. It had started to get cold, and the cave was very wet. He didn't really know where he was going or what waited for him. A subconscious whisper reminded him that the last time he heard the dragon scream, it was coming from the direction he was now walking.

"Harry held his small torch in front of him and eased down the dark tunnel. A fleeting thought struck him, *If this torch goes out, I will be in absolute darkness with no hope of getting out of here.* Panic threatened to paralyze him, but then he thought, *If I don't go forward, the princess will be trapped in darkness forever.* So, he pulled up his sagging pants, tucked his cowardly heart in them, stuck out his chin, and fell forward into a hole in the tunnel floor. He screamed and thought he heard a laugh but was too frightened to concentrate, as the hole became a slide of small rocks and hard bumps. His feet acted as brakes, and his rear end anchored him from tumbling head over heels out of control. He only fell a few yards and even managed to keep the torch lit, but he was cut and bruised and sore and angry. He stood up in the pile of gravel he had brought with him dusted off the small pieces of rock covering his clothes and embedded in his arms. As he reached around back to brush off his pants, he discovered a huge hole where his britches' bottom used to be."

A stream of giggles and snorts reminded the old man to be careful. He had a room full of impressionable kindergarteners and didn't want to focus them too much on a bare-tailed warrior, so he quickly added, "And was glad his mother couldn't see him now. She would complain about how he was always ripping up his clothes, that they didn't grow on trees, and couldn't he be more careful."

A small voice replied, "Isn't that the truth? I wonder if his mom was kin to mine!"

"That sounds just like my mom too: 'Take off your shoes. Don't bring in dirt,'" another little pigpen echoed, mimicking his mother's squeaky nasal tone.

"Anywaaay…" the old man growled, forcing down his own temptation to comment on the nature of mothers, and increased his voice volume for just a moment till things quieted. "Those thoughts quickly vanished as Harry finally noticed where he had landed. He looked around, stilled by what he saw. He blinked wildly for a few seconds and backed up, actually falling on the rock pile he had just slid down. He finally stood up and held his torch in front of him as high as he could. The dim torch light reflected off small pieces of crystal that lined the cavern walls. In front of him Harry saw a huge cavern, and on the floor of this room lay a very large pile of…"

"Gold!"

"Human bones?!"

"Treasure?"

The brigade of story-riveted children, who ate boogers like adults ate popcorn, stood wild-eyed, shouting out guesses.

The old man laughed and answered calmly, facing each one and each guess. "No, it wasn't gold."

"Hmmph."

"No, it wasn't human bones."

"Are you sure?"

"Yes, I'm positive," the old man answered quickly, then added, "and it wasn't treasure."

"It has to be treasure!" a little girl on the back row insisted. "Because everyone knows that a dragon has treasure."

"You're right, he does, but it's not in this room. Anybody else?"

Sarah slowly raised her hand.

The old man looked at her. Suddenly the air around him grew icy cold, raising the hair on his neck. He gulped and then goaded the little girl's name out of his mouth. "Sarah," he finally squeezed from his lips.

"They were dragon bones, piles and piles of dragon bones."

The old man sucked in air, forgot to let it go for a moment, then exhaled in a long, slow breath. "Yes, they were." He knew immediately he had to cover the revelation from the rest of the unwary children who would be quick to ask the wrong questions and repeat the wrong answers. He didn't understand what was going on but was absolutely certain he had to hide it.

He realized that his body language clearly hinted at something troubling him, and the children might be little, but they were extremely perceptive, so he was going to have to do something quickly, unexpected, and that would misdirect the kids' attention, but Sarah beat him to it.

She stood up and started laughing. Everybody looked at her and grinned but were also a bit puzzled.

"What ya doing, Sarah?"

"What's so funny, Sarah?"

"How come you're laughing?"

"I finally figured it out!" she giggled. "This story is from the Cartoon Program Association. I saw it several weeks ago at my grandfather's. You guys didn't see it?"

The children said, "No, we didn't know it was on TV."

"Ahh, that's not right," a disappointed little munchkin complained.

"No fun. We thought this was a real story."

The old man was relieved and also caught between a rock and a hard place. He didn't want to lie to the children, but sometimes a white lie in the right place covered a dark truth in a bad place. So he started laughing too.

"Yep, Sarah's got me. This is an old, old story, and it didn't start with me. It is actually in more than one place in cartoons and books and movies. I'm surprised it took you this long to figure it out. I've just changed some things around to make it interesting. I hope that doesn't disappoint you?"

"Nah, no," an obviously disappointed child whispered compliantly.

"Uh…"

"We like the story," Sarah commanded, gathering her childish comrades' disappointment and kicking it down the hall.

She looked back at the old man and hid behind her six-year-old countenance. She didn't give him time to think, but did give him permission, "Carry on, please."

Without skipping more than a couple of heartbeats, the old man resumed, "All around Harry, and as far as his torch light reached, were piles and piles of huge dragon bones. Some were large enough that he could easily walk through them. Others were smaller but still larger than a cow. He was confused and unsure of what to think about this dragon graveyard. A hundred questions ran through his mind and out just as quick.

"Finally, after a few minutes of walking among them, he sat down on a large boulder and thought, *Some of these are ancient. They have almost turned to stone; others, not so much. A few even have bits and pieces of armor and great golden decorative harnesses around their heads.* In the process of looking, he also found better torches attached to the cave walls. After a little experimentation, he found they still worked. They were much larger and cast much better light than the small torch he had been carrying.

"Harry walked around the old dragon bones, taking note of everything he saw, looking close at the great bands of gold and silver that wrapped around the legs and arms of the dry skeletons. Finally, he got to the very center of the graveyard. He noticed the bones were actually laid out in lines and squares like a human cemetery might be, only they had no caskets and were not buried. All the lanes among the bones seemed to lead to a center aisle, kind of like a grocery store leads to the cashiers, you understand?"

They all nodded expectantly, waiting to hear what happened next.

"He followed the lanes, which ended in front of a huge dragon skeleton that had literally turned to stone. It must have been the oldest skeleton in the dragon graveyard. He looked at it closely and noticed on top and at the back of the skull was another skeleton, a smaller one, a human one! He had to climb on top of the skeleton to get to it, but did so quickly, like climbing a small hill. Finally, Harry stood atop the huge dragon bones and looked down on the skeleton of an ancient knight. The armor on this one was far older than the first skeleton he had found in the tunnel. It had the tattered remains of a banner wrapped around it and a leather pouch at its side. It also had a sword in its hand, and as he examined it closer, he saw it also had a ring on its finger, the same kind of ring that he had found on the first knight's skeleton, his own family ring.

"He gently picked up the sword that the ancient knight had sheathed on his side. The sword was lighter than any Harry had ever held. When he picked it up, it seemed to cast a pale blue light, and the longer he held it, the brighter the light grew. This scared him. He wanted to put the sword down but was afraid to, and he didn't want to hold it because it was glowing blue. He finally decided to put it back in the sheath of the old knight, but when he tried, it kept sticking and wouldn't fit in it. So finally, he gingerly unhooked the sheath from the knight and pried open the sheath's end with his fingers so he could get the sword to go in. It slid all the way in except for the last bit, so holding the sheath tightly with one hand, Harry tried to ram the sword the rest of the way. He strained as hard as he could and pushed with all his might. The sheath gave; the sword slipped and, in the process, cut him right across his index finger. Harry dropped the sword and yelled, which echoed through the cavern. He immediately stopped screaming and cringed."

Three hands went up. The old man stopped, and they whispered, "What's cringed mean?"

"Oh… it means, ah…" The old man thought, *How do I explain cringe?* Then it hit him. "Okay, has anyone in here ever gotten a spanking?" That question brought the house down.

"Of course we have."

"Nope"—then laughter—"but I should have!"

"Yes, lots of times."

"Most of the time it's my brother. I do something bad, blame it on him, and…"

"Okay, okay. You get my point. And for those of you who have never gotten a spanking, you have my deepest sympathy. But the point is, right before your parents spatted you across your little rears, you tensed up."

"Oh yeah! That's when I start screaming like I'm on fire. My mom starts hollering, and my dad leaves the room with my brothers, laughing."

"Okay, let me try that again. Have you ever had someone throw you a baseball or a football, and you're afraid to catch the ball, so you close your eyes and get hit?"

A little girl sitting by Princess Sarah sheepishly nodded her head. "Yeah, it hurt too."

"Well that, my dears, is cringing. It means you get ready to get hit.

"Harry was afraid his scream would bring the dragon down upon him. He jumped off the great dragon's bones, looked quickly around him, and ran down the lane. Suddenly, as he drew near, he saw another small path through the dragon graveyard veer away from the main path. He had the strong impression he should run that way, so he did. And then the paths split again, and he felt like he should take the one on his left. He took it, and soon he was out of the ancient dragon graveyard and back in the narrow tunnel of the cave. He stopped panting like one of his great big wolf-shepherds back home. His breath finally eased as he listened. He closed his eyes, focused all his attention on listening, and then jumped as a thunderous roar of the dragon shook the cavern and echoed throughout. Then Harry heard the heavy steam-engine puffing of the dragon and felt the air around him turn hot. The flames could not get to him, but the dragon had followed his scent and pushed its huge snout right up against the tunnel as far as it could and was now spraying dragon flame. Thankfully, Harry had run a long way down the tunnel, which turned this way then that and back again, but just to be safe, he kept moving until the air in the cave tunnel became cool again. He could still hear the dragon's angry roars and steam-engine spray, but he was safe. It could not touch him. He sat there a moment, and then it occurred to him. *How had he known which way to run?* Just as he was wondering how he could have known, he heard a voice in his head. It said, *'I told you.'*

"Harry laughed and thought, *Great, now I am talking to myself, asking questions, and giving answers.*

"*'No, you're not. I told you,'* the voice repeated.

"'No, I told myself, and that is all there is to it,' Harry said out loud. 'I told myself!' he repeated stubbornly.

"*'Okay, fine,'* the voice said. *'Be that way if you want to, but one question… if you told yourself, how did you know which way to go?'*

"Harry stood up, holding the torch, preparing to move down the cave tunnel, but when he heard the voice ask, *'How did you know which way to go?'* he slowly slid down the damp cave wall, drew his legs up, wrapped his arms around them, and started to shake.

'Now, now. There is nothing to be afraid of… I don't want to hurt you, and I can't hurt you, and why would I want to hurt my new partner?'

"Harry didn't answer but just sat there, still shivering.

"The voice continued in his head, *'Harry? You still there? I asked you a question. Please be courteous enough to answer me. Harry?'*

"Harry wanted to run down the tunnel screaming like a pack of blithering monkeys being chased by an angry mom for stealing her homemade chocolate fudge."

"Oh man!" a little boy with a pudgy face and a guilty look shouted. "That is scary!"

The old man laughed in spite of himself, then hid it behind a series of loud make-believe coughs that wouldn't have fooled anybody over six. He was about to ask, *Does anyone know where the voice came from or what it is?* when he looked at Sarah, who sat, eyes closed, with a single tear running down her cheek, trickling into a quiet smile. She woke from the trance, wiped her face with the back of her hand, cocked her head, and whispered, "Keep going, please."

"The voice continued persistently to encourage Harry, *'Harry, you are not going mad. It's okay. I am a friend, or at least, I would like to be. Talk to me.'*

"Finally, Harry, realizing he couldn't get away or shake his head hard enough to make the calm voice stop, answered, 'Who are you?'

"*'There you are. I thought you might have run away so far back into your mind I would never coax you out. As to your question, Harry, do you remember what made you scream?'*

"'Yeah, my hand is still bleeding and stings.'

"*'Yeah, about that. I am sorry to have to cut you, but there was no other way.'*

"'Ah, excuse me? What do you mean "no other way"? No other way to do what?'

"*Well, the sword that cut you… it has a soul, so to speak. Apparently, it kind of came alive through the centuries. When a human's blood touches it without violence, and that human has a good and kind heart, and is on a quest—just like you are—that sword talks to it. Harry, I am that sword!*'

"'No way,' Harry sighed heavily. 'No way. I am talking to my own crazy head, and it's telling me it's a sword… No way…'

"*Yes, Harry, it is true. I speak, and I can help you find the princess, and kill the evil dragon, and get you home.*'

"'No way.'

"*Harry, it's true.*'

"'I'm dreaming.'

"*Nope, I'm here.*'

"Harry silently stared into space for a few moments. He felt helpless to do anything, so he just sat there wishing it would all go away, that he would wake up in his father's house, in his own bed, facing a day of chores.

"'Wait a minute!' Harry shouted to the darkness. 'Now I know you're not the sword. Because you told me you can help me rescue the princess. Well, only I know what I am doing, and I didn't tell you! So how would you know?'

"*'Good grief, Harry! I am in your head, and by the way, you have a lot of empty space up here. You really should use it more often… but to answer your question… agaaaain… I can see your memories and hear your thoughts. It is kind of like being in a library, reading all the old books and looking at the newest ones. Your newly written thoughts are telling me you are here to kill the dragon and rescue the princess, and of course, get home. You believe me now?*'

"'I'm starting to. Maybe a little, but if you are a soul, do you have a name? How did you get to be where you were, and…'

"'One at a time, son, one at a time. My name has changed through the years. It's kind of grown. At first, I was only dimly aware I was even alive. I do not know how many years passed before I started to understand some things. It is like I took on the nature, the personality, of the people who forged me, and fought with me, and carried me. Every time they fought with me and won victories against terrible things, I took on a part of the very, very intense emotions they carried. Those feelings just stuck to me, gathered in me, and then, one day, started living. The last time I was used, I was broken. It was a fierce battle against a terrible, terrible dragon. And by the way, Harry, not all dragons, just like not all people, are bad. There are some very good dragons, some wonderful dragons, and they loved the knights who fought with them and rode them into battle. But back to your question… my name is Ræðumaður. Ray-oum-aour. In your language it simply means Speaker. *I am the sword that speaks. So, I am called* Speaker.'

"Harry laughed, 'This is really good. Either I am totally mad, driven insane by the darkness, my fear, and the dragon, or I have really and truly picked up an invisible friend that lives in my head named Ray.'

"Hey! That is *my* name!" the little pudgy boy, who felt guilty about eating his mother's fudge, shouted. "The sword is named after me!"

"Apparently so," replied the old man. "Now, do you want me to keep going, or are we done for the day?"

"No, no! Keep going!" the mesmerized pack of domesticated small people yelled as one.

"Okay, okay, but we don't have much longer.

"Harry was laughing and said, 'My invisible friend's name is Ray,'" the old man continued. "The stress and fear had driven Harry to the brink of madness, and now he looked over the dark edge and just laughed. It was all he knew to do. He laughed and laughed, and then, finally exhausted, he leaned back against the cave wall and slept.

"And that is about all the time we have today, guys, but remember, we will take right up here tomorrow, so go out and have a good day. Be safe and stay out of your mom's chocolate fudge. Okay?"

"Ah, it always ends in the wrong place."

"Can't you tell us how it comes out? Does he rescue the princess?"

"I don't want to go home," a whiney, little nasal-sounding girl on the second row pouted.

"Hey, does anyone know where Thomas is?" another little boy said, getting out of his chair and starting to yawn.

"I'm not going home till you tell me: Does Harry save the princess?" the pouter resumed.

"Well, in that case, let me get you a warm blanket. You don't mind sleeping in the dark library all by yourself, do you?" the old man asked calmly, pretending to look for a blanket.

"No! I mean yes, I do! I'll go home. I'll go home," the pouter yelled, jumping up and racing out the door.

"Okay then, see you tomorrow," the old man waved, laughing.

Chapter Seven

After all the complainers left, and all the chairs were folded and put away, the old man looked around for the fire marshal, who had shown up to claim Sarah and to take the old man to lunch.

"You ready to eat?" Sarah's grandfather asked.

"Always," the old man answered.

"Well, since this is a one-horse town, and it is lunchtime, the only diner is going to be full. We can go there and wait in line, or you can come to our house and eat a fine-cooked meal. Truthfully, you really don't have any choice. Sarah's grandma insisted. She's spent all morning baking some Swedish rye bread, minus most of the rye, sweetened with molasses and honey. It is amazing. And I am under orders to march you home. So, saddle up, Partner, and follow me to the house. You will not regret it. I promise."

The old man grinned. A home-cooked meal was a rarity for him, and he wasn't about to say no. He actually couldn't say no. Sarah's grandfather had already moved toward the door, and the hungry little sleep-deprived urchin had grabbed the old man's hand and was pulling him forward. As they stepped outside and the old man moved toward his pickup, Sarah looked at her grandpa and shouted, "Papa! I want to ride with Mr. Hank!"

The fire marshal looked a little surprised, but quickly shook it off and answered, "Well, Sarah, don't you think you should ask if Mr. Hank is okay with you riding with him?"

The old man suddenly remembered his pickup passenger seat had not been seen in years and was piled with layers of old books, newspapers, and McDonald's coffee cups. He was pretty sure his truck didn't stink anymore because a rat had found all the leftover hamburger pieces and devoured them. There was no way he was going to let anybody, especially a child, ride with him. They would have to sit on top of the pile. He wasn't even sure the seat belts could be found, or wouldn't fall apart from dry rot, and he was pretty sure they wouldn't reach high enough to strap her down on top of his rotting pickup mulch pile.

"Sarah, I am sorry but…" he began balking.

"It's okay, Mr. Hank. Grandpa's old truck stinks too, and if Grandma didn't gripe at him all the time, it would be as bad as yours. Besides, look! The library dumpster is right beside your truck."

Sarah's grandfather started laughing and said, "I'll help you, Hank."

Hank rolled his eyes in surrender and said, "Fine. If it stinks, throw it out; that includes anything from the bottom. If you see anything important, but dated five years ago, throw that out too."

The old man slowly shook his head and looked at the beaming snaggle-toothed mystery innocently prodding him. He shrugged his shoulders and opened the side door. After a hard pull to get it to come loose, an embarrassing cascade of garbage fell onto the pavement. Sarah dived right in, and the old man started shooing her away.

Kenneth kept saying, "It's okay. It's okay. You should have seen mine." Five humiliating minutes later, the passenger's seat was cleaned out. Some trash went into the dumpster and the rest behind the seat. The story time princess was perched and buckled in, and the old man's blood pressure was starting to go back down.

As they drove out of the library parking lot, the old man suddenly realized he didn't know what to say, but considering who was with him, that was not a problem.

Sarah started slowly as though she too was having a hard time with the words, "I don't know what is going on, Mr. Hank. Last night I cried and cried, and it was scary. And the other day, when you asked about the discern-ornament, I knew..."

"What?!" the old man gasped. "I never told you what the disc was called! How did you know it was the discern-ornament?" He looked at the child and almost ran a stop sign, causing the truck to shriek to a halt. He quickly shoved it into reverse, and a car behind him honked a warning to stop him.

Sarah began to cry. She might have acted preternaturally mature for her age, but sometimes she was just six, and this was one of those moments. "I am scared! I don't know what is happening," she sobbed in great panic-stricken wails.

The old man pulled the truck aside and parked it. He reached over instinctively, then hesitated because he was unsure if it was appropriate to hug the distraught little girl. Sarah had no such misgivings. She unsnapped the seat belt and jumped into the old man's lap, wrapping both arms around his neck, sobbing, and gasping. "What... is.... happening... to me?" she sniffed between sobs.

The old man held her close and patted her back. "I'm not sure, honey, I am not sure." Then a voice in his head whispered, *Liar.*

After a moment Sarah straightened up, moved back into her seat, buckled it, and said, "We can go on now."

The old man looked at her and laughed, "Yes, your imperial highness."

She cocked her small head at him and huffed; then she continued on with her previous conversation as though nothing had happened.

This time the old man interrupted, "Sarah, let me say something first, just to make sure you and I are seeing the same things... okay?"

She nodded, then wiped her nose with the back of her hand and looked for a place to wipe her hand off, finally deciding on a mostly clean spot on his truck seat.

"You seem to suddenly know things about the story, like what is going to happen next, and what the back side of the discern-ornament looks like, and you are having dreams about the dragon." Sarah nodded again, slowly urging the old man to continue. "It is almost like you are looking at memories, like you remember things about the story. Is that right?"

She sighed and said in a small, six-year-old voice, "I think so."

The old man leaned back in his seat and was quiet a long time. He didn't know what to ask her next, and it was too late anyway. They had arrived at the country house where Sarah lived with her grandparents.

Sarah burst out of the truck and ran to the front porch, almost kicking the black country cat that owned the front yard. "Get out of the way, Hagar!" she fussed as she shouted for her grandparents. "Mr. Hank almost got into a wreck. He tried to run a stop sign and a car honked at him!"

The old man's face reddened, and he was about to argue, when it occurred to him, Sarah was providing an excuse to cover for the time their conversation took. Her uncanny ability to deflect unwanted questions and lead people down safer paths was disturbing.

The old man was still blushing when he reached out a hand to greet the greying fire marshal, who admitted, "Sarah doesn't have any secrets. Whatever pops into her head comes out her mouth, never stopping in between. To be honest, I am glad it's you and not me!" He laughed.

"Thanks a lot, friend," the old man chuckled, then added, "but if this lunch is as good as you say it is, then the six-year-old mauling is worth it."

"Oh, it's grand. Let me introduce you to my cook, housekeeper, and"—Sarah's grandmother walked into the room right at that moment, and the fire marshal's tone instantly changed into praise—"and the most beautiful creature in this part of the county, my wife, Grace."

"Good to meet you, Hank. I heard you speak the other day at the library. I wanted to hear more of your story but yours truly there"—she pointed at her husband—"kept sneaking out with Sarah to get to the library before I could catch them. He said he wanted to make sure she got there in time for the story, but I think it had more to do with hot coffee at the doughnut shop."

Sarah walked up, heard her grandmother mention the doughnut shop, and started, "Oh, no, Grandma. It is apple fritt—" when her grandfather grabbed her up into his arms and interrupted with, "It's time for you to get your hands washed, young lady."

Grace, laughing, said, "I heard her! Apple fritters? The greasiest mouth-soaking bits-of-cardiac-stopping poison in the county!"

But the fire marshal, to escape further harm, had retreated down the hall with his secret-spouting granddaughter.

The old man was left standing with Grace and tried vainly to keep the smirk from seeping through his lips. When the fire marshal's wife looked at him, she said, "No worries. I'll work all that fat off him. You ready for lunch?"

"Yes, ma'am," he replied, suddenly aware of where Sarah got her ways.

Once everyone was seated at the table, the fire marshal bowed his head, then looked back up at his granddaughter and asked, "Sarah, would you like to pray?"

She responded immediately and began:

"God is great. God is good.

Let us thank Him for our food.

By His blessings we are fed.

Give us, Lord, our daily bread. Amen."

And then, before anyone could raise his head, she added, "And Lord, please make my bad dreams go away, and also have mercy on Thomas and Mr. Hank as he gets ready to fight the dragon again. In Jesus' name, amen."

Sarah's grandmother looked quickly at the old man and then back to her husband. The old man hesitated, shook his head, and let the moment pass, but for a few minutes he struggled to hear the conversation at the table because the phrase "fight the dragon again" astonished him.

The fire marshal, however, didn't skip a beat. "Thank you, Sarah. You are a good pray-er."

Sarah's face, stuffed full of mashed potatoes, replied in open-mouthed-potato glory, "Voor vwlcom."

The old man's chuckle was followed by a giggle from Grandmother Grace. The fire marshal tried hard not to succumb to the little girl's antics, but failed miserably and had to back away from the table to keep from choking on a roll he had used to try to stifle his outburst.

"Okay," he choked, trying fruitlessly to get his speech back. "Let me tell you our story." His speech picked up speed as he hurried to cram his words into the time he knew was allotted. "Grace can fill in the gaps, and I am sure Sarah will contribute her insights. The truth of the matter is, I probably won't get to talk at all before they grab the story and run with it, but at least I can introduce it." Both the grandmother and the child stiffened, their eyebrows raised, and the firefighter knew his bravery was going to cost him if he didn't deflate the moment. "Because they are so much better storytellers than I could ever be at filling in details—unwanted and unneeded," he whispered loudly, still treading where angels had long ago retreated.

"Yes, well," Grace began, "at least we get the story right. The way you tell it, Sarah appeared on our doorstep like some fairy story waif!"

"What's a waif, Grandma?" Sarah asked, cocking her head in a movement the old man had become well acquainted with.

The fire marshal answered, "It is a homeless, orphaned child, Sarah, a baby so precious that its parents feel totally unfit to raise it and give it up to the best home the baby could ever have."

The old man listened to the gilded definition and realized the fire marshal had worked on that answer for a while.

"Oh," Sarah replied, then got that faraway look in her eyes. The old man realized she was looking at memories. A perplexed look crossed her face, and then she spouted, "I think my parents were a king and a queen."

The old man answered, "Well, I think you are right, little one. They would have to be, because you are a princess."

Grace looked at the old man and nodded. "Well-spoken, Mr. Hank. I totally agree, and her grandfather and I are so incredibly grateful the good Lord has allowed us to be in her life, to love her and look after her. She is definitely our princess."

Sarah radiated. Whatever was going on in her life, whatever it was that haunted her heart, the old man was certain she knew she was loved and adored.

"But…" her preening grandmother Grace declared, leaning over and stroking Sarah's hair, "she is also very tired, and now very full, and needs to take a nap."

Usually Sarah would argue and grumble and stall at the word "nap," but this time she surrendered, nodding. "I sure do." And then, in a quieter voice she added, "I hope I can sleep and not go back there."

The old man stared hard and thought, *Go back where, Sarah?*

Grandma Grace hustled Sarah off to her nap. The old man watched the two leave, but right before they left the room, Sarah ran back into the dining room and hugged the old man. Then she moved to her grandfather and hugged him. As she started to leave again, the old man said, "Wait a minute, Sarah." He looked her in the eye and extended his hands; she walked back to him and grasped them. The old man continued in a raspy voice, "Sarah, when I was a little boy, I remember I had bad dreams too. One night I woke up screaming and raced to my parents' room. They woke up and comforted me, and then my dad picked me up and carried me back to my bedroom. He lay down beside me, nestled me close, and then said, 'Son, I want you to understand, before anything gets to you, it has to come through me, and it's not getting through me.' Your grandpa and grandma and I are all here. They love you, and I kinda think you're okay for a smart-aleck little ragamuffin."

As she looked at him, her eyes narrowed and a fake frown gathered across her face.

"We are praying for you. And I know that you have really big guardian angels. So, you can be at peace and you can sleep, okay?"

Sarah's eyes glistened; she sighed, nodded, and then walked back to her grandmother and left the room with her.

The fire marshal looked at the old man and said, "Would you like to move to the living room? We need to talk." After settling down in some overstuffed leather chairs, the fire marshal continued, "Thank you for that. She has really taken a shine to you and loves your stories, or at least, in this case, story."

"You're welcome. She is a very special young lady."

"We know. As you have probably already assumed, Sarah is not our real granddaughter. We have children, but they are all grown and have moved away, though they haven't started their families yet. Sarah is actually our foster child, although on a permanent basis. You see, I found her at a fire."

The old man leaned forward, riveted to the fire marshal's story.

"A little over three years ago, we were called to a huge fire at a large warehouse across town where a lot of rich people had stored their wealthy belongings. Four stations from around the county were called. Any other time, in a town this small, in a sparsely populated part of the county, four trucks would not have been called, but the city commissioners and their connections… well, you know… so, we were hard at it. After a long, hot night, we had the fire contained, and then the weather decided to cooperate, and it actually began to rain, so the fire was out. As the fire marshal, it was my job to go through the ashes and determine cause. I was poking through the usual places: electrical boxes, wiring, et cetera, and I was beginning to suspect arson. I could smell sulphur but couldn't find any hint of a chemical accelerant. We found two bodies almost burned to ash because the fire was so hot and had lasted so long in a focused area. While trying to collect their remains, I kept hearing a baby cry. At first, I thought it was some type of morning bird or maybe even a lost kitten, but it kept on.

"I couldn't tell if the cry came from within the ruins or under them. I started looking for a basement hidden under the debris; then I saw a movement out of the corner of my eye. I turned toward it and was shocked to see a toddler, a little girl, covered in soot and shivering with the cold. When she saw me, she began to wail and walked toward me, arms outstretched, crying her eyes out. I guess she was trying to get my attention and has held it ever since. I didn't know how she got there. She was dressed in the tattered and burnt remains of some type of green cloth. If you have ever seen Depression-era photographs of children draped in flour sacks, this was kind of like that. The cloth was coarse and burnt, and it was all she had on. I wrapped her in a blanket and took her to the hospital. They kept her overnight and treated her for exposure. Grace and I watched over her, and when Child Protective Services came, we applied for guardianship, and since Grace is on the board and was in county government, it wasn't hard to attain. We have had Sarah ever since. We've looked everywhere for her parents, but no one came forward, and she had no fingerprints on file. We even had her DNA checked. The closest match was found in Eastern Europe! How she got here, who her parents are, and where they come from is a mystery. We have no idea. But to be honest, Hank, I am also glad. We love that little girl. She has renewed our lives and filled this house with laughter and sometimes a little cussing and hollering, but it's happy."

"She is an amazing child. That is for sure," the old man replied, then hesitated, his face reflecting his unspoken question, and the fire marshal seized on it.

"What is it? What's on your mind?"

"Well, I don't mean to pry, but I am curious. Did Sarah describe her dreams to you? Did she say anything about what she saw or was afraid of?"

The fire marshal sighed, leaned back in his overstuffed leather chair, and stared at the old man. His face was blank, and the old man thought, *I will never play poker with this man.* After a moment of deliberate and apparently extremely thoughtful reflection on the old man's question, the answer started to come, and then Grace walked back into the room.

"I finally got that little tootle-butt to sleep. She was afraid if she closed her eyes, something would get her. Finally, she fell asleep with me holding her. For a long time, I didn't know if I should set her down on her bed or just hold on to her. When she finally didn't seem troubled and was at peace, I put her in her bed. Apparently, I have walked into something interesting because you, my dear, have *that look* on your face."

The fire marshal cocked his head at his wife and squinted, as if to say, *What look?*

"You know exactly what I mean. We have been married thirty-eight years, and I can read you like a dog-eared book. What is going on?"

The old man waited for the fire marshal's reply. The fire marshal exhaled quickly in ultimate surrender and answered, "Hank asked me a question. And if I answer it, I am pretty sure it is only going to lead to more. So, I am preparing for that."

"Oh," she responded quietly.

"Look, if you feel like it would be better not to discuss Sarah's dreams, I understand. You have a responsibility to protect your daughter, and her privacy is included in that protection. I am sorry I pried," the old man said.

"No," both grandparents responded at once; then Grace stopped and looked back at her husband.

"Sarah is a very special child," he began.

"That's obvious," the old man agreed.

"More than we even know. For a while now, I have begun to wonder about things that I didn't before. When she was a toddler, we didn't notice so much, but now, we face a new question almost daily. She knows things that she shouldn't at her age, things we didn't tell her. She tries to hide it sometimes, behind her precociousness, but when she is home and relaxed, well, sometimes it's like talking to someone much older, especially the last few weeks, especially since you started telling your story at the library."

Grace continued with the revelation, "We are starting to believe that..." She paused as though afraid that speaking the words would cement them.

"That what?" the old man begged.

The fire marshal looked at the old man and said, "You see it too, don't you?"

This time it was the old man's time to draw back into his thoughts, but he sensed that he was in a safe place and could be honest, at least to a point. He could reveal he sensed things in Sarah without revealing what he was beginning to suspect about her.

"I do, but I am not sure what I am seeing. I have seen a lot of strange things in my time. I mean a lot. I used to be a... hummmm... how can I share this... I kinda worked for a group of people that looked into... strange things. I know that is only going to raise more questions, but this is one of those situations where..."

"If you tell us, you will have to kill us?" Grace offered, only half joking.

"Ha," the old man snorted, "not quite, but, well anyway... we are both going to have to trust the other. I am going to trust that you are good parents that love Sarah, and although you might not understand what you are seeing, you still love and want to protect her. You are going to have to trust that I know some things that might not fit into the way you have been taught to see the world. So… far… at least."

"Uhhh," Grace groaned, "kinda sorta thought things might lead to this, especially lately. I really don't want to be the first one to open this keg, and since, if you really do have experience working with a group that looked into such things, perhaps you should be the first one to pull back this curtain we are all staring at, and noticing shapes behind, but are afraid to pull apart?"

The old man looked at the grey-haired couple staring back at him. A you-got-me-and-now-what-am-I-going-to-do-about-it look spread across his face, hiding behind a slight smile. "Well, I think Sarah is experiencing memories that may not be from her own recent past. I am pretty sure she is not from here."

"As in from where?" the fire marshal asked. "Another planet?"

"I don't think so," the old man responded slowly, seriously considering the question. "There are several possibilities, everything from split personalities with one of those being a… spirit."

"You mean possession?!" The fire marshal sat up on the edge of his chair, concern locked into his jaw.

"No…" the old man continued, "not like what you're afraid of, and that is just one option. Sarah's brain might be acting as a receiver, picking up images from another time. She could be incredibly empathic and seeing into another universe that coexists alongside ours and that occasionally breaks into our own. There are many different possibilities, but I am sure of this, she is gifted. Whatever seems to be provoking or creating or releasing this insight—for lack of a better word—has just begun, and things are going to get stranger before they get better."

"I don't know if you have told us a thing we didn't already know, or at least suspected," the fire marshal said, scratching his head.

"But he has organized it for us and helped us to realize we're not crazy, and Sarah is not... is not, what, I don't know... normal doesn't fit, and it is okay if she is not normal; normal is boring. Sarah is okay. She is special, not in a broken way, but a brilliant and gifted way. I don't know what we are going to do about her, but it doesn't matter; we love her."

"Well, one thing you could do is answer my first question. What has Sarah told you about her dreams?"

"You tell him, Grace. You remember details better than I do, and if you leave anything out, I will fill it in, okay?"

Grandmother Grace nodded and was about to start when the fire marshal began speaking, "There is really not a whole lot to tell. It all happened in one night. We went to bed around ten, our usual time. Sarah had gone down at eight thirty, her usual time. As we passed by her room on the way back to ours, we did what we always do, stuck our heads in the door to check on her. We heard her groaning, which was unusual, so we opened the door and walked in. We kept the lights off and just drew close to her bed. We listened for a few minutes. The groaning didn't stop; then it turned to whimpering and she began to scream and cry out. That is when I reached down and picked her up. When I touched her, she cried out and woke up. At first, she didn't seem to know where she was, and then things got really strange. You want to take it from there, Grace?"

"Hummph. Thanks a lot. Leave the weird to me, why don't ya? Well, fine. Sarah was talking, screaming actually, in her sleep, but it wasn't in English. I don't know what language it was. This went on for some time, so while Kenneth held Sarah, I grabbed my smartphone and recorded some of it. You want to hear it?"

The old man wanted to say, *No need.* He already knew what language it would be, but answered instead, "Of course I do."

"Thought you might." Grace pushed the right buttons, and Sarah's voice came through the phone.

"Pūķis atstāj mani, tu mani nevari nomirt. iet prom. Harija man palīdzēt palīdziet man harry Ak Dievs nē! Harijs atgriezies atgriezties Harija!"

"It just repeats over and over like she was stuck in the dream."

The old man's chest tightened and pains ran up his right arm. His breath came in gasps and the room began to spin. He moved back into his seat and closed his eyes, but not before Grace, who was an RN, noticed his physical response and grabbed him.

"Hank, you okay? Get me a wet rag, Kenneth!"

"I'm fine," the old man lied, his breathing coming in gulps. He could feel the blood running back into his face. Pushing out words he said, "I just wasn't expecting... to recognize the words. They are old Latvian. My grandparents were from Latvia. I am supposedly a descendant of royalty there, or so I have been told." Lies poured out of the old man's mouth, programmed by years of rehearsal, so that even in the most traumatic of moments, their shield would hold. The problem was the older he got, the more he struggled to remember what was fabrication and what was the truth, but at the moment, a little truth and a lot of lie kept problems at bay.

"So, you recognized the words?" the fire marshal asked.

"Yeah, most of them. They are definitely an ancient version, but I understood them."

There was a long awkward pause as the old man stepped back into thought. It was interrupted by Grandma Grace. "Ahem… you understood them? Well, good. Would you be interested in sharing their meaning with the rest of us?"

The old man looked at Grace and blinked. It had not occurred to him that he would be asked to translate, and now when faced with it, he was wondering how he could get out of it, not share too much, or how much was too much, and a score of other frantic thoughts. He even considered using the tired expression "I would, but then I'd have to kill you" but passed over it quickly. Sometimes the truth wasn't a bad idea.

"Yeah sure," he finally answered. "To the best of my recollection they translate something like… 'Dragon, leave me. You are dead. Go away.' And there is more, but I am having a hard time with it. Sounds like she is calling for someone to help her, but…" and then he lied, "I am not sure who."

The lie the old man told was embedded in enough truth to slide by. Essentially, it was an accurate translation minus one word. But that word was explosive and would open up more questions than he was prepared to answer. So he deliberately didn't mention the name, Harry, that Sarah called out.

Chapter Eight

The next library story day, the old man tumbled out of bed. His feet hit the floor; then he groaned as his back reminded him that it was a little slower than the rest of him, insisting on the over-fifty oh-dang-my-spinal-discs-just-shifted dip. A few steps later, it came together, straightened out, and he could walk upright again. By then he was headed to a hot shower and the inevitable shave. Soon after, he was puttering down the road in his antique pickup.

Things had changed at story time, at least for him and Sarah. The rest of the kids still thought it was just a great story, at least he thought they did. He wondered if Thomas would be there today. He hoped he would. It would be awful if that poor, overregulated young man was not allowed to continue to participate. The old man knew that if he could have that kid for a few weeks, the young man's whole destiny would change. He also knew that would never be an option, and the thought grieved him.

Pulling into the library parking lot, the old man noted the familiar cars parked in their familiar places, and then he also noticed an unfamiliar one, a black Crown Victoria, older model, classic edition. Those cars evoked either a here-lies-a-cop, or on the other side of the coin, a here-there-be-monsters kind of presence. They were a favorite of old-style gangsters, and the old man was interested to see which had come to visit.

As he walked through the door, there was an immediate and almost overpowering sense of dread. Something evil this way walked, of that he was certain. He had not yet met the Reverend Laden Long, but the old man was intimately acquainted with the aura that radiated wickedness. He walked into the informal den where his audience typically cavorted and detected a dismal blandness in the air. His body reacted to the sense of heaviness that pervaded, and nausea started to climb up from its dark hollow in his stomach. Looking around, he saw Thomas, pale and fragile, standing next to his grandfather. The boy was stiff and out of sync, lacking the childlike restlessness that usually romped through the library.

The children were still busy but unusually quiet, as though they were actually in a traditional library hounded by a rigid old woman whose demand of silence hid her inability to arouse the genius of childhood. The old man kept looking for his rowdy minions to charge him with a thousand questions, ridiculous by adult standards but essential logs on a young imagination's altar, but they did not burst upon him, and he was surprised. He continued looking for his favorite mystery munchkin. Finally, he found her back in a corner, as far away from the intimidating figure of the dark reverend as she could physically get.

When the old man saw that his little princess was cowering, and that his kingdom of childhood wonder was under siege, the nausea in his stomach backed down, whimpering like a cur, tail tucked between its mangy legs, and in its place, courage arose, sheathed in cold anger. It was escorted by a spirit of wholeness, and had the old man understood it, he would have realized the power that felt like anger, but under rigid control, was also shepherded by Holiness—sheer, unadulterated, undefiled light. Immediately his mouth opened and words catapulted forth like an ancient Roman ballista aimed at a dark dragon. He walked across the room, stood in front of the Reverend

Long, and said, "You look awfully familiar, but it must have been a while since we've met because I can't quite place it. How are you? My name is Hank."

The old man stuck out his hand and Reverend Long reached out to grab it. A brilliant white smile etched its way across Long's face, like an unfamiliar stream cutting a path through dry places. The reverend's grip was powerful and intended to intimidate, but the old man's hand was cut from oak and trimmed in callus. As they gripped, it was like a cobra's head caught in a mongoose's mouth. Surprise and dismay rippled across the mask that served as a face of the reverend. He tried to squeeze a little harder, and then eased his grip in such a nonchalant manner that no one noticed the first round had been fought, and the old man was ahead.

"My name," the Reverend Long replied, slowly, "is Reverend Laden Long. I am the steward of St. George's."

"Saint George the dragon slayer? Now that is an occupation that didn't have much of a retirement plan," the old man laughed, wondering why in the world he had just said that.

"No, it didn't. Those old myths do tend to reflect good moral principles though, don't they?"

"Well, depends on what myth and what principle, I suppose. You have any particular ones in mind?"

"I was thinking about the one typically associated with Saint George."

"I guess I am not familiar with that one," the old man said, sensing a rusty gate starting to close in behind him.

The reverend laughed and then said, "You know the one: do not meddle in the affairs of dragons."

"Oh, *that* one! Yes, I can see the wisdom in that, but my favorite is from an old, old book you might be familiar with, considering your vocation. 'Michael and his angels fought with the dragon; and the dragon and his angels fought, but they did not prevail, nor was a place found for them in heaven any longer.' You know that one, don't you? Seems between the two moral principles we share that the conclusion to the matter would be *dragons* need to be careful what they consider their affairs because if they don't, *angels* will whip their ass. It's good to see you, Reverend Long. Will you be joining us for story time?"

The old man was unaware that the atmosphere in the library had changed. He probably would not have noticed for several more minutes but was made forcibly aware when a rubber ball flew through the air and hit Reverend Long in the chest. The old man pretended to scowl and looked around for the culprit, even though he knew immediately who had thrown the ball and wasn't about to expose her. "I am sorry, Reverend. Seems the party has started, and I need to corral these babes."

"That's all right, Hank, I was just leaving, but just so you know, Thomas's time here is almost up as well. He will be moving to another state soon. His mother is not happy about it, but she has known for a long time this day would come. A child's absence always leaves a vacuum until something else comes along and fills it. Have a good day. And oh, by the way, considering your love of old books and quotes, why don't you look up Daniel 7:25? It might be of interest to you. It all depends on the season, doesn't it? Good day, sir."

The old man was taken aback. He knew of and was never fond of that passage in Daniel 7. It was something about the saints being given over to the beast. He would have to look it up for the context, but even so, it left a dark ring around his heart, and fear threatened to break over him. He had won the first round, but now the aftermath lingered, and the enemy, that old serpent Fear, was an insidious opponent. The old man felt the room start to spin.

His adrenalin spike was over and now he was paying for it. He felt light-headed and thought he might faint but caught himself before anyone could notice. Even though his body was weakened by the exchange, his eyes never left the dark reverend as he walked through the crowd of children who unconsciously moved away from him like snow from an iron plow. He couldn't believe what he had just heard. On the surface it was innocent enough, but only so. The Reverend Laden Long might have just told the old man something horrible. As he tried to keep his cringing thoughts from flowing down their blood-soaked path, a small hand reached into his own, and then Sarah cupped her hands to her mouth as the old man bent laboriously down to hear her.

"You will stop him. You always have." Then nonchalantly, like a mouse asking for a cookie, she continued, "But now it is story time!"

The cloud lifted and chaos, in its glorious life-giving form, resurrected. Children laughed and shouted. Gathered chairs were tossed into a wobbly line. Little rear ends tried to sit in them but only managed glancing touches before spindly legs cast them off again.

Finally, the old man gathered his wits enough to begin the story. "O…kay!" he uncharacteristically shouted into the ears of his little flock, who also uncharacteristically settled down and began to listen. "When we last heard from Harry, he had discovered Speaker, the living sword. He had run from the dragon and was leaning up against the sides of the dark tunnel."

"Yeah, he was asleep."

"He was afraid he was going crazy. My dad thinks my mom has done that."

The old man's thoughts hid behind wide eyes and raised eyebrows at the last revelation, but he continued, "Yes,

Harry was asleep, but he was also dreaming, and in his dreams, while in the cave, he would visit with the princess. As he dreamed, he felt drawn down a new tunnel, swirling with wind he could actually see. It circled him and outlined the dream walls he wandered through as he reached out to the princess. Finally, he arrived and walked into the light her small fire cast on the dark cave walls that surrounded her.

"'I have been waiting for you!' the princess said as she turned to meet him. 'Where have you been? Why haven't you tried to rescue me? I am struggling so hard, and you haven't come. I thought you were dead! I heard the dragon roaring a few hours ago; then he visited me and said he had killed you and burnt your body to ash. I told him I didn't believe him and asked him to show me your body. When he didn't answer right away, I hoped it was because he was lying, but then he answered softly, like an old friend. He kept asking me why I didn't like him and wouldn't I like to be free. He told me all I had to do was ask him, and he could change me into a dragon; then we would be free to soar the heavens together. I screamed against him, and he left, but Harry, I am weakening, and the dragon knows it. Get me out of here! Please free me! Come get me!'

"As Harry listened, he longed to run to the princess and hold her. He knew her anger was fueled by fear and felt there was nothing he could do about it. Then it occurred to him. Maybe he could run to her, or at least walk closer, and hold her. I mean it was a dream, but she was dreaming too. At the same time, it kinda wasn't a dream if they were both in it and really talking to each other through it."

"Hold on! Hold on! Is this going to get moooshy?! My mama doesn't want me watching or listening to anything mooshy, like kissing. I think that's because it causes cold sores!" the little redheaded girl on the second row protested.

"Yeah, that is right!" another young man, a gap-toothed warrior with a face full of scattered freckles, agreed. "Your mama is my aunt, and I still remember what *her* aunt, which I think was my great-aunt, said at my cousin's wedding. It was kinda strange. She told my cousin to be very careful on her honeymoon because kissing causes cold sores! My cousin, the one that was getting married, just stared at my great-aunt, who had never been married, and started crying. Her face turned red, and her body shook, and she ran off before she could fall down! So *obviously* kissing is dangerous!"

The old man was at a loss. The innocence of youth. Glorious naïveté. Imagination without bounds or experience to rein it in, and oh, how funny it could be. He was about to go on with the story when the discussion moved along quicker than he could corral it.

"Kissing does not cause cold sores. It causes baaabies!" an older boy, about seven and fully experienced in life, added, grinning.

"No, it doesn't. The stork brings babies."

"No, it doesn't. There is a baby fairy that is cousin to the tooth fairy. I know for certain because my dad lost a tooth and told me that's how I got here!"

The old man ducked his head in his hands and began to convulse. He was trying hard to hide his laughter, but the dam was cracking.

"Oh my goodness!" The old man's daughter laughed as she moved into the discussion and said, "I hate to interrupt story time, but would anybody like some hot chocolate? I need to take orders if you do, and then Dad can get back to his story. Okay, once again. Who wants hot chocolate?"

The happy chorus of me-me-me! stopped the interesting conversation, and after a moment or two of does-it-have-mint-in-it? and I-don't-want-any-with-whipped-cream, and then a discussion about the merits or lack thereof of the said topping, the old man finally got back to the story.

"So, the princess was crying and Harry wanted to hug her and comfort her. He cautiously moved toward her and reached out to her. She saw him coming and reached back, and for a moment, the two young people simply stood in their dreams and held each other."

Sarah looked up at the old man with an incredibly wise look on her weary face as she leaned forward and said, "I remember that." Then her face changed, she blinked, and a six-year-old's eyes stared back.

The old man sighed and thought, *I do too*, then he wondered, *But who are you? Is the princess speaking through you? Or are you the princess?*

"Well, is everybody settled back in? Okay now, where was…"

"They were hugging," the seven-year-old sage on the back row laughed.

"Yep, yeah, that's where we left off. Harry had never hugged a girl before, and even though it was a dream, it really wasn't. The thought occurred to him, *I am hugging a princess!* And then he thought, *And I really don't care. She is dirty, and scared, and I really hope you can't smell in a dream because I know I have swamp mud all over me.* He looked at himself and saw he was clean in the dream and laughed to himself, *Thank you, God! Now I know this is a dream for real!*

"Princess Sarah looked at Harry and said, 'Yes, it is, but it's not either, and it's okay. Even if you do smell like a skunk that bathed in a sewer, I would still hug you.'

"'Can you hear my thoughts?' Harry asked, shocked, thinking them toward the princess.

"'Of course I can, Harry. We are in a dream world, and we got here through our hearts' imaginations. But it's still real.'

"'Wow!' Harry said, and then he heard it again, the sound of the dragon huffing along the tunnel that led to the princess's dungeon.

"'I will be back, and it will be very soon. Please don't give up hope. I have a friend now, and he has beaten dragons before. So, don't give up ho...' Harry was going to say 'hope,' but awoke before he could get the word out. He looked around and he was still in the tunnel. It was still dark, and he was still alone. Then he heard it again, the roar of the dragon, only this time, it was a lot closer.

Chapter Nine

"'*She is pretty,*' a voice in Harry's head said.

"'AAH!' Harry jerked and then calmed. 'I forgot you were there. It's going to take a while to get used to this.'

"'*It always does. It's not easy for me either, you know. I was asleep for... good grief, I don't know how long I have been dormant.*'"

An eager hand shot up, and the old man didn't skip a beat, "Dormant means asleep. It is usually associated with winter, and it is what plants do when it gets cold outside. They go dormant. Are you good with that?"

The little towheaded boy on the middle row nodded quickly as his wide eyes beckoned the old man to continue. Then he stuck his hand up again. "Uh, Mr. Hank? I wasn't asking about the word, I was asking to go to the bathroom."

"Ah, man!" an angry, childlike hornet's nest replied in unison.

"*Now?*" the buzz grew stronger. "Can't you wait a little longer?"

The anxious blond instrument-of-discord quickly shook his head and said, "Nuh-uh! My grandma decided everybody in the family needed a spring cleaning. I thought it was chocolate candy, and *noooo*! I can't wait!" the poor boy yelled as he ran straight into the ladies' bathroom.

The whole audience erupted with, "He went in the wrong bathroom!"

The old man's daughter, quick on the draw, ran right after the cramping culprit, stopped at the door, cracked it a little, and whispered so low every little ear in the house leaned forward, "Mike, are you okay?"

"Yeah, I made it, but oh just barely…"

The place howled and rocked, and the old man joined in saying, "That's not right. That's just not right!" But nobody paid attention.

Finally, after the glowing, red-faced young man returned to his seat, the squirming slackened and the story recommenced.

"*What year is it?'* Speaker asked.

"'Excuse me?'

"*What year is this?'*

"'Well, as of yesterday, it is May the eleventh, the year of our Lord 1206.'

"*'Oh my gosh! It has been over seven hundred years since I went to sleep! But by the looks of you, and the haphazard way you've organized your brain, and the fact you barely know how to read, a lot has changed. Has the empire fallen?'*

"'What empire? The Franks ruled for a while, and the Pope hasn't called for a crusade in several years.'

"*'Mercy!'* the old sword whispered. *'They did it! The Germans and the Gauls finally drove us back and broke us. I bet it was those wretched Celtic dragons that finally broke our backs. I can see it in your memories. Some old man came by your home. Your father fed him a night or two, and he paid you in stories. He was a scholar, and you don't even remember this, do you?'*

"'No, I'm sorry, I don't, but if I don't remember, how can you?'

"*'Doesn't matter, boy. Right now, you have a dragon to kill and a princess to save before she turns on you.'*

"'What! Turns on me?'

"*'You heard me, and you're seeing it, too. Weren't you listening to her? Didn't you see it in her eyes, hear it in her speech? The dragon is making progress in turning her. She grows fearful and angry. Both of those feed the dragon's spells. He thrives on them, and then uses them against her. We have to move soon.'*

"Harry sat on the side of the cave tunnel, the torch flickering close to him. He stared wide-eyed into the dark. *She is turning,* he whispered to himself. *She is turning!*

"Okay, children, that is enough for this morning."

"Nooo! You can't stop there! You just can't!" the whole pack howled. "What happens next? Can you give us a hint? Pleeease, pretty, pretty please!" they echoed, like a flock of angry crows. "Just a little… Does she turn?"

The old man looked around the room, a half scowl across his face. Wherever his gaze turned, a silence fell. Finally, when all was still, and you could hear the faint panting of a dozen little breaths, he said, "I forgot."

The squawking and yelling and even crying was so loud that the elderly lady next door to the library thought her hearing aids were squealing, so she took them out and thumped them on the table.

The old man laughed and laughed, and the children squalled and pouted until finally he said, "Okay, okay… Harry saves her. She doesn't turn… completely… but it cost Harry, and that is all I am going to say till tomorrow!"

"No, no!"

"Wait!" one brilliant-memoried herald called out. "Tonight is the night for the weekly update with our families. We started it last week, and they all want to attend, remember? So, you can start from where you just left off tonight! Yeah!"

The old man heard the trap slam behind him, knew he was caught, and laughed, "Okay, okay. Tonight it is, but you must go home, help with your chores, and be nice to your siblings."

"I don't have any siblans, and if I did, my brother would probably eat them because he sticks everything in his mouth! My mother says he's a little eatin' machine. Dad said he's better than the dog because the dog leaves some things alone. So, I am sure I don't have a siblan, or whatever you called it."

"Okay then, go home and take a nap, be nice, play sweet, and bathe before you come tonight. Got it!"

They did. "Especially Mike!" one little girl whispered, loud enough to cause the next-door neighbor lady to check her hearing aids again. "Because he stinks!"

As the old man's daughter stepped between the would-be combatants and hustled them out the door, the old man sank down into his rocker, sighed, and closed his eyes. He was starting to enjoy the moment when he heard movement in front of him. He opened his eyes and was not surprised to see his favored child.

The old man looked at her and waited. Her grandfather wasn't usually late. Her face was blank. Then it changed and the eyes looking back at him were pain-filled. "I don't know what's going on. I am having dreams during the day. In them, I see the story. I feel like I am in the story. How did I get there, Mr. Hank? I do like the princess, though."

She blinked and switched. Suddenly someone else was looking back through her eyes. "I'm still here, Harry. I am starting to remember. He followed us. Somehow, he came through the stream. I remember you fought so hard. You beat him, but he came back. He is here now." She blinked again. Her voice changed, her body language shifted, and a terrified six-year-old girl stood in front of the old man. "He is going after my grandparents, Mr. Hank! Grandpa knows more than he lets on. He may be able to push him back, but he can't hold out for long."

The old man didn't have time to think about what he had just seen. One minute, Princess Sarah was there, then blink, and little Sarah was there. All he could do was stuff his heart back into his chest, push back his fears, and move. "Do you know where your grandpa is, Sarah?" He gasped. "And how has the dragon come for him?"

Sarah began to cry. She wiped her nose on her arm and said, "Thomas let him in. Thomas let him in." It was all she could manage. Her hands came to her face and she moved into the old man's arms. "He didn't want to. He fought, but he had no choice. The dragon knew how to use him…"

The old man held the little girl close and then pulled her back just a bit and looked at her. "Where is Thomas now, Sarah?"

Sarah whimpered and started to weep harder. The old man persisted, "Where is he, Sarah?"

"He went away, Mr. Hank. He had to. The door opened, and they took him, and then the dragon came through." Sarah blinked again. The old man felt the tension in her body ease; then he felt her sigh. She lifted her head, and Princess Sarah stared back at him. "He died, Harry. The dragon used its host and slew the boy. Now the dragon is in full possession, and he is coming for me."

A grim mask covered the old man's face. Warrior eyes, cold, hard, and strong, stared back. "We will kill this beast." He took a deep breath, and his spine stiffened. The old man straightened up and said, "But this time, he isn't facing a peasant boy. I've learned a few things, acquired a few friends. I will ride him down."

Princess Sarah looked at the old man and whispered, "As always, my love, as always." Her body shook, and little Sarah was back. "We really like you, Mr. Hank. I am not afraid anymore. The princess keeps me brave. So, come on! Let's go get Grandpa!"

Chapter Ten

Twenty-four hours earlier

The Reverend Laden Long laughed. Like a snake shedding its skin, he discarded his coat and threw it across the threadbare couch that sat in the dusty living room of the old house. He had brought his daughter with him. She was in the basement. She knew what she was required to do but was grieving the thought of doing it. Laden Long was a Satanist from a long line of them. His family had been sacrificing their first-born for centuries. Every time they did, prosperity came to the remaining family.

He had conveniently forgotten that for some strange reason, it didn't last long, and ultimately a new sacrifice had to be made to bring the family back out of the poverty and debilitating diseases that inevitably caught up to them. Long had taken the life of his first-born. He had not even winced when the knife struck and the fire consumed the boy. He had been there when the new family line had been established, the insurance that prosperity stayed near. He had told his daughter repeatedly what must happen, what had always happened, and why it needed to happen.

She remembered her brother but also loved the money his blood bought. She had been conditioned from birth to do what was about to be done. The Reverend Long was embarrassed by her weakness now, but also knew her emotional pain was part of the sacrifice. His heart was darkened. It had to be because of the mockery he made every Sunday of another sacrifice.

There was nothing left of the man except hunger and arrogance. Long's encounter with the old man had shaken him, but now, after tonight, he knew that he would be unstoppable. And the old man and that brash little girl would make another wonderful payment that would unstop the flow of riches that would pour out on him and those who served him.

What the dark reverend didn't know was that a new player was in town, one with an old quest and ancient vengeance. It was a deeper evil than Long's family had ever known, a primordial one, vested not with avarice, but with power and the insatiable need to control. That evil was behind the veil, held in check, waiting for the blood of an innocent to flow and unleash him. Gradually, through the ages, he had been using the Long family, preparing for this night. Year after year, sacrifice after sacrifice, the patient dragon had waited. It had been careful to ensure that Long's family would be equipped to handle the change, that a body, able to carry the anointing, would be prepared.

Reverend Laden Long did not know that death was coming for him too. He did not know that his soul was about to reap the earnings of his family's crimes. The dragon was about to consume and replace him. The time had come. The consummation and possession had been insidiously moving forward all Long's life. Little by little, Long had given up his humanity. Now, the last vestige would be torn from him by an evil of his own making. The sacrifice of Thomas would open a gate by which one would leave and another enter. The Reverend Laden Long laughed. Had he been able to peer behind the invisible curtain of the spirit world, he would not have been so joyous, for there another serpent smiled, and it laughed too.

Long reached into the back of his clothes closet to find the hidden door that led deeper into the closet. He pulled out a robe: ancient, deep red—blood red, actually, to better hide the stains—and streaks of embroidered gold thread representing the reward of avarice. The robe, like the man who wore it, was a mockery, a wicked attempt to mimic, to counterfeit a glory it could not manifest. For centuries the members of Long's family, and others like them, had worn such robes. He knew his daughter would also be wearing one.

Long placed the robe on his bed, stepped into the bathroom, and laid aside the rest of his clothes. As he stepped into the shower, he noticed his skin condition had worsened. The doctor labeled the scaly rash ichthyosis vulgaris, an inherited skin condition that occurs when the skin doesn't shed its dead skin cells, causing dry, blotchy patches on the surface of his skin. It was also known as "fish scale disease" because the dead skin accumulated in a pattern similar to fish scales, or as he liked to think in his case, dragon scales. If he had known what he really had, and how it was preparing his body, he would have ripped the skin off his own flesh with his fingernails, but he didn't know, and after his hot, soothing shower, he donned the wicked cloak and proceeded down the stairs to the basement.

***

Thomas stood shivering, naked, and tied to a large wooden stake cemented deep into the basement floor. His mother had insisted he drink some nasty-tasting hot tea. It didn't taste anything like the rich cocoa he drank at the library, but she was his mother, and he had gotten used to her stringent ways and awful-tasting concoctions. He was also extremely aware, from painful experience with her, and even worse, his grandfather's strap, that if he did not obey instantly, he would regret it for a long time.

His mother had bought many new bed sheets over the years because blood stains didn't come out well. So Thomas stood rigid, although drugged, as people began to gather in the large basement. At first his foggy brain was ashamed that so many people could see his nakedness, but the thought soon left, pushed back by a growing sense of fear. Even in his bewildered state, Fear's pointed barbs had begun to prick him. As Thomas stood there, he tried to focus his eyes. It was hard, but he kept trying and began to see that the people all gathered around him were folks he knew. People from town, members of the church he attended, a local police officer, the animal control lady, his mom and grandfather.

As Thomas continued to stare through his drugged state, he also noticed a face he had never seen before. It belonged to a young man who wasn't dressed like the others. Everyone else had on red robes, but not this young man. He just wore jeans and a long-sleeve denim shirt. As Thomas stared at the young man, he began to hear the singing of the people in the room. It was really more like saying the same thing over and over again, softly. He knew it wasn't regular singing because there was no music. They just kept repeating and repeating the same words.

Thomas saw everyone begin to move slowly around the pole where his mother had tied him. She had promised that if he stood very straight and still that he would not have to stay there long this time. Sometimes, she had tied him to the pole and left him for hours, once overnight, but this time, she promised that it would not take long. He wished he felt better and could see more clearly. He wanted to listen to the singing but couldn't really hear it very well. His confused mind realized it must have been the hot tea his mother made him drink. Sometimes, when she made him drink it, it caused him to get foggy-headed, and then, in the mornings, after he woke up, he would have the worst headache.

His mom had promised him, as she tied the familiar ropes around his slender frame, that this would be the last time he had to do this. She looked troubled, and when he asked her if she was okay, she said she was. He didn't believe her though and tried to make her feel better by telling her that, in the morning, he would fix her breakfast. It was just him bringing a bowl of cereal and orange juice to her bed because he was too young to be allowed to cook. But he loved doing it for her because she was his mom. She looked at him funny and her eyes got all teary; then she covered her face and ran up the stairs. Thomas had searched his heart to see what he could have possibly said to hurt her feelings but couldn't think of what it could be. As this last thought slipped away from his drugged mind, Thomas saw the young man move closer to him. He liked the man. He had a kind face and looked strong. His hands were callused like Mr. Hank's at the library. The young man knelt down and spoke to Thomas.

"You didn't say anything wrong, Thomas. You just reminded your mother of what was right."

"Then why did she start to cry and run away from me?" Thomas asked, puzzled.

"You reminded her of her big brother, Thomas, and how much she misses him."

"Oh." Then Thomas looked around and noticed the singing had stopped, and the people had quit moving in a circle. They just stood as still as statues. It was like a movie he saw once where everyone was turned to stone until the hero came and freed them.

"Why did they stop?" Thomas asked.

"They stopped because they can't go where you're going. I am taking you on a beautiful trip."

"I probably need to ask my mom first," Thomas replied dutifully.

The young man stood up and tousled Thomas's hair. "I will see to that, and we don't have to be gone any longer than you want to be."

As the young man stood, Thomas realized his ropes had fallen to the floor, and he was no longer naked, but dressed in play-clothes so bright they sparkled. He smiled, looked up at the young man, and said, "Okay. But I don't want to be gone so long Mom worries about me."

The young man sighed, took Thomas by the hand, and pointed to a beautiful door that had opened in the dark basement. Thomas looked through the open door and said, "Wow, look at that!" then, hand in hand, walked through the door with the kind young man.

***

As the mutilated body of the little boy sagged over the ropes that bound him to the sacrificial pole, his grandfather laughed and the people in the room celebrated with him. Reverend Long stopped celebrating, however, when the darkness behind the still-warm body of his grandson began to deepen. Long watched, mouth agape, as a scaly claw pushed through the darkness like a shark's fin breaking through ocean waves. The first claw was followed by another, and then the huge head of a horrible dragon roared into the room. Reverend Long's dark revelry quickly turned to terror as the laughter died in his throat. He tried to scream, but only a hoarse half-human cry broke out. Long wrapped his fingers around the stair balustrades as his feet flew off the ground. Hot sucking flames encircled his legs, drawing him down; his skin blistered as his clothes burned away. His fingernails broke loose, leaving a bloody trail as he was pulled along the fragile stair rails. With a loud crack, the wood broke as his tormented wails scraped the walls of his throat.

Time stopped and for an instant the screams were silenced. The huge serpent that had used an innocent's blood to break its ancient chains smiled at the burned and broken body of the counterfeit clergy. Then, with one razor-like claw, it sliced him from top to bottom, grabbed his writhing soul, threw it into the flaming pit, and took its place. As the creature pushed into the remains of the clergy, the body began to spasm, to change, to heal. In a moment, it was completely whole. The companions of the reverend who had participated in the sacrifice were standing wide-eyed and trembling. Their mouths opened, but nothing resembling words came out. The new reverend smiled and then, with a hungry leap, was upon them.

What Laden Long never knew, because no one was available to tell him, is that when you conjure evil dragons or demons, a vacuum is created. If something comes out, something else has to descend. A vacuum has to be filled. If the one sacrificed is pure, then, although his blood is powerful enough to open the gate, his soul cannot descend into the darkness, so someone else must take his place, usually the most wicked available, and in this case, that was Laden Long.

Chapter Eleven

As the old man and the library's reigning scamp turned to leave, the door opened and the fire marshal walked in.

"Grampa!" Sarah yelled, ran toward him, and leapt into his big arms.

"Hey, tootle-butt. What's the deal? It's not like you haven't seen me in years. I got held up. Seems there was a terrible traffic accident down the road." The fire marshal looked at the old man and mouthed *we need to talk* behind Sarah's back, who hadn't let go of his neck long enough to let her grandpa breathe.

The librarian, who saw the fire marshal's silent request, looked at Sarah and said, "Sarah, I have something to show you. Come with me while your grandpa and my dad talk for a minute."

As the two walked into an adjoining room, the fire marshal leaned into the old man and in a quiet voice said, "Hank, the accident I just mentioned involved Reverend Laden Long's daughter and grandson. Apparently, they wrapped their car around a tree, causing the vehicle to explode. Not sure how that could have happened. In real life, automobiles are not supposed to do that. I'm going to have to investigate as soon as the flames are out and the bodies removed."

The old man gasped. "You're talking about Thomas and his mother, aren't you?"

"Yes, and I don't know how to tell Sarah. I am pretty sure she is going to take it hard."

The old man stared back at his new friend and sighed. "Kenneth, she already knows."

The fire marshal's eyes widened. He blinked rapidly, shaking his head. "I am not surprised. She senses things like this all the time. What did she say to you about it?"

"She told me that the dragon slew the boy and came through the door made by the sacrifice. Those weren't her exact words, but they convey the meaning. I don't think the accident killed Thomas. I am pretty sure it was only after he had been killed that it occurred. As to his mother, I have no idea, but the car accident is a cover-up, of that I am sure."

The fire marshal shook his head slowly, then looked at the old man and said, "I suppose you've seen a lot of things like this since you used to work for a group that investigated them?"

"More than I ever wanted."

About that time Sarah came back accompanied by a very disturbed librarian, who said, "Sarah just looked at me and said, 'Thomas and his mother are dead. Thomas went to Heaven, but his mom did not.' After that, I thought maybe I should bring her back to you."

Both the old man and the fire marshal knelt down to be on eye level with Sarah. Her grandfather spoke first, "Honey, you know about Thomas?"

"Yes, sir," she answered quietly, "I do. I saw it in a dream. The dragon came through the door after the bad people used Thomas to open it, but the young man fooled them. He took Thomas before they could hurt his heart, and then he unlocked the door so the real dragon could come through it and eat them. They were surprised about that," she stated so innocently it was disturbing.

The old man snorted, "I bet they were! Got a little more than they bargained for, didn't they?

"Sarah, do you know where this happened?" the old man continued.

Sarah stared hard at the floor like she didn't want to answer the question.

Both men saw it, and her grandfather asked first, "Sarah, why don't you want to tell us where Thomas was hurt and the bad people eaten?"

The old man shifted from his knees to sitting down and whispered, "What's wrong, honey?"

Sarah looked up, tears glistening in her eyes, and whispered, "Because if we go there, he is going to hurt us." Then she leaned into the men and sobbed.

As the old man and the fire marshal held Sarah close, the old man heard a familiar voice, *"Don't you think it would be better if, instead of crawling into a dragon's lair again, you forced it to come to you?"*

The old man flinched but quickly caught himself, regained his composure, and then thought back, *I haven't heard from you in a long time. Good to hear your voice. I would ask you where you've been, but I happen to know. And yes, by the way, I do think it would be better to confront the dragon in an arena of my own choosing than his. What do you have in mind, Speaker?*

"Not now," Speaker said. "You take Sarah home so the fire marshal can examine the accident and be sure to tell him to look for sulphur residue."

Humph. Yeah, I'm sure that will be there in abundance.

"Hank, you okay...? You kinda went blank on us there for a moment," the fire marshal asked, concerned.

"Huh?! Yeah, I'm sorry, just had a major flashback. Sometimes old voices flare up and remind me I have been here before." The old man marveled at how the truth could deceive if worded just right; then he volunteered, "Would you like for me to take Sarah home so you can get to the scene?"

"I was hoping you would ask. Yes, sir, if you don't mind, and if you want to feed her, I am sure her grandmother would be grateful as well. Let me call Grace and let her know you are coming."

"Sure. Absolutely," the old man replied, thinking, *Kenneth, you are as shrewd as a serpent yourself. You trust me, but you are also guarding your granddaughter by ensuring that Grace knows we are en route. You're a good grandpa!*

"There is something I need to ask you, Kenneth," the old man added. "When you search the wreckage, will you look for sulphur residue? It will probably be obvious, but just in case it is not... well... I will be surprised if you don't find it."

The fire marshal stared back at the old man for a moment and then answered, "I was kinda expecting it myself. We need to talk some more when I get home."

"Yeah, we probably should," the old man replied. "There is so much going on here, and I have come to the conclusion the more you know, the better you can be prepared." *Up to a point,* he rationalized.

When Kenneth called his wife to let her know that Hank would be bringing Sarah home, she insisted that Hank stay for lunch instead of bringing a greasy hamburger to "warp his guts," as she phrased it. As the old man and Sarah headed toward her grandparents' farm, the fire marshal left for the grizzly scene of the accident.

The old man's truck stuttered into life, and as he looked over to the little girl strapped into his passenger seat, he realized he didn't know who he was addressing now. Was it the six-year-old queen of story time or his ancient princess?

Speaker, who, above all beings, was able to read his mind, answered, *"Both, I think... There seems to be a merging, an integration occurring between the two personalities. They are both Sarah—the little Sarah, and the big Sarah. One has been hidden, lying dormant, and as a result, the other grew naturally like a normal child would. Now, they are merging. In the wisdom of modern day, you would liken it to a multiple personality disorder in the process of being reattached or assimilated with their alters, and by that, I mean the different fractured personalities are being merged back into one."*

The old man, silently listening to the ancient inner voice that had guided him sporadically throughout his life, replied, "Oh," out loud.

Sarah looked at him and said, "He still talks to you, doesn't he? I am starting to remember more and more, and I remember the sword you called Speaker. It bonded with you, didn't it? Together you were able to defeat the dragon. He is still with you, isn't he?"

The old man gave Sarah a sideways glance and laughed quietly. "Yes, he is, and we were just discussing you. I asked him which one of you, my six-year-old munchkin, or ah, well…"

"The ancient princess you grew to love?" Sarah interjected sadly.

"Yeah, I guess…"

She smiled back at him, one eyebrow raised in an expression he had missed for ages. "No guess to it, peasant boy!" And then her expression softened, and she asked, "What did Speaker say?"

"Apparently, he is well read in current psychology," the old man started but was interrupted.

"Of course, I have read everything you do and retain all of it, whereas you do not. I know everything you know and more."

"He is also as rude and as interrupting as ever," the old man continued.

"Must be hard having two voices in your head," Sarah mused.

"Are you experiencing anything similar? The speaker seems to think, both... of what...? Of you? I guess the six-year-old Sarah and the ancient princess."

"Watch it, buddy!" Sarah growled.

"Huh?"

"Are men always this clueless?" Sarah's six-year-old voice asked. She blinked and shook her head, and the mature princess responded, "Always, my dear, and as our beloved Hank carelessly mentioned, I am ancient, so I would know."

Four personalities located in two bodies began laughing as the old truck continued rolling down the highway.

After a few moments the old man grumbled, "Okay, this is not working. It is time to get serious."

A six-year-old face with twinkling ancient eyes looked back at him and calmly responded, "I am working. Now what did the speaker think we ought to do?"

"I can take it from here," the spirit of the old sword answered inside the old man's weary brain.

And just how the hell are you going to do that without involving me? the cranky old man protested.

"I talk, you translate, and no worries about my hearing the princess. It's as simple as that," the speaker continued.

The old man turned toward the squirming six-year-old and griped, "Speaker wants to answer you directly through me, with me translating." Then the old man laughed. "So now, the wheels have turned. I get to interrupt him. This should be fun!"

The old man heard a voice in his head grunt, *"Humph!"* and then begin. *"Tell her the trap idea is a good one, and that a diversion would also be a good idea."*

The old man obeyed slowly, "Speaker says traps and diversions are going to be needed."

His six-year-old passenger looked back at him. "What does diversion mean?"

The old man sighed. This was going to be a very long conversation. He hoped the fire marshal was having better luck at figuring things out.

***

The fire marshal hesitated before getting out of his truck. Firefighters and paramedics were hovering around filing reports and waiting for him to investigate so they could conclude their grizzly work. He stared at the accident scene, noticed smoke still curled up from it, and sighed. He hated combing through the still-warm ash of broken lives, especially when he knew the people the bodies used to be, and especially when one was a child, a playmate of his own granddaughter... but somebody had to do it. He was trained and had years of experience. Most of the time he could tell as much in five minutes as a forensic specialist could in a two-hour autopsy. It was called experience. Combining the context of the accident specifics, he could usually be fairly accurate. His observation didn't carry the weight of a specialized autopsy report, but it usually nailed the important parts. Today he hesitated, then climbed out of the truck, put on his protective gear, and walked over to the crash site.

Donning his breathing apparatus and gloves, the fire marshal could still smell the stench of the burned corpses through the filters. He steeled himself for the investigation. Suffering and pain were so powerful. People without good shields did not become first responders.

The fire marshal had powerful shields, some natural, some cultivated. After the initial shock of horror, they slipped into place. His eyes hardened, and his observational skills heightened. The first thing he noted was the position of the smaller body. Neither sex nor age could be determined due to the extensive burns, but the fire marshal did notice how the body was strapped into the car. The seat belt had jammed, so it wouldn't give any slack. He cut the belt, freeing the small body, and then placed one hand under it and the other behind the head and neck, moving it for a better view. He noted that the chest cavity, although burned nearly through, revealed broken bones and a major gash; not a tear from an explosion, but a long thin cut that even though partially burned, clearly had not been caused by the accident. His verdict? The smaller individual was dead before the car crashed.

After a few more minutes of close inspection, the fire marshal shifted his investigation to the larger body. He moved over to the other side of the car, pried the door open, and began his observation. This body was obviously female. Her face was burned, making immediate identification impossible, but what was obvious was that the head had been hammered from the side, not from a collision with anything in the front. His conclusion was the same. This victim was also dead before the car collided with the tree.

The question was how the vehicle hit the tree and exploded if both occupants were dead before it crashed. Most investigators would immediately presume it was impossible, regardless of what the bodies seemed to indicate. Dead bodies don't drive cars; therefore, they would rule that the driver must have been alive before the accident. No other possibility would seem to exist.

Kenneth Linscomb, however, was not a normal investigator, at least not in this situation, knowing what he already knew. He was about to back carefully out of the vehicle when he glanced over at the smaller body. From this angle he noticed something he had not seen before. He walked back around to the passenger side of the car and bent down low. This time, with gloved hands, he gently pried open the slit that ran the length of the body's chest cavity. His eyes widened and he gasped! The body's heart was missing! He shook his head and looked again, but it was clear. The arteries and muscles that would normally have held the small heart had been severed with almost surgical precision. *Damn! What is going on?*

A fireman heard his gasp and moved in close to help. "You okay, Kenneth? Everything all right?"

The old fire marshal caught his breath, his shields slipped back into place, and he yelled back, "Yeah, I'm fine. It's just hard when it's a kid, and especially when you knew him." With that, he quickly covered the chest with remnants of the clothing and thought, *I need to talk to Hank.*

Chapter Twelve

After a conversation shortened by the limits of the drive to her grandmother's house, Hank pulled into the driveway and said, "Now as far as anyone else knows, there are only two people in this truck. So, no one forget that, and pipe up out of turn, and really confuse things. Okay?"

The speaker responded, *"Don't you think you're stating the obvious?"*

The princess, looking though a six-year-old face, nodded, then Sarah blinked, shook her head, and said, "I really like her."

Hank grimaced, nodded, and thought, *This can't be real. I am an inmate of an asylum living out my delusions. I have a voice in my head that is a thousand-year-old sword and a six-year-old at my feet who thinks she is a medieval princess. Help me!*

Sarah looked up at him, smiled a snaggle-toothed smile, and took his hand. "Come on! Grandma is cooking, and I am hungry!"

The old man looked back at her and heard, *"Well, if you are insane, at least you're in good company."* Then silence.

The old man was still shaking his head when they walked through the front door.

"Good to see you again, Hank," Sarah's grandma said as she hugged Sarah and shook hands with the old man.

"Good to see you too, Grace."

"Well, come on in, wash up, and get ready to eat. I didn't have time to throw together a really big meal, but most people like bacon, lettuce, and tomato sandwiches, so I hope you do as well."

Hank looked back at Grace and winced.

She caught the expression and stopped. "What?"

"Well, I'm allergic to tomatoes, and pork gives me migraines."

Grace paused and looked back at him, her eyes narrowing. She tilted her head as she studied him. Hank withered before her glare. His snort gave his secret away, and this exposure was complete when Sarah chimed in, "Grandma Grace, he is teasing. He loves tomatoes and used to raise pigs!"

They both turned to look at Sarah, whose princess-personality quickly retreated, leaving the six-year-old façade to face their stares. "What? What did I say?"

The old man recovered, laughing, and confessed, "She's right, Grace. I'm only teasing. I *love* BLT sandwiches and have it on good authority that you could sling mud in a pie plate, and it would come out tasting wonderful. So, forgive me. I am a terrible tease."

Grandma Grace looked at him with an *I-thought-so* smirk across her face and said, "Oh, that's fine, Hank. It's not real bacon anyway. It's made out of soymeal," and walked off to fix the sandwiches.

Hank looked back at her, saw her shoulders shaking, and knew she got him! He glanced toward Sarah, who just shrugged as if to say, "Hey, my grandma is tough!"

Lunch was filled with pleasant conversation, and the old man was grateful for a moment of respite from the worries of dragons and ancient princesses. He was about to leave when the fire marshal got home and the old man realized his reprieve had been short.

"Glad you're still here, Hank. Please tell me you ate all the bacon."

"Yep, sure did. There was one last piece, but when I realized it wasn't enough for a sandwich, I decided to go ahead and eat it to save you the misery of having only one piece left."

"Don't let him mess with you, Kenneth. I knew you were going to be late, so the moment I heard your truck enter the drive, I threw a couple more pieces on. Yours will be the freshest and hottest of anybody's."

The fire marshal paled. He swallowed hard and looked at his wife. "I just got back from a fire, burn victims. I would rather not have any bacon. It's just, you know, honey."

Grace rolled her eyes and her hand covered her mouth as shock threw a dark veil across her face. "Oh gosh, yes! I am so sorry. I wasn't thinking. I knew better. I just forgot."

The old man looked at Kenneth, eyes widening. "Oh my! I didn't know. I am so sorry!"

"It's fine. I am used to it. After a few days, the smell gets out of my nose, and more importantly, out of my head, and I get back to normal, but right now, not so much."

About that time Sarah walked in the room, looked at the faces of her guardians, and said, "But dragon meat smells really good, and I will be glad when you guys have some ready for a meal!"

All three of the adults in the room stared at the little girl. A heavy silence held for an awkward moment. Grandma Grace recovered first. "Well, we will do our best, dear. Now why don't you get ready for your nap while your grandpa, Mr. Hank, and I have an adult talk?"

"Grandma, I know you love me and mean well, but if it's okay with you and Grandpa, and of course Mr. Hank, I think being here listening to you figure out how to defeat the evil that has come into our town will be a lot more comforting than me laying in my bed staring at the ceiling, listening to my fears."

Grace stepped back, stunned by Sarah's retort, but was bailed out by her husband, "You may be right, Sarah, so why don't you come sit in my lap while we talk about this. If there is something you don't understand, then you ask. Okay?"

"Yes, sir, and if I get sleepy, I'll just nap right here with you holding me."

"Sounds like a plan," the old man responded to the fire marshal.

Grandma Grace had stepped out of the room to regain her composure. Her granddaughter's very adult-like voice, countenance, and even word choice had stunned her. When she came back in, she carried hot cups of Earl Grey tea on a tray. Once everyone was served, she sat down, looked around, and said, "Bring me up to speed. I have a feeling I have missed some important details of what's going on."

The fire marshal looked at his wife and said, "I'm trying to remember what you know and what you don't. Let me start with the most recent. Thomas and his mother were found dead in a burning car off Highway 279 a few hours ago. I just came from investigating it, and this hasn't been officially announced yet, so…"

Grace shifted in her chair, instinctively becoming more official, and nodded. She had been married to the fire marshal for close to forty years, knew the protocols, how he would lay them aside to talk to her, and how they would both put them back in place as soon as the conversation was over.

The fire marshal continued, "After investigating the accident, I am convinced both Thomas and his mother were dead before the car exploded."

"Whoa!" Hank cried.

Grandma Grace closed her eyes and whispered a sad prayer.

"I was expecting it, but even so, it's hard to grasp," the old man replied softly.

"What is going on around here? This is crazy!" Grace cried. "He was just a little boy." Then remembering Sarah, she asked, looking at both men seated in front of her, "Are you sure she needs to be hearing this?"

"Sarah knew it before we did," the old man responded. "She even knew *before* it happened, and I'm pretty sure she knows who did it. The only surprise to me is that Thomas's mother was also killed. I wasn't expecting that."

Sarah, whose face had hardened as much as a six-year-old's could, calmly addressed her grandmother, "Thomas saw an angel, Grandma. He left the room before the bad people could hurt him and went to Heaven with the angel. Then the angel surprised the bad people by letting the dragon out of its prison. He let the dragon eat those people; then the dragon hid inside Thomas's grandpa. It's a smart dragon, but my other Sarah knows him, and she and Mr. Hank are going to fight him, just like they used to. Aren't you, Mr. Hank?"

Grandma Grace shuddered at her granddaughter's words. Confusion spilled across her features as she turned to the old man and waited. The announcement had gotten the fire marshal's attention as well. All three of them looked at the old man, waiting for his response.

The old man's neck tightened and his head drew back stiffly. The truth was he didn't know how to reply. He had just recently come across the whole truth himself. As he paused, trying to get his words right, the sword that lived inside him whispered to him, *"Ask them where they want you to start. Don't assume they know enough to ask the right questions. Start with theirs. Be honest, but don't lay all your cards out."*

"I don't know everything, but I may be able to help you some. What is it you want to know?"

Grace blurted out, "Everything! I want to know why my six-year-old granddaughter talks like an adult one minute and a six-year-old the next. I want to know how she could possibly know Thomas was going to die, and about angels, and why she spoke Latvian in her nightmares, and how she knows you. Who *are* you?" As Grace spoke she grew louder and more frustrated, almost shouting by the end.

Sarah hopped out of her grandpa's lap and walked over to her grandma, looked her in the eyes, and said, "He is okay, Grandma. He really is. He saved me a long time ago, and I know he would lay his life down for me because he did it before. Please trust Mr. Hank. He is a good man." Sarah had taken her grandmother's hands in her own, then leaned in and hugged her. "Trust him, Grandma. It's okay," she whispered as she held her tight.

The fire marshal also walked over to his wife and granddaughter and held them both in his long arms. After a moment they broke and all looked back at the old man expectantly.

"Sarah and I did not always live in this time," Hank began. "We have, as she said, fought this evil manifestation before… centuries ago."

Grace's mouth fell open and Grandpa Kenneth's eyes widened.

"It's true. It really is." The old man nodded. "The story I have been telling the children in the library is not a fairy tale. The timing is ironic, however. I had no idea when my daughter asked me to help her with summer story time that my story would renew itself. Nor did I know that Sarah even existed, or that the dragon would come back to torment us.

"But back to your questions. First, who am I? I am Harry. After battling the dragon, I fell, broken and burned, into darkness. I still don't understand how I got here. The last thing I remember was fighting the dragon that had abducted Sarah from her father's kingdom. I thought I had killed it, but then I passed out from my wounds. When I woke up in your time, a continent away from my home, I was alone. It took me years to discover when and where I came from. What I could recall from my past seemed more like fanciful old stories than memories. I was as shocked as you were to discover that *my* Princess Sarah was manifesting in *your* little Sarah. I was even more shocked to realize that the dragon was alive and had followed us through time."

Grace's face hardened. "I want *my* Sarah back! Whatever spirit is trying to use her to relive its life, you can't have her!" She turned to stare adamantly back at the six-year-old in front of her.

Tears began to flow freely down Sarah's face. She looked back at her grandfather, who was also stunned, and then at Hank, who opened his arms. She ran to him, shaking. The old man continued, "It's not like that, Grace. Your Sarah *is* my Sarah. Of that, I am sure. They're not two spirits fighting over one body. Kenneth, you told me you found Sarah after a fire, a little girl wrapped in old cloth. Isn't that correct?"

"Yes, yes, it is," he said, leaning over and nodding.

"Did you keep the cloth?" The old man subconsciously held his breath, waiting for the answer he hoped would bring proof to their dilemma.

"Yeah, we did. It was quite unique, old even, with unusual symbols on it."

"Has Sarah ever seen it?" the old man asked again, continuing to hold his breath.

"No, she hasn't," Grace answered. "We thought it might be better to show her when she was older." She scoffed, shaking her head, "That's ironic, isn't it?"

"Can you get me a piece of paper and something to write with? I want to show you something that might help you understand what has been happening. And would you mind letting me see the cloth?"

As soon as he was given the paper, the old man drew a simple symbol on it. The one Sarah had drawn the week before during story time. Grandma Grace entered the room, holding a small cardboard box. In it was a bundle, sealed carefully, in a transparent garment bag. She was about to take it out of the box when the old man stopped her.

"Before you open that, look at what I have drawn." They both leaned over and noted the symbol. "Sarah drew this last week. I was telling the story and stopped to have the kids draw what I had just described. She drew what she had heard me talk about, and then she also drew the other side of the coin, which I had not described!"

Grandma Grace held the crayon-scrawled drawing of the symbol close and said, "I still don't see what this has to do with anything. I want my Sarah back."

The fire marshal looked at his wife. "Give him a minute, Grace. It's going to be all right. I feel it."

"Thank you, Kenneth. I'm grateful for your patience." The old man turned to Sarah and said, "Sarah, have you ever seen the garment that your grandparents have in that bag?"

Sarah looked back at the old man and said, "No, I have not."

"Now, please answer one more question."

Sarah nodded. "Okay."

"What was the color of the dress you were wearing when I rescued you from the dragon?"

A gentle smile brushed Sarah's lips as she thought back. "It was green, dirty, and tattered, especially after I tore the hem out to bandage your wounds."

The fire marshal and his wife both gasped; then Grandma Grace drew out the garment, carefully unfolding it. It was burned and torn at the hem, and it was green.

Sarah rushed over toward it. "My dress! It's my dress!"

The old man continued, his eyes glistening, "I am not sure of this, but it is the only thing that seems to fit the facts. I believe that Sarah was also transported through time. Only, for some reason, her body was changed back to a child as she was swept along. She lost her memories and woke up in the ashes of the fire you were investigating, wearing the tattered remains of the dress you now hold in your hands. You see, Grace, your Sarah is my Sarah."

A tight smile slid onto Grace's lips. The old man watched as her face contorted. She gripped the edge of the table as anguish fought with truth for control. Grief postured for release, and hot tears swam in the fray. Finally, faltering words slipped from her in sad whispers, "I've lost my baby. She's leaving me. I didn't have her long enough." Her head bowed, she held her face in her hands and cried, "I don't understand. It can't be. Oh, Kenneth, what is happening? Am I going crazy?"

Sarah rushed to Grace, wrapping her small arms around her waist. Grace lifted her up and Sarah buried her face in Grace's neck. "Grandma… please don't cry. I love you. It's me, Grandma. You're not going crazy… and if you are, I am going with you. I need you. Grandma, please, please… it's me. I can't do this without you. You're my mama. Please." Then Sarah began to sob, and Grace hugged her tighter and wept with her.

For a long time, they just held each other. The men were afraid to break the sacredness of the moment. Then Grace sighed, looked up, and said, "Well, I don't know about you, baby, but I feel better."

Sarah laughed, wiping her nose on her hand. Grace looked at the act and scolded, "Sarah, I don't care if you are a thousand years old and some type of fairy princess, you're still my granddaughter, and if I have told you once, I have told you a hundred times—do not wipe your snotty nose on your hand!"

The fire marshal and the old man heehawed in chorus, but were halted in mid-breath by the stern voice of Grace, "And if any of you old men start mocking us women about our crying, the fur will hit the fan. Have I communicated in such a way as you understand?" she added, continuing to stare down her nose through her wire-rimmed reading glasses.

The old man was about to snort but caught the fire marshal's facial expression and strangled the laugh before it was born.

"I hear ya, Grace. I hear ya. But the question still remains: Now what? What are we going to do?"

The old man scratched his head and said, "I think we need to carry on as though we're not aware of the murders, since most people don't know what's happened. You haven't even had time to file your report. The last official word on Thomas was that he was moving out of state. If we go ahead with story time tonight, I don't think the dragon will risk exposing himself in public. So, continuing as normal may be the safest play for the moment. I have a friend I need to talk with, and then I will get back to you. Now, I need to get going. See you tonight."

Hank looked at Sarah. "The truth is out there now. I know you will want to tell your grandparents more, and feel free to. What hasn't been said is probably not something I even remember. Right now, this storyteller needs a break, needs to talk with himself, and needs to get the story time version of this fable. So, see you tonight. Okay?"

The Sarah he used to know looked back through the eyes of the little girl and nodded, then quickly winked, letting him know that she would be careful. What her grandparents didn't know, they could not accidentally reveal. Who would believe them anyway? So why risk being taken from the people she loved because some Child Protective Services employee heard her grandparents were nuts, or worse, risk the story getting out and back to the dragon. She was tired and needed a nap. Sometimes it was good to be a six-year-old.

***

Before Sarah reached the stairs that led to her bedroom and the nap she craved, her grandmother's strong hand clasped her shoulder. "Not so quick, young lady." And then Grace frowned and said, "Are you a young lady?"

Sarah turned toward her grandmother and answered, "To you always, even if you live to be ninety, and I make it to seventeen."

"Ha!" Grace cackled. "That's something else we need to work on—your math skills. But don't think you're getting out of here until I hear the rest of the story. I am claiming my rights as a curious woman and your guardian. Now sit back down while I get you some cookies and a glass of milk; then you can tell me all about it."

Sarah rolled her eyes and slyly winked at her grandfather, who had included himself in the moment and also wanted to know more. Her grandmother brought a small plate of chocolate chip cookies and a cold glass of milk and said, "Start."

Sarah sighed. "Okay. My father was a very busy king…"

Chapter Thirteen

Story night at the library

The old man couldn't nap that afternoon. The speaker never slept and, now that he had begun talking again, wasn't inclined to quit. The old man did nod off a few times, but his daughter called to check on him right as he had fallen asleep. They talked long enough for him to assure her that he was fine, and then he drifted off again. Finally, the rumbling in his belly reminded him that he probably ought to eat something lest he embarrass himself and his assorted crew of candy crunchers. He ate a can of chicken noodle soup filled with so many crackers it was dusty, took a quick shower, decided not to shave, and got dressed. As he pushed the latest trash out of his truck and was about to drive away, he stopped, walked into his garage, popped open an old army locker, and removed a long bundle. "I sure hope I don't need this," he heard himself say. Then another voice joined in, *"But if you do, you'll have it. Besides, the closer I am to it, the more I can help you."* Throwing the bundle into the truck, the old man got in and drove to the library.

The host of children had a hard time settling that night. They squirmed, and chatted, and fussed, and then finally gathered close to their storyteller. The old man was also restless. In spite of all that had transpired, all he had rediscovered and remembered, and even with the threat of death and dismemberment hanging over his head, he was excited.

A few years ago, he had started to believe that he must have made up the story rather than lived it. He was tempted to see a counselor but knew he would be placed on drugs that would steal his memories. It might mean peace, and maybe he wouldn't be plagued with nightmares from a time out of this time so far away, but nightmares were a small price to pay to remember the good things. So he decided to keep his memories, fight his doubts, and just keep living. Now, in a remarkable way, by telling the story, he was forced to relive the memories. It amazed him when he first started telling the story how easily it had slipped from his lips, how vivid the memories were. The realism crept into the story, even the redacted version he told the babes that gathered at his feet. He enjoyed how their faces reflected their captured imaginations and was sad that tonight would be the end of the story, or at least the part he could tell.

So once again the old man settled in, his bones creaking as they positioned themselves in the old rocker. A small hand touched his arm and the six-year-old queen of story time laid her head against his shoulder. He was glad she was there but also fought back sadness. This was not the life they should be living. They should have been allowed to grow old together, not this abomination of him being an old man and her, a first grader. But before the sadness could drown him, he began the ritual of meeting the eyes of each child who had become dear to him. They gazed back and smiled, a room full of snaggled teeth and bright eyes.

As his eyes lit upon Sarah, he tipped his head toward her. She grinned back, then leaned in and whispered, "Grandma Grace heard the story this afternoon and told Grandpa and me to go on without her. She needed some time to herself to process things."

The old man nodded his understanding and then noticed how close the children had gathered. Tonight, they had slipped out of their little chairs and moved toward him. His eyes twinkled as they hovered close. He had learned to love every one of those booger-eating, snaggle-toothed little knotheads. When he had first started with story time, he couldn't wait to be done with it; now he didn't know how he was going to live without it.

His urchins must have also sensed this was the end, and apparently felt that the closer they could get, the longer the story would last. Their parents hovered around like chickens guarding their brood. The old man took a deep breath, cleared his throat, and was about to begin when the library door, clanging and rattling with the bells his daughter had attached to it, opened. Reverend Laden Long sauntered in.

The old man's eyebrows cocked in surprise, but he brushed them back into place quicker than a mongoose could strike a cobra's neck. The speaker's voice, deliberately cold in the old man's mind, said, *"Well now, look-a here. The devil's come to church. Good thing you brought me along, isn't it?"*

The old man thought back, *I am not going to hack his head off in here! I might get blood on the children, and besides that, I would never hear the end of it from Sarah. She wants to skin him herself.*

"Well, you're going to have to say something quick. He sees you've noticed him. Look closely. He is trying to veil his eyes, but your discern-ornament keeps him from hiding from us."

What do you mean? the old man asked Speaker. Then he saw it as the man neared. The eyes of the reverend were slitted, serpentine. He could hide everything else about him, but the dragon could not hide the windows of his soul from the old man.

"Nod to him like you're not aware, and then begin the story. Hurry, before he senses something," Speaker demanded.

The old man turned his attention to the children at his feet and then asked his typical opening question, "All right now, where were we? What happened last in the story?"

Amongst the confused chorus of conflicting cries, a pretty little redheaded girl on the front row calmly raised her hand. It was such an unusual gesture that the old man ignored the ruckus and smiled down at her. "Hush, everyone!" he growled in a friendly way. "I want to hear from Luwanda. She has been very polite and not bawled out the answer like certain other little heathens." The old man looked down at her grinning, rewarding her sweet calm.

"My uncle said he has heard this story before. He told me that the dragon was really a good dragon and just lonely. He wanted the princess to marry him, but mean old Harry stole her away."

The old man looked around the room and saw the Reverend Long's wicked smirk; then he quickly looked back at the innocent one in front of him and asked, "Who is your uncle, my dear? I think he and I have heard different versions of the story. I am sure his intentions were to help you understand, but I have to say, I think he is a little confused. You see, in my story, the dragon is selfish and does not care who he hurts so long as he can get what he wants. Your uncle is right about one thing, honey. The dragon does want the little girl."

The speaker's voice in his head yelled at him, *"Princess! Not little girl!"*

The old man thought back, *I said exactly what I meant. I want him to know I know what he is up to.*

"Oh."

"My uncle is right over there," the little red-haired girl beamed, pointing at a burly man in fashionable clothes, seated a few rows back. She waved to him, and he waved back. The old man looked at the uncle, thinking he was definitely going to talk to the man after story time. The old man nodded to the uncle, and for the first time noticed his serpent eyes glaring back. The old man quickly blinked away his surprise and casually scanned the room for more serpentine eyes like the uncle's.

The speaker calmly spoke, *"I count five of them. Of course, I am limited to your eyes, but I would be willing to say that at least twenty percent of the adults in this room are not our friends."*

Not missing a beat, the old man continued speaking to the little red-haired innocent, "But the dragon doesn't love the princess, honey. I promise you that. Now let me continue. When we last heard from Harry, he was speaking with the sword named Speaker that could speak to Harry using just his thoughts.

"Harry answered the sword, 'But what now? How do I rescue the princess? I am not even sure she is the princess anymore.'

"The speaker answered, *'She is still Sarah, princess of her father's kingdom, Harry. But she's struggling. She doesn't want to be a dragon. She doesn't want to be selfish and hurt people, and even though she may get a little dragony, and maybe even turn a little greenish, and even sprout some scales, she will still be a good person as long as she keeps fighting to be. If she gives up, well then, you have to let her go because then she will have completely turned into a dragon, whether she looks like one or not.'*

"Harry scowled." At the mention of the word *scowled*, fourteen children tilted their heads in sync. The old man, in spite of being surrounded by veiled enemies who were intent on his destruction, laughed, "I see you might not know that word? It means, well..." He looked up and saw the expression on Reverend Long's face, and taking advantage of the moment, pointed at the reverend and said, "Why, it looks just like Reverend Long's face right now." Every urchin head in the room pivoted, staring at the counterfeit clergy caught before he could react in the spotlight of their innocent eyes. The old demon's glare intensified under the scrutiny. The old man, concerned his little flock might be frightened, discovered to his amusement that his courageous little princess was lightning on greased wheels as well.

"Ewwww!" Sarah whispered in mock fright. "He does that so well!" Several children, catching Sarah's innocent and fearless manner, echoed her response.

"Wow! That looks mean!" a little freckle-faced boy, sucking on his perpetual Tootsie Roll Pop, chimed.

"No, it doesn't!" another fearlessly naïve candy cruncher added. "He's just helping Mr. Hank out and doing that on purpose."

The old man, sensing the timing was perfect, said, "Yep, that's what a scowl looks like. Thank you so much, Reverend Long!" and then, "Let's all give the reverend a clap for his help in telling the story."

The room exploded with mirth. The old man's flock loved to clap, and of course, several had to holler, and then a couple of the rowdier boys on the back row had to have a clapping contest. The old man looked at each one with the slightest hint of an arched eyebrow and said, "You can clap, or you can listen, but you cannot clap while I am telling the story. Now, which will it be?"

Silence, like a guillotine in its track, fell across the crowd. They shifted, sat down, and were soon staring intently at the old man, anxiously waiting for him to continue.

"Harry scowled. 'I will never let her go. I will fight the old dragon down every dark place in this gloomy lair. If I must, I will grab him by the tail and haul him into the light.'

"The speaker corrected, '*Harry, we are not talking about the dragon. We are talking about the princess. If she chooses to become a dragon, there is nothing you can do.*'

"'That's not true. I can win her back—help her heal her heart. I will die before I let her go.'

"The speaker persisted, *That's just it, Harry, if she becomes a dragon, she will be the one who jabs a sword into your heart.*"

The old man heard a sniffle and turned to see ancient grief clothed in tears streaming from Sarah's eyes. She was seated directly in front of him, so no one else was privy to her pain. The old man looked quickly away, wiping memories back like a stray hair, and then without a breath, continued.

"Harry paused a moment, stared into the endless dark tunnels, and said, 'If that happens, I will forgive her endlessly, and bare my heart to her a hundred times if it takes that to win her back.'"

The old man looked up and noticed the fire marshal also had a stream of tears quietly cutting trails along his tanned face. Their eyes met, and the old man knew his friend understood.

"Then Harry said, 'I appreciate the warning, but it hasn't happened. I still have time to rescue the princess. Tell me what to do.' Forced to trust this voice in his head to help him navigate his way through a maze of dark tunnels into the dragon's den, the words of the speaker haunted him. Could he have come so far only to lose the princess now because she had lost the battle for her heart? The dragon's power was more than the physical strength of a monster with a huge body. His most dangerous power lay in his ability as an evil tempter, a master manipulator, who could get anyone to do whatever he wanted if he just talked to them long enough. Harry feared that the princess had already spent too much time listening to the dragon's lies. He didn't blame her. Young, alone, and enslaved, all the attempts to rescue her had failed in the violent deaths of the men who tried to save her.

"Harry thought, *That would make me feel awfully hopeless and very lonely.* He started to wonder what chance he had to save the princess if all those great knights had failed. If she had already started to turn into a dragon, why would he even want to try? After a while, Harry realized he was tired and hungry. He couldn't remember when he had last eaten or slept. So, he said aloud, 'Speaker, are you there?'

"*'Of course I am, Harry. Where else would I be? You have the sword now, and we share a blood bond. I will be with you, whether you want me to be or not, for the rest of your life. What can I do for you?'*

"'I am tired, and I want to rest and eat something. Is there time?'

"*'I don't know if there's time or not. If you mean—will the princess turn into a dragon if you stop to sleep and eat—I have no idea. But I also know this: if you don't stop to eat, you will not have enough strength to continue your mission, and then the princess will fail because you will not be there to rescue her.'*

"Harry nodded, moved over to the cave wall, and slid down it. He scrounged around in his knapsack for a bundled piece of jerky—that's a kind of dried meat for taking on long hikes," the old man explained without missing a beat. The older members of his audience snickered, but his young fans took it as a matter of course and skipped right along with their storyteller.

"The meat was hard to chew and spicier than he liked, but it was all he had, so he kept chewing and swallowing until sometime, in between bites, he fell asleep. In his dream, he drifted down the dark tunnels barely able to see. He was, once again, moving toward the princess. Harry prayed she had not turned into a dragon, that somehow she had held on. The tunnel he followed led into the princess's dungeon. As he entered the chamber, he could see her huddled around a fire, shivering, futilely trying to stay warm. Harry cautiously whispered, 'Sarah… Sarah.'

"She startled as he entered the cave but said nothing. For a moment she just stared at him, then said, 'Why do you keep coming back? Leave me alone! He is going to kill you like all the rest. No one can stop him. No one can help me. He wants me to change so he can marry me, and I have no choice.' Sarah began to pace, stopping to twirl her hair. 'Surely it won't be so bad. I think I would make a fine dragon.' She turned toward Harry, and he was shaken to see that her face had small scales like a fish, her eyes were slitted like a snake's, and her skin had begun to turn dragon green."

The eyes of the little ones, who were gathered close to the old man, widened. Some visibly shivered. One little girl scampered to her mama to cuddle but didn't take her eyes off the old man. Even those with dragonish eyes leaned in. Some had never heard this part of the story, especially from the old man's point of view.

The old man continued, his voice intense. "The fear within Harry wanted him to turn and run back down the tunnel, make his way home, jump in his bed, and pull the covers over his head. But in his heart, he knew if he didn't find a way to save the princess and stop the dragon, it would deceive her into betraying him to his death.

"So instead of running away like he wanted, he stepped forward and said, 'When I stood in the marketplace with everyone laughing at me, only one person came to my aid. She stilled the mocking crowd, and she covered me— rescued me from my shame. Now it is my turn. You are the heart of your people, Princess! They love and respect you. The dragon has stolen the heart of my country, and he has slain the brave men who warred with him to bring it back. I am from a long line of warriors, men and women who restore that which is stolen, who look evil in the eye, and do not back down. Sarah, you were there for me. Now it is my turn to be there for you. I am here to fetch you home, and if I have to kill the dragon with one arm and drag you home in the other, I will do it.' Harry paused, slipped out of his warrior mode, and winced. He could not believe he'd said all that. *Sword, were those your words?*

"*No, Harry, that was all you. Those words came from your heart. I just unlocked them and set them free.*'

"The cold stone eyes of the princess stared back at Harry. Her pale, green face was void of emotion. Harry wondered if she would transform in front of his own eyes. A wave of dark despair slammed against his heart, almost overwhelming him. He looked away. His shoulders started to sag and his ancient borrowed armor felt like it weighed five hundred pounds. Forcing himself to watch, he looked back. Sarah blinked. Her expression changed. It softened, her eyes rolled back in her head, and she slid down to the floor. Before she could fall and hurt herself, he caught her and eased her down. Her body started to jerk, and then spasms swept through it. She rolled and groaned, and then she let out a huge breath and blinked again. As Harry watched, she changed. Her eyes relaxed, and the narrow vertical slits of a snake changed back to the normal eyes of a person.

"'Princess Sarah? Can you hear me? Sarah?'

"Slowly her eyes began to focus. She looked up at him, and as he held her, a soft smile crept across her lips, and then she whispered, 'Thank you, Harry. Thank you. I was changing. I don't want to be a dragon. I want to go home, but I don't know how long I can hold out. Please hurry.' Then, as though realizing that he was holding her and thinking how awkward he must feel, she sat up, dusted herself off, then forced herself to stand on wobbly feet. 'Do you know how long it will take? Do you have a plan? Please tell me you have a plan.'

"Before Harry could answer, the speaker warned him, *No! Harry, don't tell her a thing. She can't be trusted. She's too close to the beast. What he can't read of her mind, he will persuade her to reveal.'*

"Harry gulped, then answered the princess, 'Not yet. I don't know. Soon. I won't give up. I am coming for you.' Then he felt his body start to drift away. The dream was ending, and he was swept back into the tunnel. 'Noooo!' he groaned. He watched in despair as the princess reached for him as he faded away. The look on her face told him she could not endure much longer.

Chapter Fourteen

"Harry sat in the dark tunnel, not wanting to open his eyes. He knew he was awake, but he didn't want to face the day... or night. He had lost track of time in the cave. The speaker said, *'Sitting here is not helping her. I have a few things to show you, and then we attack. You need to move. Get up. Get going.'*

"'Can't,' Harry spoke out loud, 'the torch is out, can't see a thing.'

"*'Not working, Harry. The torch went out hours ago. My flame is what has been lighting your way. I am here, the light is on, and we must go. Now get up.'*

"Harry slowly forced his aching body to slide up the cave wall. When he finally stood, he opened his eyes and realized the tunnel glowed pale blue. The light came from the sword, sheathed at his side. *Is this real, or have I just gone crazy?*

"*'Well, my friend,'* the speaker replied, *'if you're crazy, you're in good company. Now, let's move!'* The sword led Harry back the way toward the dragon graveyard.

"When Harry realized where they were going, he asked, 'Why are we going back to the cavern where the dragon bones are?'

"*'You need some tools—armor, spurs, and things of that sort. You cannot take on the dragon as you are. One breath of his fiery spray and you would be sadedzinātais vējš.'*

"Harry shook his head. 'What did you say? I don't believe you said that!'

"*'Never mind, forget I said anything. Just trust me. We have some things to pick up.'*"

"Wait! Wait!" a chorus of curious children cried. "What does sady-zina-vej mean?"

A sly look crossed the old man's face. He had deliberately thrown in the word to spark his urchins' outcry. He loved teasing, provoking, and even—God forbid—educating them. "It is an old cooking term from the country the sword came from. It means, well, let me ask you: Have you ever had a wiener roast? You know, where you put wieners on a coat hanger and burn them outside over a campfire?"

"Oh yeah!" one of the restless boys in the middle of the pack barked. "We did that in Cub Scouts. We put wieners on a stick or a coat hanger and burned them to a crisp; then we put them in a hotdog bun with ketchup. I ate too many and threw up four times!"

The whole nursery of avid Oscar Meyer fans howled at that remark, and a deluge of puking stories threatened to flood the moment. The old man bent over and curled up, pretending to throw up. Everybody moved out of his way; then he straightened up and smiled. The small crowd laughed and drew closer to him again. "Okay, okay. Settle down. Just trying to get your attention so I can get through this story. It ends tonight, and we have a lot left to tell, so get quiet and let's see what happens next." The old man was a master storyteller. He had taken communication courses in college and knew that in order to keep the attention of a modern audience, especially children, he had to create a commercial break about every seven minutes. That interlude of burnt wieners and puking stories was the commercial. The children were now ready for the story to continue.

"'So, what are we looking for?' Harry asked as the speaker led him down a path enclosed on either side by ancient dragon skeletons. They were various sizes. Some were as large as a big horse, others as large as a school bus, and the largest of them was larger than his village house! Most of the skeletons had tattered banners draped across their backs. Occasionally, Harry saw one with a saddle-like harness for a rider, and for a few, the rider was buried with the dragon. For some strange reason, Harry was not afraid. He could sense that the dragons that lay in this ancient cemetery were honorable creatures, and was sure if he asked the speaker, the old sword would confirm it. In a remote section of the cavern, Harry came upon the bones of an old dragon and its rider. Layers of dust and cobwebs covered the rider's armor, and the banners which lay across the ancient beast were in shreds, ravaged by the great length of time they had been in the cave.

"*'Harry, this is what we have come for. Climb up atop the bones and haul the skeleton of the rider down. He doesn't need his armor now, but you do.'*

"Harry scowled, groaned, and grumbled, but moved forward through the maze of old bones, putting a foot here and a hand there until he climbed to the top. He looked at the rider's skeleton, still enclosed in armor, bent down, and started to pick it up, when it moved! Harry screamed."

The old man shouted, "Ahhh!" for effect and caused a startled ripple of gasps and "Ahhhs!" from the children, as well as some of their parents. Garnering a few glares in the process, Hank couldn't help the chuckle that escaped.

"Wah-ha, Mamma!"

"Oh, goodness!"

One old man in the back yelled a four-letter word. Every non-dragon-infected mom in the place jerked her head around and, in hoarse whispers you could have heard next door, yelled, "Shush!"

Sarah, who had been listening intently and remembered the incident, jumped up. "Hey, it's not what you think… it's just a bat!"

A blanket of peer-energized pressure fell on the children; the story time princess had cast her royal authority over her friends, and they shushed. A few nervous giggles squeaked out, and a pigtailed girl on the back row whispered, "Are you sure?"

To which the little monarch replied, "Yep, I know this part. It's not time to be *scared* yet, but..." Her voice dropped a notch, falling to a whisper, "But it's coming." Then she sat down and said, "Continue, please."

The old man smiled proudly and sighed. *She still commands and doesn't even know it.*

To which the speaker replied, *"I'm pretty sure she knows it. I think she just hides it but knows when to break it out, and just as quickly, stuff it back. She is a princess, remember. They are taught these things from birth."*

The old man looked down on the little girl seated on the floor at his feet. She looked back with the most innocent smile; then he saw the twinkle in her eyes.

Wow! he thought. *She does know it!*

"I told you she did. Princess Sarah is reigning and ruling," the old sword laughed.

Harry shook his head and continued on, "Well now, you guys okay? I didn't mean to scare you too much. Sometimes I just can't help myself."

A storm of "sure-you-dids," laced with "it's okay" and sprinkled with laughter and "Hurry up and tell us what happened!" urged him on.

"As soon as Harry bent over to move the skeleton, a bat flew out. As a matter of fact, several bats flew out. He jumped back, fell off the dragon skeleton, yanking the rider's armor with him, and landed on top of a bundle of rumpled and tattered banners. The banners broke his fall for the most part, but he felt a sharp pain in his backside."

The room of awestruck little booger-eaters tilted their heads and scrunched up their eyes trying to understand what had just happened. The old man pointed to his own rear end, and the crew of munchkins smiled.

One whispered voice declared, "He got something stuck in his butt!"

A gaggle of snickers swept across the rug but halted like a hound dog running into a tree when the old man harrumphed, clearing his voice.

"Harry jumped up, banged his head on the low-hanging spinal bones of the dragon, and howled. He heard, *'Oh, you found what we came for!'*

"'What is that?' Harry asked, rubbing both his bottom and his head. 'All I managed to do was frighten a bat, fall into the bones of a long dead dragon, and land on something sharp.'

" *'Yep, that is exactly what you did. Those sharp somethings are... spurs... dragon spurs to be exact! Dragons don't like them, but the smartest of them will admit they do help.'*

"'Help? Help what?' Harry asked, still rubbing the place where the spur had stuck him.

" *'Yeah,'* the speaker continued, *'those spurs have two functions. Number one, if a dragon rebels against its rider, the rider can hold on with them and force the dragon to obey. Number two, if the dragon is exhausted, like in the middle of a battle, the rider can gently touch the side of the dragon and those spurs will supernaturally give the dragon strength. So, a bad dragon gets a spike, and a good dragon gets help. Pretty powerful things, aren't they?'*

"'Sure,' Harry responded. 'But who's going to be riding a dragon? I sure don't need 'em.'

"There was a long pause from the speaker, and Harry began to feel uneasy. Cautiously, Harry said, 'Speaker, I am not going to be riding a dragon.'

"No answer came from the sword.

"'Speaker, I am not going to be riding a dragon!' Harry said forcefully, and then hearing only a long, extended period of silence from the old sword, Harry began to look for assurance and questioned in a small voice, 'Right?'

"This time the speaker answered, *'Well, Harry, about that…'*

"'What!?" Harry bellowed.

"The speaker went silent.

"He could read Harry's thoughts often better than Harry could, so he knew exactly how much Harry was afraid of heights, and fiery dragons, and wondering why, oh why he was where he was, doing what he was doing. So, the speaker paused to make sure he spoke to Harry in words that would calm him.

"When the sword realized they didn't have enough time for Harry's fears to calm, he laughed, *'Well, it keeps life interesting,'* and then just went ahead and told him, *'Harry, you're going to have to climb up very high, walk through a dark, twisting tunnel that leads you out high over the dragon's head, jump and fall several feet through the air, and hope the dragon doesn't see you and swallow you whole.*

"*'Once you land on its head, if you live through the fall, dig your spurs into its thick hide and hold on while it bucks like a wild horse. Be sure to hold on tight with these spurs because the dragon is going to fly out of the top of the cave, into the night, roaring in anger. Hope that your eardrums don't burst because of the beast's roar, and cling even tighter with your spurs when the dragon spins upside down and whips around trying to throw you off. During these dragon gymnastics, you need to be stabbing the dragon and praying that its flames can't burn through this old armor and barbecue you.*

"*'Finally, you must find just the right spot below the dragon's head, above its shoulders, stab it—I, of course, will be there to guide you—and then continue to hold on as it spins in nauseating circles all the way to the ground, where it will crash with such fury and flame that you will be crushed and burnt to small cinders unless you jump off right before it crashes. Did you get all that or do you want me to repeat it?"*

The faces of the old man's audience varied from grinning in unbelief to gasping in fear. The Reverend Laden Long, who coincidently was born with the strangest mark on his neck right below his head and above his shoulders, squinted with angry, lowered lids. He had always thought it was a birthmark, but when he examined it in front of the mirror, it had always reminded him of an old scar. Now that Laden Long was fully possessed by the dragon, the old man's story brought back angry memories. The reverend had the strangest compulsion to crack his neck and rub the old scar. Funny how it itched.

"As the speaker had been describing what Harry had to do, the poor boy's mouth dropped open, his eyes widened, his breath came in quick pants, his knees grew weak, and he slipped to the floor. As the speaker continued, Harry's heart beat faster and faster. When the speaker got to the part where Harry had to jump off the dragon's back before the serpent hit the ground in a fiery crash, Harry slumped over and fainted.

"Hey! Harry! Harry? This is not the time to be napping, boy! Get your scraggly face up! Harry, come on! We're in this together. Look, I know you're there. I can hear your thoughts, kid... come out. Come out! Harry? Look, screaming down dark tunnels of paranoia isn't going to help..."

A score of little heads pivoted on little necks, eyes scrunched, hands shot up, and the old man stopped and said, "I sense that there is a question." A floor full of scrubby fingers rose to the sky, and then the shouts began:

"What's a pair of noia?"

"What's wrong with Harry? Is he sick?"

"Why did he faint? My mama fainted when my little brother was in her tummy. My daddy said that's because my brother stepped on something he wasn't supposed to. Can men faint, too?"

"He was *skeered*, wasn't he?" the boy with more freckles than skin sneered.

"Is he going to wake up?"

"Is something after him?"

The storm of curiosity pelted the old man like thunderstorm hail on a pickup.

"Okay, okay! Hold it! Give me a second to answer... No, Patty, men do not have babies... it's not a pair-of-noia, it is paranoia. Now here is what happened. Sometimes, when people get really, really, really scared, their mind will shut off a minute. They just kind of turn off the TV in their head and stare at a blank screen. Harry was terrified of high places. The reason he was so afraid is because when he was little, he climbed a tree and made like a flying squirrel, except he didn't fly, and landed on his face. It knocked the breath out of him. He broke a rib and had a hard time breathing for a day or two. So, the last thing in the world Harry wanted to do was to get on the back of a bucking dragon and fly up into the sky. But do you know what?" The old man looked around the room, holding the gaze of every little person. "I bet he does it anyway. What do you think?"

"My money is on Harry!" Sarah said, standing to her feet. "Everybody who believes Harry can do it, stand with me. Hurrah for Harry!" The room broke into shouts and laughter and applause. Finally, the old man shushed them all back into place, gave Sarah an I-wish-you-hadn't-done-that look, to which she just shrugged and smiled.

The old man started back with the story, "The speaker sword said, *'Screaming down dark tunnels in fear...'*" He looked around the room to ensure they all realized that he had replaced *paranoia* with the word *fear*. They nodded in accordance, and he continued. "*'...isn't going to help. It won't help the princess. It won't help your people, and it won't help you or me, for that matter. So, gird 'em up, boy!'* The speaker searched through Harry's mind, looking for his essence. Finally, he heard a squeak in a dark room of Harry's soul. A door creaked open, and a small beam of light shone across Harry's imagination. The sword was the only one who could see into this deepest place of Harry's heart. What he saw was Harry... but not the peasant boy Harry, not the young man who wrestled piney woods rooters and fell in murky stinking swamps or griped about walking down cobweb-filled dark tunnels. No, what the sword saw was a man who looked like Harry because he *was* Harry, but he was also more. His face shone like he had bathed it in sunlight and not bothered to dry off. His eyes were fierce but gentle, his smile still belonged to shy Harry, but his heart had changed. The speaker, who thought he had seen just about everything that could be seen in the hearts of warriors, was a little surprised because he had never seen this.

"Stunned, the speaker stumbled over his words, *'Ha... Ha...rry? Are you okay?'* and thought, *This being looked like Harry, but was it really Harry? I mean, it had to be Harry. It was in Harry's mind and body, but oh my, what stepped out of that dark place in Harry's heart sure wasn't what went in.'*

"The speaker waited for Harry to say something and was rewarded with a gentle smile. *'Yeah, Speaker, it's me. I am ready now. We can do this.'*

"*'Harry, what happened? Where did you go?'* The speaker's curiosity bubbled up.

"Harry awakened and was standing to his feet. *'I don't know, Speaker. I fell down into darkness. I felt like I was being torn apart by a thousand fears; then I heard a voice. It was powerful but pleasant. A man's voice said, "Leave him alone." Suddenly the fears hushed. My heart got quiet. Then the voice said, "Come up here, Harry." I looked up. The darkness had gone away, and I could see clearly. I was in a large room, kind of like the huge cavern where the dragons and their riders lay, like this room, I guess.' Harry laughed, looking at the cavern around him. 'Maybe it was this room but a long, long time ago, or maybe a long, long time from now. It wasn't dirty, and there were no bones.

"'I looked for the one calling me and saw, at the far end of the room, a throne, and before me a red carpet, the color of dark blood. It led to the throne. I felt like I was supposed to walk down the carpet, but I was uncomfortable walking on it, so I took my shoes and socks off and walked down that red pathway barefoot. Finally, as I drew closer to the man who called me, I noticed that the great hall had other people in it, even dragons, but they were not evil. They were magnificent, powerful beasts. When they looked at me, I saw intelligence in their eyes. Standing beside them were hundreds of riders clothed in brilliant, beautiful colors.

"'As I walked down the red carpet in my bare feet, I realized I looked like a homeless person compared to those splendidly clothed riders. The nearer I came to the throne, the worse I felt. I saw how dirty I was, how torn and tattered my clothes were. I was aware that I hadn't bathed in weeks, and thought I could smell myself. I slowed down my pace and almost stopped. I was close enough to the throne to see a king, but not close enough to make out his features. I knew I was out of place in that great hall. I felt so unworthy, ashamed, and unprepared to meet the great king. I wanted to run away and hide, but as I turned aside to look back, I saw that the dragons and their riders had closed in behind me and were also walking toward the throne. I couldn't tell if they were backing me up, or keeping me from running, or both. The closer I got, the worse I felt.

"'I found myself able to make out the features of the king. He had dark hair and tan skin, like he had worked in the fields with regular people. His grey beard and dark brown eyes were framed in a strong but friendly face. Though he wasn't smiling, he wasn't frowning either. I tried to keep walking toward him, but I could barely move. Finally, I fell to my knees, bowed my head, and wept. I don't know why. It was like layers of shame, and filth, and all the bad things I had ever done or thought were laid out in front of this king. I can't explain why I felt that way. I can only tell you that I did. I was half-blind from my tears. I couldn't stop crying. Then I felt a hand on my head and heard that voice again.

""'It is time, Harry."

"'I was dazed and didn't understand what the King meant, so I just looked up at him.'

""'It is time for you to step into your destiny. This is your commissioning. This is the moment you receive your mantle, your marching orders, and lastly, the ability to do what I am asking you to do. Receive your anointing, Harry!" the rich, deep voice boomed. I heard it, and more significantly, I felt it. I felt the energy that ran through his hands as he laid them on my shoulders, tingling like electricity. It didn't hurt. It felt hot, though, and I began to sweat. I felt my face get hot, and I know I must have turned red. My body began to shake, and then the most humiliating thing happened. I had multiple seizures, not the kind associated with disease, but more like hiccups. I couldn't stop. My body would spasm. I bent over at the waist and I began to wail. I felt helpless and powerless, but after a few minutes, I felt good, really, really good. I don't know how to explain it. I just felt good. Emotionally, physically, any way a person can feel, I felt wonderful. When I opened my eyes and looked around, I was back here. I saw the door, walked through it, and here I am.'

"The ancient sword, which was bound to the young man, was very quiet. Since Harry had no face or body to address, just a voice in his head, he could only feel the presence of the sword, so he knew it was still there, but it was silent. After a moment, it spoke. *Harry, I didn't realize. I mean I should have known, but to be honest it's been such a long time that I forgot, and that is a terrible thing.'*

"Harry sat in the dark of the tunnel, his face lit by the blue light coming from the sword and sheath he had draped across his knees. If anyone could have heard him, they would have thought they had stumbled across a madman lost in the tunnels and driven mad from fear. But no one was there to watch, and so no one could see the expression on the boy's face. Curious, and patient, and powerful, he waited in the darkness. 'Forgot what, Speaker?'

"*I forgot to tell you that every dragon rider must be commissioned. They have to be called by the King. He has to embrace and empower them. Yours is a sacred duty.'*

"'Well, it's easy to see why you forgot. I mean, I don't look like a dragon rider, I don't want to ride a dragon, and I don't even have a dragon to ride. I don't think that jumping from a high place to land on this evil critter's backside, holding on for dear life, and then finally sticking a sword in it, qualifies for riding. Wild hog riding, possibly, but not like what I just saw in that great hall. Those dragons were good. They were friends with their riders, partners, if you will. They were not enemies, so I am not sure what I just experienced is what you think it was.'

"*Well, sir, hmm... somehow that very response proves my point, Sir Harry... hmm.'*

"'I tell you what, Speaker, let's not use that title... I am Harry, just plain old Harry.'

"The speaker laughed to himself and thought, *We shall see.*

"To which Harry replied, 'You know, Speaker, I can hear your thoughts, too.'

"They both laughed. *Harry, the reason we came here was for you to get some things. One you've already found, the spurs. The second fell with you onto the floor. If you will crawl over there and pick it up, we can dust it off and get acquainted with it.*'

"'I hope it fits, and all the buckles are not rotted. I'd hate to put it on and then get into a brawl with the dragon only to have him swat me and knock this cumbersome conglomeration of armor off.'

"'*Oh, it will fit, Harry. I guarantee you. It will fit.*'

"'And just how do you know that?'

"'*Watch and see, Harry. Watch and see.*'

"Harry was about to argue with the speaker when they heard a roar so fierce Harry's body vibrated as the scream tore through the silence. He had forgotten that the dragon graveyard was easily accessible to the evil dragon that lived in the caves, but that roar reminded him!

"'*He smelled you, Harry. Pick up that armor and run!*'

"Harry grabbed the bronze-colored armor at his feet and ran as hard as he could through the tunnels, following the speaker's directions. The floor shook with the pounding of the dragon's feet. He must have caught Harry's scent early and snuck up on him. Harry could hear his steam-engine panting close in on him. Then all of a sudden…"

The old man looked around. His audience, both adult and child, were seated on the edge of their chairs or gathered up close; a few of the children were even hugging one another. Everyone was waiting and then the old man laughed and said, "That is all we have time for tonight, folks. Kids, we'll have to take it up again in the morning! It's getting close to some of your bedtimes. And for you old folks, like the fire marshal, the nightly news is about to come on."

"Nooo! You can't stop there! Does he get away from the dragon?"

"How does he get away?"

"What happens next? This is not right!"

The adults were laughing, but the frowns on a few faces revealed they agreed with the children. Ending the story at this part was not nice. Then there were the serpent-eyed adults who seemed to perpetually frown, unless they were wearing a beaming façade of a smile. One of those, the Reverend Long, was moving toward him, his hand out to shake the old man's hand. The old man was not particularly inclined to shake a dragon-possessed man's hand, so he drew his hand to his face and pretended to have a runny nose. He looked at the reverend innocently and said, "Sorry, Laden, my nose started itching and running. I'm embarrassed, but I probably shouldn't share this with you, if you know what I mean."

The big, bright smile flickered like a windblown candle and was replaced by a frown that transitioned into a sneer once the reverend saw that only he and the old man were close enough to hear their conversation.

"Interesting mythology, Hank. You tell a good story. It even sounds familiar, although I don't think I've heard it the way you're telling it. In the version I recall, the dragon was the victim robbed of what was rightly his by conquest."

"Well now, that is an interesting take on the story," the old man replied. "The dragon kidnaps a princess, murders the men sent to rescue her, and then complains when somebody wants to steal her back? That is funny! And what an amazing term, *right of conquest*. Seems to imply that if you have might, you're in the right. I don't think I ever read that in the Good Book."

Hank saw a small group of people gradually drawing close to him, each one infected with the same slitted eyes as the reverend. He didn't back down, until he felt the small hand of his favorite princess grab his. He didn't take his eyes off the reverend but wished Sarah wasn't standing in the line of fire.

The Reverend Long, or the serpent possessing the Right Most Reverend, looked down at Sarah, smiled, and reached out to stroke her hair. With a steel gaze she stopped him mid-reach. "You touch me, and I will bite your finger off, spit it out, and scream. Then my grandfather will barge in here and beat you to a pulp. Have I communicated in such a way as you have understood?" she said, smiling innocently.

"My, my, you've grown up. Or perhaps I should say *caught up*. Haven't you, Sarah? I remember when you were different."

"No more games," the old man growled. "You know how this ends. I beat you before, and I will beat you again. Only this time, I will finish the task. Does your neck itch, dragon?"

The reverend stepped back, blinked, and then released the veil that he thought hid his eyes. "It's a different time, Hank, or should I call you by your given name, *Harry*. I will not be denied. I *will* take the princess. She *will* submit to her dragon nature; you'll die a bloody and painful death, and just like last time, she'll lick your blood."

Sarah stiffened and bowed her head. The dragon's words reminded her of her failure and crashed against the hope that had strengthened her heart.

The dragon's speech coiled out of the clergy's body, hissing now that it had been revealed. The voice held nothing back. "Thatsssss right, little dragon princesssssss. You remember, don't you? You liked it too. You were turning because you wanted to be mine."

The old man had enough. In the presence of manifest evil, the dormant part of him, which he didn't bring out because he was never sure he could tuck it back in later, burned. Before the dragon's last words had barely left its mouth, Hank struck. Five old, gnarled fingers balled into a callused fist. Then in a display of speed that surprised even Hank, it collided with pent-up fury into the dragon's brazen teeth. The possessed body of the reverend flew across the room. The people who had stalked closer to support their master surged forward but slammed into a wall and stopped. They didn't move. Like still frames of a movie clip or old photos, they were motionless.

The old man, who had been expecting to be tackled, looked behind him to see a young man, dressed in jeans and long-sleeve denim shirt. The young man smiled and said, "I am not going to hold them long. If I were you, I would take Sarah and her grandfather and leave the library. This is not the place for the last confrontation, and the King doesn't like to remove all doubt." He pointed to everyone else in the room. "So, nobody manifests here tonight, and no one dies." And then in a tone of regret he added, "Regardless of whether they deserve it or not."

Old man Harry grabbed Sarah in his arms and moved as fast as his arthritic legs could carry him. He saw the fire marshal standing in the corner, oblivious to the fact that, just across the room, time had stopped. The fire marshal saw him carrying Sarah and didn't hesitate when Harry said, "It's time to go." As quickly and calmly as they could, they hurried out of the library.

Chapter Fifteen

The old man looked at the fire marshal and, before he could ask questions, said, "Not here. Not now. Let's get to your house where we can talk."

He put Sarah down and was about to get in his truck when she said, "Grandpa, I'm gonna ride with Harry, I mean Mr. Hank."

The fire marshal laughed at her slip and said, "I think we all know who he is now, Sarah, and to be honest, I don't know what to call him either. I'll meet you there. Be careful. No more accidents today."

She nodded and crawled into the old man's pickup.

"Things are moving a little fast," old Harry mused. "My secret's out, I guess. To be honest, I'm not sure what you should call me either. I have been Hank Ferguson for sixty years, yet I am also very much Harry the young man who rescued you over a thousand years ago. It is a little confusing."

Sarah leaned into him and rested her head on his shoulder.

"You know, you really ought to put a seat belt on," he said, looking straight ahead.

Sarah laughed. "We have been targeted by a dragon that wants to kill you and kidnap me, and you are worried about a seat belt? As to confusing—try merging a six-year-old personality, who still likes to watch cartoons and color, with a thousand-year-old medieval princess who could turn into a dragon if she doesn't behave herself. Frankly, Harry, I don't think you know what confusion is."

Harry snorted, then sighed. "And I really hope I never do, because this is difficult enough. Now, however," he continued, releasing a long breath, "now, I am not sure what to do. I am pretty sure the dragon, or reverend, or whatever the hell that beast is… oops, sorry, Sarah, didn't mean to cuss."

"Aheeemmm, that was a really bad wooord," a little voice chirped beside him. He looked down at her, wondering which Sarah was manifesting, concerned that he had offended. A sharp nudge in the ribs freed him from that fear.

As they started to make the turn onto the road that led to her grandparents' house, they could see through the open pasture that the porch light was on. Harry was about to turn down the long drive when the speaker interrupted his thoughts. *"Harry, something is not right. You are being watched. Text the fire marshal before you drive down this road. Tell him to turn the porch lights off! Do it now!"*

The old man was quick to obey, turned off his truck lights, and stopped the truck in the middle of the dirt road before the turn to the farmhouse.

"Harry, what are you…"

"Shh! Something is wrong. Speaker is warning me."

"Grandma and Grandpa!" Sarah cried. "Are they okay? Are they hurt? Did the…"

The old man ignored her. Honed in on his task, he began to text: **Kenneth, this is Hank. Not trying to be too cautious, but we are being watched. Is that you in the house? If it is…** Then he stopped. *What can I ask him?*

Sarah, who was carefully watching his screen to see what he texted, piped in, "Ask him what my favorite storybook is."

Old Harry quickly texted: **...turn off the porch lights and tell me what Sarah's favorite storybook is.**

Seconds after sending the text, the porch lights on the farmhouse went out. After a few more seconds, Hank's phone beeped. The message read: **Sarah's favorite storybook is *Harry Bear and Barry Hare* by Wm David Ellis. Come on in. We have coffee and hot cocoa for Sarah.**

Both the sword in his head and the girl to his right started talking at the same time.

"Something *is* wrong. I hate cocoa!"

"Harry, you need to get out of here... but text him back."

The old man quickly tapped the oversized keys on his senior citizen smartphone: **Right answer, but don't want to endanger you further, so spending the night elsewhere. See you at library tomorrow with fresh clothes for Sarah, and her favorite breakfast, egg burritos with lots of onions.**

"I hate onions and eggs," Sarah whined.

"I know you do. It's to let your grandparents know that we know something's wrong." The old man pressed send, and the text was delivered. He started the truck but didn't turn on the lights until they could no longer see the farmhouse. Then he turned on the running lights and finally, after a mile, the headlights.

Sarah was frantic. "Where are we going? Are Grandma and Grandpa okay? Does the sword know if they are okay? Has the dragon hurt them?" She was close to panicking.

Understanding her fear, the old man answered as slowly and calmly as he could, "Sarah, the sword thinks, and I agree, that your grandparents are safe, at least for the night. I told them to meet us tomorrow to say goodbye, that we needed to leave for a while, and to bring you some more clothes. Even if the dragon and his followers realize they were tricked, if they want to capture us—well, capture you; they just want to kill me," he interjected, "—they will have to keep your grandparents alive for bait. Those dragon people know we are going to be at the library tomorrow, so they will have to bring your grandparents, unharmed." *Or at least I hope and pray so,* he thought.

Sarah's sharp panting breath slowed down. She exhaled a long, slow, cleansing breath. "Okay, okay… sounds right. What now?"

***

In the farmhouse with the fire marshal and Grandma Grace

"All right, we did as you asked!" the fire marshal reprimanded. "Get out of our house!"

Three prominent citizens of the community, people who had been acquaintances, guarded them. They had never been friends, but people you waved at when you saw them in town. As they stood in front of the fire marshal, he noticed that their faces, now unveiled, were pale green with patchy, scaly skin. Their eyes were bizarre. Instead of normal, round human irises, they were yellow and slitted like a snake's. Even their body movements were different, smoother, and they flowed through the room. The leader, a sergeant on the local police force, laughed, walked over to the fire marshal, and slapped him across the face. Blood trickled from his split lip.

Grandma Grace, who was tied in a chair in the room, screamed, "Kenneth!" then turned to the sergeant and glared. Had she not been such a churchgoing Southern lady, she would have cursed the man. Then she thought, *Well, if I think it, I might as well as say it.* "You weakling. Hitting a man when he is tied up! How many times do I have to flush before you go away? When we get out of here, he is going to tear your head off, and I am going to let him!"

"Ah! Oh! My goodness! My poor ears," the sergeant laughed, then moved toward Grace and slapped her. "Keep your opinions to yourself."

The fire marshal spit blood from his busted lip and said in a tone that sent chills down Grace's spine, "You know, I've been furious with this woman many times, but I have never struck her. And if I can control my temper, you should have controlled yours. You've made me angry. The last thought you have before I break your neck, with Grace's permission, of course," he said, nodding toward his wife, "will be 'I wish I hadn't done that.'"

The sergeant looked hard at the old marshal, measuring the stare that promised a bad end, then shook his head and in a still-gruff tone, but without another display of violence, said, "Yeah, like that's going to happen." He turned to his companions. "Duct-tape their mouths shut. I need to call the reverend and see what he wants to do with them. They might live through the night, and then"—he walked over to Grace and stroked her hair—"we may just get to eat them. We'll see."

As the sergeant pulled his cell phone out of his pocket, the house shook and a hot wind whirled through the screened farmhouse windows. The captors paled, a strange look on light green skin. The sergeant's hands began to shake, his mouth grew dry, and he grabbed a bottle of water and drank it down. Finally he had calmed enough to speak, "He's here. Go out and greet him, Melba."

"I don't think so. You're the fearless leader. You greet him," the tall brunette quickly responded.

The sergeant gulped down the bile that threatened to embarrass him and, turning to the other kidnapper, motioned to him to greet the dragon. The man remained silent and shook his head.

"Fine, I'll do it then!" the sergeant barked; then turning to Grace and the fire marshal, he said, "You two better start saying your prayers. You're going to need them."

The fire marshal stared back, his mouth duct-taped, but his thoughts free. *I am always praying, buddy, and, unlike you, I am not afraid to meet my God.*

Grandma Grace was also thinking. *Oh, my friend… I have it on good authority that you are the one that should be praying because you will soon be standing before the One who tamed that dragon of yours a long, long time ago.*

***

The sergeant opened the screen door and stepped out onto the front porch. The lights were still off, but no one needed them. The sky over the secluded farmhouse was lit with red flames. A dragon twice the size of the farmhouse was descending, its fiery breath lighting its drop. The sergeant trembled, waiting for his master to land. He watched in fascinated terror as the dragon flapped its bat-like wings. The creature reeked evil. Its eyes shone like cauldrons of poisoned lava, its scales shimmered, reflecting the red tint of its flame. Then with a thud, the earth compacted beneath its great mass. As soon as the serpent's claws gripped the ground, it cast out a furious spray of flame that encircled it, momentarily hiding it from view. The effect only lasted seconds. As it died down, the figure of a man formed. When the inferno had completely dispersed, the Reverend Laden Long stood there, steam rising off his clothes. He stared at his trembling disciple and watched as the sergeant bent down to one knee, head bowed. The reverend approached him and calmly asked,

"Where is she? You captured her and killed the old man, right?"

The sergeant didn't look up. A pool of warm water formed around his feet. "No, sir, she did not come to the farmhouse," he finally gasped out.

The reverend's golden, serpentine eyes narrowed. "What do you mean?" he asked in a voice that would freeze blood.

"She never showed up, Master. The storyteller texted the fire marshal checking to see if it was safe to come in. We monitored the whole conversation with a knife to the throat of the old woman, assuring the fire marshal would behave. We censored every word. It didn't matter. The storyteller and the girl told the fire marshal they didn't want to endanger him or his wife, so they went elsewhere for the night. That's all we know, sir."

Reverend Long looked down on his trembling underling and sneered. "The sword told him. I'm sure of it." He walked into the farmhouse. "Oh my! Look who's all tied up—I do love puns—the fire marshal and his lovely wife, Grace. I would ask how you are, but it is rather obvious. What you need to ask yourselves, however, is do you want to be roasted like a chicken over a pit, or can I just kill you quickly and be done with it? You're going to die, no doubt about that, just slowly or quickly? The choice is yours." Then he laughed. "Just kidding. You have no choice at all. It is my choice and that choice will be determined by your behavior. All you have to do is answer my questions. Where is Sarah? And where is the old man? It's that simple. I will start with you, Grace... may I call you Grace? I am going to anyway."

The reverend turned toward Grandma Grace, stooped down, and ripped the duct tape from her lips. Grace yelped as the tape ripped off a thin layer of skin. She licked her lips, looked the dragon square in the eyes, and said, "That was not nice." Her husband snorted beneath his own tape. He had heard that tone of voice before and knew the dragon had better not give his wife an inch, or she would ream his butt all the way back to perdition.

The demon's eyes narrowed and a sneer slid across his lips. Grandma Grace held his stare. Her expression did not waver; then she answered, "We do not know where he is, you old serpent. Hank didn't tell us. I think he saw we were... *tied up* and didn't want us to give anything away. So, what can we tell you?"

Reverend Long stepped back, reluctantly agreeing with his captive. He continued to stare at her, thinking. A heartbeat passed, and then the reverend motioned to the woman who held the fire marshal's phone. "Let me see the texts."

The middle-aged woman tossed her long brown hair over one shoulder and looked up at the reverend from under her lashes. She was tall, fashionably dressed, and carried herself well. It was obvious that she was enamored with the reverend. She reached into her pocket, grabbed the phone, and handed it to the clergy. "Yes, sir," was all she could bring herself to say. Her eyes sparkled in idolizing worship.

The reverend flipped through the texts, carefully reading each one. He flipped back again, reread them, frowned, and then turned to the sergeant, who was not beaming in idol worship but shivering in terror, his eyes fixed on every move the cleric made. The sergeant came close to shrieking but bit into his lip instead. He quickly grabbed a handkerchief and was daubing his mouth when the dragon turned to him and, in that same cold tone, said, "Right under your nose. He warned them right under your nose, with you watching his every move."

The sergeant's eyes grew large with fright. His heart pounded. "Look here, you fool," the reverend continued, pointing to the cell phone screen, "Hank Ferguson texted the fire marshal, asking if he was safe. The fire marshal was only minutes ahead of him and the girl. Why would Ferguson think that they would be in danger so soon after leaving them? Someone warned him, and I know who it was. I wasn't sure he was still around... but the sword still speaks." The clergy turned toward the sergeant and smiled. "But that does not free *you* from responsibility.

"Notice what the crafty fire marshal says next... 'We have coffee and cocoa for Sarah'... both of those have caffeine. You don't give a six-year-old caffeine before bedtime. He was warning them off, and they got the message. See their response... 'We don't want to endanger you further, so spending the night elsewhere, see you at library tomorrow. Bring favorite food... eggs and onions'... Have you ever been around children, sergeant? They do not like onions; onions are an acquired taste. You failed me, sergeant. Now, what should I do about that?" He turned to the woman, who was still looking at him in admiration, smiled, and then said, "Please follow me, dear. I need to think, and your company would be appreciated." He bent over and kissed her hand. Her eyes brightened in fanatical reverie. He clasped hands with her and took her outside. "Sergeant, come with us."

As they walked out under the stars, the sergeant trembled with fear, barely able to move. He tried to calm himself by lighting a cigarette, but his hands shook so much he couldn't do it. The reverend smiled at the woman, patted her hand, and said, "Stand here, please." He stepped back about twenty feet, took a deep breath, and exhaled. Flame spewed from his mouth and curled around him, briefly hiding his form. The dragon stepped out of the fire, and a quick draft of wind instantly extinguished the flames. Towering over the woman, he bent down and opened his mouth. Terror instantly replaced the woman's smile. She barely had time for a short, muffled scream as she disappeared down the throat of the beast. Flames curled back around, and once again, the Reverend Long stood in a burnt circle of grass. He wiped his mouth and walked over to the sergeant, who lay curled on the ground in a fetal position, weeping.

"Now, now, sergeant, somebody had to be punished. See here, be glad it wasn't you... this time. So, get up now and do your job." Then in a stern, hypnotic tone that broke through the broken mind of the man, "Get up and guard those two! They are bait for my trap. And change your clothes. You stink. Now go." The demon's voice had cast a spell on his minion, forcing the brokenness to dissipate, leaving him calm, drugged, but functional. "I will be back in the morning; then we will go to story time to finish this story. Goodnight, sergeant." With that, the reverend stepped back, breathed out, and in a flurry of flame, clothed himself in dragon and flew away. The sergeant stared into the night sky for a long time, then walked into the farmhouse to shower and change.

Chapter Sixteen

"I'm not sure where to go," Harry said. "We can't go to my daughter's house. They will probably be watching there, and I don't want to endanger her in any way."

"You didn't seem to have that same problem endangering my grandparents!" Sarah fumed.

Harry looked back at the ancient princess pontificating from a six-year-old's body. He wanted to bite back and say he hadn't endangered them. She had. But he knew that even though true, it would not help. In a calm voice he answered, "Your grandparents are your protectors, your guardians. Your life means more to them than their own. They would lay down their lives if they had to. My daughter has no idea what is going on. She is not prepared for this."

Sarah's fear-based anger turned to shame. She bowed her head a moment, regaining her calm. Her thoughts shifted to another topic that was extremely important to her. Her face showed she had a question. Before her mind was ready to ask it, she forced herself to relax, hoping Harry hadn't noticed.

He had. "Go ahead, ask," he prompted.

"Well, Harry, you have a daughter, and that is fine. I mean, you probably thought you would never see me again, and why would you? I understand that, I really do, but that also means you have a wife, and—this is foolish. I am six years old going on 1,244."

The old man gawked in confusion. "Huh?"

"Is she still alive?"

"Well, I hope so! She's the librarian. Keeping her alive is why we're not going to her house, and by the way, I thought you were five."

Sarah pulled back, made a fist, and punched the old man smack in the arm.

"Dang, Sarah, what's your problem? You asked me a question. I gave you an answer, and you slug me?"

"Harry, Hank, Ferguson, or whoever... You know exactly what I meant, and exactly why I hit you. I wasn't asking about your daughter. I was asking about her mother. And for your information, I celebrated my sixth and 1,244th birthday two weeks ago."

"Oh," the old man laughed. "Well, the truth is, I never met her mother. I don't know who she is. My daughter is adopted."

"Harry, you don't have a wife?" Sarah said, sitting on the edge of the seat and turning to face the old man.

"I didn't say that."

"Well, who is she? Where is she?" Sarah asked, leaning back against the seat and folding her arms.

"Uh, she isn't," he answered cryptically, deliberately not giving away any information.

"Haaarrrrryyy!"

The old man laughed again. He was enjoying this exchange. Sarah sounded like a cat, one minute purring, the other hissing. He hoped he knew, based on her tone of voice, just exactly when he would have to cough up the truth.

The truck cab grew quiet as Harry drove down the road, thinking of where they should go. They needed someplace private, someplace protected, someplace the Right Reverend would never think of going.

Sarah was also thinking, *This is miserable and ridiculous. He doesn't want to tell me about his wife. He used the phrase "She isn't," so she must have died. He adopted, so they must not have been able to have children, and he doesn't want to be reminded. He must have loved her a great deal. He really is a good man.*

"Harry?"

"What?"

"I'm sorry about your wife. You must have loved her a great deal. I am sorry you couldn't have children. Did you tell her who you really are? If so, what did she think? Did you tell her about me?"

The old man shook his head, frowning. Even in the dimly lit cab, Sarah could see his reaction. Finally, he said, "Sarah, I never married. There was never a wife."

Sarah leaned back in the truck seat again.

"Put your seat belt on, please," the old man requested quietly.

Sarah moved across the seat, over to the passenger side, and snapped the seat belt. She looked back at Harry and whispered, "Why? Why didn't you ever marry, Harry? You were young. I was as good as dead. I don't understand." *Yet, maybe I do.*

The old man struggled to get the words out, "I don't know. It just didn't feel right. I got close a couple of times, but it was never… right, never the same. I tried to love. I had opportunity, but it's like my heart wouldn't let go… of that princess I met in the market so long ago. There was no room for anyone else, because I could never forget…"

"Oh, Harry." Even though a part of her had wanted him to say just that, Sarah began to cry. "How many times have I failed you? I betrayed you. I lost you. More than a thousand years separated us, and I couldn't find you. Now we are just as far apart as we have ever been." Suddenly her face changed, and a look of shock held it. Her eyes blinked, and then she said, "Oh, dear God! Harry… I remember… oh, I remember after you had driven the dragon into the ground, and it was breathing its last. I heard it speak. I heard it in my heart. It cursed us. That evil beast said, 'Your love will never leave you, but neither will you have it… till it does.' It cursed us, Harry. It cursed us, and now it wants to kill us."

The old man listened. He didn't say anything for a long time. "I don't know what to do, Sarah. I don't know how we got here, I don't know how to change things. I don't even know a safe place to go tonight."

As Harry was talking, the speaker interrupted. *"Harry, you are still the dragon rider. You still carry the anointing of the King. And there are two things I need to tell you, three actually. First, an undeserved curse does not come to rest. It just won't stick. Second, the blessing the King imparted to you breaks the yoke of bondage. Third, I know of a place within a few miles of here that will be safe from the dragon. He cannot enter there. You and Sarah will be safe. Be at peace, and rest tonight because tomorrow is story day and you need to be ready."*

"He spoke to you again, didn't he? What did the sword have to say?"

"How did you know that? How do you know when he is talking?"

"Well," she said in her six-year-old voice, "you put on your listening face." Then her 1,244-year-old self manifested, and she continued, "And you get this very focused, faraway look in your eyes. That's when I can tell the sword has spoken. So, what did he say?"

The old man shrugged his shoulders, understanding her reply, and answered, "He said you and I are stronger than a dragon's curse. We will find a way to break it, and that there's a place up ahead…" The truck headlights lit on a sign, and Harry laughed, "Of course! This is perfect."

"What is perfect, Harry? Quit doing that. I don't have a clue what's going on. You're having a private little conversation with your age-old invisible friend, and I have to go potty—sorry, old habits die hard—use the restroom."

Harry laughed as he turned into the parking lot of a country church. The sign read *St. Patrick's Lutheran Church, visitors welcome.* "I am an elder here. I have a key. Come on, I know where some blankets are, and if you're nice, I'll even show you where the bathroom is."

The old man stepped out of his truck, waited till Sarah crawled across the seat, then helped her out. They walked to the front doors of the old church. It was a typical church building built in the late-nineteenth century. Constructed entirely of wood, as it was hard to find stone in the middle of East Texas, the people who originally built it had been more interested in what happened *inside* it than its exterior siding, but it was lovingly maintained. It probably had at least forty coats of paint on it. With a hide like that, the old guardian had no need to fear weather, and as to the tornados that blew through from time to time, they had only peeled its roof on occasion.

The preachers often claimed it was because *the Lord would pass over His own.* The old man kind of believed that and wasn't interested in pressing the theology. He needed some passing over and wasn't of a mind to mess with what was working. As they entered the sanctuary, the old man realized something he had never noticed before. In the dark, the church looked a lot like the great hall where the dragons and their riders had stood, and where he met the King. He thought, *That's just a coincidence. All buildings shaped like a hall will look like a hall.*

As they walked down the aisle, Sarah noticed the great windows and the stained-glass art held in place by lead lining. Each window told a story. As she walked around the room, studying each window, she came to one and stopped. The legend of Saint George. She felt Harry walk up to her and place his hand on her shoulder. She looked up at him and asked, "Is that a light behind the windows?"

Old Harry looked down at her and said, "What?" Then he looked at the window she was pointing to and saw the glow. It wasn't lit by a brilliant light, but it stood out, like a nightlight in a dark room would cast a small glow, enough to push back the gloom. The window of Saint George was shimmering. Harry took a seat on one of the hard, wooden pews and stared intently at the stained glass.

Sarah whispered, "Can you feel it?"

Harry most definitely could, and smiled. "Yep, I can. I think we will be safe here tonight."

Sarah agreed, "Absolutely," then snuggled in close to the old man. "It's in the walls, you know."

The old man sighed, and for the first time in days, rested. He looked up at the glowing window and scanned all the other stained glass, his eyes finally resting on the centerpiece of the sanctuary, an old cross, which hung behind the choir loft on the baptistery wall. It was also lit. He stared at it for a while, then spoke softly, "Thank you."

Chapter Seventeen

The morning sun shone brightly through the stained-glass windows. One mischievous ray moved slowly across the old man's cheek till it danced on his eyelids, sending a signal to his unconscious mind that it was time to wake. Apparently, the same ray decided to skip Sarah. She slept soundly on. The old man had slept fitfully in spite of the blanket of peace that rested on the sanctuary. The pews were too narrow for his broad shoulders to lie on, so he slept sitting up. It was uncomfortable but he would have been lying if he had said he had never slept in that position in church before. He dreamed of dragons, and blood, and swords, and screaming children. It was hard to rest in the middle of those nightmares, but now it was time. Sarah was covered with a blanket with her head using his lap as a pillow and the rest of her stretched down the cushioned pew. He tried to gently pry her head up and slip out. He was halfway through that procedure and about to congratulate himself when she opened her sleepy eyes and said, "Where ya going?"

"Well, if you must know, I am going to visit the men's room, and then I'm going to dig out my armor, put it on, drive into town, and kill a dragon and its demonized followers. What are you doing today?"

Sarah sat up, rubbed the sleep from her eyes, and stretched like a cat. "Well, I'm hungry. A growing girl needs her breakfast. After that, well, I thought I would tag along with you and hand you things when you need them. If it got dark, I could hand you a flashlight, or hold it while you cleaved a few heads. I will try to keep it out of your eyes, but hey, you know six-year-olds, we get distracted…"

"Hum… you think it is going to take us all day to lop off a few heads?"

"Don't know, but it's best to be prepared!"

With that Sarah got up and trotted off to the restroom.

The old man snorted, enjoying the banter. As he made his way down the paneled hall to the restroom, he also realized that even though he had loved the heart in front of him for over a thousand years, the time they had actually spent together was probably less than a day. Any relationship manual would say love at first sight—or in his case, first fight—was iffy at the least, and dangerous at best, so what was he doing? Then he remembered the first time he met her in the market square, how she had covered him and tried to protect his pride. She was royalty and could have had him flogged, or worse, for even touching her, but she didn't. She was a woman… then. He looked at the six-year-old that nuzzled up to him and thought, *Sarah is a little girl, a very young woman, who, when she was an older woman…* He laughed out loud. *This is nuts! Absolutely nuts! I am going to wake up in a drugged stupor and find myself in an asylum.* "Whew!" he sighed. *Or I am going to get up, go to the café, put my armor on, and either kill or be killed by a dragon disguised as clergy. Good grief… could it get any more confusing?*

Then he heard the speaker's voice, *"Harry, be careful what you ask!"*

Sarah trotted back into the sanctuary from the restroom where she had tried to freshen up. Her eyes were puffy and she was crying. "I can't help it. I am so worried about Grandma and Grandpa… what if?"

"Sarah, your grandparents are some of the most loving and gracious people I have ever met. I would like to get to know them much better," he slowed down and whispered, "but I don't know if they are still in this world or not." Sarah grasped her head in her hands with that statement. The old man continued, "But Sarah, I do know this… wherever they are, they *love* you, and want you to live… and survive. Giving way to your fears right now is not the way to ensure that. Now try and think of something else, anything else. It is morning. Are you hungry?"

She nodded and then looked up at him with red eyes. "My grandpa says when he gets real hungry, that his big gut is trying to eat his little gut. I know how he feels now. Where we going to eat?"

"I have a special place downtown where I often eat in the morning. Let's go there. But first, I am going to put on my armor."

"You brought your armor with you? I didn't even know you still had it."

"It's a long story, but the short version is I woke up with it on and was convincingly reminded it had certain qualities… one of which landed me in the mental ward of the hospital. If you remember, I didn't have a whole lot of time to practice before I had to use it."

"What do you mean 'convincingly reminded'?" Sarah asked, curious.

The speaker intruded the old man's thoughts, *"This ought to be amusing. Are you really going to tell her that story?"*

The old man rolled his eyes and answered, "She is 1,244 years old; she only *looks* like a first grader."

Sarah heard the old man respond to the speaker and protested, "I do not *look* like a first grader!" Then she frowned, looked down at herself, and sighed. "Okay, maybe a little." Her eyes twinkled as her face lit up in inquisitiveness. "The speaker is talking to you again!"

"Yes, he is. Now, do you want to know what happened or not?"

"Oh, most definitely, but can you tell me on the way to breakfast?"

"Honestly, I could, but then you'd want to see it, so hold your taters and let's get the armor."

The old man started to walk down the aisle of the church. Sarah grabbed his hand and walked beside him, still asking questions, "Did you hide the armor in the church?"

"Nope."

"But you brought it with you?"

"Yep."

"In the truck?" she persisted.

"Well, of course it's in the truck, silly. If I brought it with me, and I don't have it on, it has to be in the truck, right?" he answered again, tight-lipped, enjoying every minute.

She kept on, "In the back of the truck?"

"Yep."

She hopped up on the sideboard of his old Ranger and scrutinized the back of the truck. "Where?"

The old man dug into his pocket and drew out a key. He opened the tailgate and hefted his cranky body into the pickup bed. He crawled over to the cab on whining knees, placed the key in the lock of the huge toolbox that was anchored into the truck's bed, and opened the lid. Sarah peered inside. She didn't see anything but hammers, saws, pieces of copper wire, and plumbing supplies.

"There's no armor..." She was about to say "in here" when the old man started pulling out the tools, moving everything out of the box.

Once the toolbox was emptied, he inserted another key into a small inconspicuous slot that could have easily been mistaken for a scratch or oil smear. The lock clicked, and the old man pulled up on the key to reveal a hidden shelf, just large enough for a fingerhold that he could pull up. "Dang thing gets heavier every time I dig into it," he complained. Finally, with a lot of tugging and grunting, he got the lid out. Sarah peered into the hidden compartment. Inside was the bronze-colored armor she had last seen over a thousand years ago.

"I don't know who made this," Harry began. "On the surface, it looks like German armor. It is, as you can see, brown with horizontal rings overlapping like fish scales. The helmet is open-faced and lightweight, with a hinged peak projecting out over the forehead like some kind of beak. Its detachable shin guards are held with leather straps…"

Before Harry could finish his detailed description of the armor, Sarah interrupted, "Looks like a bug, a big, scaly cockroach."

The old man looked back at the little girl who stood on his pickup truck runner wearing a most sincere expression. He couldn't tell if he was looking at a naïve six-year-old or an irritated and very hungry 1,244-year-old. He finally decided it was an agitated mix and proceeded with his lecture.

"Are you sure we can't have this conversation on the way to the café? I haven't eaten in twenty-four hours and my blood sugar is getting low. Or at least I think it is. That is what Grandpa always says when he is harassing Grandma about dinner." At the mention of her grandparents, her face clouded and her eyes began to glisten.

The old man cast a steely gaze back at the six-year-old, who was vainly trying to look innocent, and replied, "Remind me again. You didn't turn into a dragon, right? Because right now… oh, wait a minute. I forgot you're a princess, and you aren't used to *not* having your way… Excuse me, Your Highness. I was just trying to keep both of us from getting killed, and then, while I am at it, figure out a way to kill a dragon and rescue your grandparents. Sorry for inconveniencing you."

He turned away and continued to pull out the bronze armor. Sarah became quiet. He was trying to untie a leather strap but kept failing to loosen it. Frustrated, he turned back around to face her. Tears were streaming down her cheeks, a heartbroken look across her face. With trembling lips, she said, "I'm sooorrrrryy... I didn't mean to complain. I'm just scared... I'm scared for my grandparents and scared for you, and for all the rest of the children who are going to be at the library."

The old man looked at her and then crawled back across the truck bed toward her. He held out his arms, and she hugged him. She was shaking, sobbing, and trying to talk. He just held her.

"Okay, it's going to be okay. We are here for a reason. And, we are together. There is too much going on, too many things coming together for me to believe this is all going to end poorly. Have faith, Sarah. Hold on. We'll get through this." He felt her body relax as he hugged her close.

She sighed and drew back. With a twinkle in her eye, she asked, "Now can we go get something to eat?"

"Yes, but first, help me get into this armor."

"You're putting that on now?"

"Yes."

"Over your clothes?"

Exasperated, Harry looked at Sarah and explained, "What I have been trying to tell you is that this armor is... I hate the word *magic* because I have a feeling this isn't magic, but science, which some wise crone once said appears to be magic to a culture that doesn't understand the science."

The speaker interrupted, *"I think you are referring to the words of Arthur C. Clarke. What he actually said was 'Any sufficiently advanced technology is indistinguishable from magic.'"*

"And just how do you know that?" Harry stopped in mid-sentence and asked his invisible friend.

"Harry, I remember everything you read, and everything you hear. I confess that sometimes, when you aren't using your body and choose to sleep, I borrow it and read. I've read every book in your house, including that old encyclopedia in your attic."

"Is that why I wake up tired some mornings with my eyes burning?"

"Gripe, gripe, gripe. But just think. You have immediate access to an incredible amount of knowledge anytime you need it."

"Why, after sixty years, am I just finding out about this? Why didn't you tell me sooner?"

The speaker paused and said, *"Well, to be honest, I don't know. The truth is you were fighting dragons or other types of evil critters, so I just didn't think about it. I wasn't trying to hide it from you. I just didn't think you cared to know."*

"Harry, you have that I-am-talking-to-the-speaker look on your face, and since I am not privy to that conversation, do you want to tell me about your armor so you will be happy and I can go to breakfast?" Sarah interjected.

Harry looked at the tyrannical munchkin in front of him and laughed, then continued, "As I was trying to say... this armor has capabilities that make me wonder two things, and I have no idea which of the two is correct, but I can only think of two possibilities. First, I believe the armor is the product of an extremely advanced civilization, either from the future or, and I tend to lean this way, from a civilization that lived and died on this planet a long time ago. Either way, it has some amazing qualities. It can adapt to the body size of the person wearing it. It can cast a veil over itself so it becomes invisible, not only invisible to the eye but intangible to touch, hiding from both visual and tactile observation.

"It also has the ability to defend itself by adapting to the threat. It can deflect sword, spear, and bullet. It can also withstand great heat—necessary when fighting a dragon. And, if its wearer, in spite of all those defenses, gets wounded, it has the ability to attach itself to the wounded area, send out small thread-like tentacles, and stop the bleeding. Finally, it's a source of energy and can reenergize its wearer in battle. It's an amazing technological feat.

"A few years back, I scraped off a small piece and took it to a prominent laboratory but never let it out of my sight. The scientist, who studied it over a twenty-four-hour period, concluded it was advanced nanite technology. I had to steal the sample back, which I could do because I was wearing the armor. And perhaps best of all, after you put it on, it is thought-activated."

"Hmm, okay, that is pretty awesome. I just have one question?"

"Yes, we are going to go eat. Just let me put this on, and we can go," Harry grumbled.

"That's not what I was going to ask. I want to know how you go to the bathroom with all that on?"

"Get in the truck. Just get in the truck. You are the most exasperating, aggravating, question-asking 1,244 six-year-old I have ever known."

Sarah giggled and crawled over the driver's seat of the cab, still talking, "But I want to know. Also, Harry, does that thing get hot? Harry, where are you?" Sarah looked back through the cab window to see the old man sitting on the tailgate with one leg out of his pants. He was trying to get the armor over his work boots without having to take them off, but he wasn't having much luck. His bright blue boxers were slipping, and the top of his rear end had started to shine. She quickly turned around, snickering. Her revelry was cut short when the old man opened the driver's seat door and slipped in, completely dressed. As he slid the key into the ignition, Sarah asked, "Do you have it on now?"

"Yep."

"Wow! That is amazing. You really can't see it, can you?"

"Nope. I'm hungry too, so let's go. Did you bring any money?" Harry asked.

"Huh? No, I don't have any money!"

"How are you going to pay for your breakfast?"

She folded her arms and put on a pouty face. Things got quiet again in the cab. The old man let her stew for a few minutes, and about a mile from the café parking lot, a shocked look of comprehension crossed his face. His eyes widened, and he turned toward Sarah. "Wait a minute! You don't expect me to buy your breakfast, do you?"

A big grin lit up the cab. The transformation was instantaneous, and the old man wished he had brought sunglasses. "I tell you what. When we get there, you sit in the cab while I go in and eat. If I have anything left over, I'll get a doggie bag and bring it back."

Sarah's smile fell from her face and was replaced by narrowed eyes. Before the old man knew what happened, she had balled up and hit him. "Ouch!" He laughed so hard he choked, and then had a hacking fit, almost running off the road before he got it under control. "Okay, okay, you can come in. How do you like your eggs?"

"I don't want eggs. I want pancakes, with bacon, and milk-coffee."

"Hmm, typical six-year-old," the old man muttered as they pulled into the parking lot of his favorite café.

The hail-pocked crimson-colored sign in front of the café read *Jamie's Café, You Stab 'Em, We Slab 'Em,* in big white letters. The tagline was meant to be funny, but some locals took it seriously and were known to bring fresh roadkill in to be fried up or made into gumbo. The café was in the very rural place of Moab, Texas, and was built from huge pine logs that looked like a rustic cabin with a wrap-around porch and a handicap ramp. Inside, it had the same log siding, and picnic tables were arranged in rows for the guests. The old man had been frequenting the place for years, and everybody knew not to sit at the table on the east side of the café between seven and nine every morning except Sundays because that was his "reserved" spot.

The owners, Barry and Jamie Dinker, were as different from each other as they come. Barry was a Kiwi from New Zealand, a sophisticated man with a calm demeanor and a dry wit. People around those parts called him the tractor-whisperer. He would listen to an ailing tractor by taking a long-handled screwdriver, placing one end on the tractor frame and the other to his ear, and diagnose a tractor like a physician would an asthmatic.

His wife, Jamie, was his polar opposite. Born on the opposite side of the world from her husband, she continued the traditions of her heritage, as a pure redneck woman. Long and lanky with bottle-blond hair, she had an opinion about everything and, as much as it pained Harry to admit, on occasion she had been right. She was loud yet had the hearing of a jackrabbit, listening to all the conversations in the small restaurant while frying sizzling bacon in the back kitchen. Barry had to continually scrape the cussing off the walls due to Jamie's distinct gift for saying exactly the most provocative, aggravating thing at just the right time.

Once, when the old man asked her if she were interested in attending a Bible study, she answered, "No way! I never discuss religion with anyone I like." After he quit laughing, the old man shrugged his shoulders, chalked it up to sophisticated redneck philosophy, and left.

Sarah scampered into the café, walked over to the old man's table, and sat down like she had eaten there forever and had stock in the place. The old man slowly walked in behind her, nodding to everyone he knew, most of whom were nameless, as he only knew them as the people he nodded to at Jamie's each morning.

The old man moved toward his table across from the usual group of old men he did know, who always sat in the same chairs, at the same table. Several times through the years, they had asked him to join them, but he always declined, saying if he sat with them, he couldn't listen to them, and he preferred to laugh at them and take notes so he could use their examples in the Sunday school class he taught—examples of what not to say and how not to act. The old men always laughed but never knew that he meant exactly what he said. He had actually referred to them several times in his Sunday school lectures.

"Weel now! Who is this here young lady?" Jamie bellowed from behind the counter. "You're way purtee-er than anybody this old man ever sat with before. What's your name?"

Sarah slipped into her I-am-a-pretty-little-princess role, and the curtsey in her voice was nearly audible. "My name is Sarah. I am six years old. And my grandpa thinks I'm a princess."

"Well, you sure are, baby girl. Now don't let this old man you're sitting with growl at you. You keep him in his place, ya hear?"

"Yes, ma'am."

"Now, what can I git for ya?" Then, turning to her harried husband, she screeched, "Barry, you ain't got no coffee over here yet? What's wrong with you? They been in here for five minutes!"

Barry walked up, as solid as a rock and as calm as the sea after Jesus stilled it, cantering in a Kiwi accent that had escaped the influence of twenty years of East Texan dialect.

"Gud morning there, Hank. What can I get you this morning other than your usual coffee? And what can I get for you, young lady? Don't I know you? You're Kenneth's granddaughter. Oh yah, I remember you. How's he doing today?"

Sarah grimaced, but caught most of it before it pierced the fear she had been pushing aside. "He is good. I'm eating with my great-uncle this morning."

Harry mumbled under his breath, "Great-uncle my rear end..."

"Well, I see that. And what would you like?"

Harry and Sarah gave their orders, and Barry limped away to give his boisterous wife the order.

Sarah's 1,244-year-old side manifested and said, "I have tried my best not to think of Grandpa Kenneth and Grandma Grace, but when that man asked, I almost lost it. I'm so terrified I'm shaking. While we were at the church, I could push it aside. I just felt like they were okay, and when we were driving down the road last night trying to hide, I kept it under control. But..."

About that time, Jamie brought their order. Hank said his usual, "Wow, that was quick!" and was about to comment on the size of Sarah's pancakes when he looked up into Jamie's eyes and flinched. They were serpentine.

Chapter Eighteen

"Before you have a jerking spell, hang on, Hank. It ain't what it appears to be. Not everybody who…" And then she bent down and did something totally out of character; she whispered. That in itself was enough to cause the old man to blink and pull back. She slapped him on the shoulder and continued, "Stop it, old man. That damned ol' reverend may have left a mark on some of us, but he done shot his mouth off for the last time. I didn't know his fancy talk and twisting Scripture would lead to this. I wasn't there when they did what they did to Thomas. I wouldn't have it. Then he went and ate—*ate*, mind you—my cousin Melba Jean. I am having none of it. Neither are a lot of others who were under his spell. We want out. And the way I hear it, you're the key to that door. You ain't all you seem to be, are you, old man? Ha! At least I hope not cuz you ain't a whole lot to look at, if you know what I mean…"

Sarah's body stiffened, and the old man reached across the table and subtly squeezed her hand.

Hank growled and said, "What do you want, Jamie? Why are you telling me this?"

"Well, here's the thang, Hank. The reverend is expecting those of us who were his followers to be at the libarie today to ambush you and take Sarah. By the way, Sarah, your grandparents are safe fer now. Laden didn't tell everybody everything, but I, at least, know that. I don't know where they are, but I know he's bringing 'em to the libarie. There won't be a lot of kids there. None of the children belonging to the reverend's flock'll be there, and some of us tried discreetly to warn other folks. But no one went out of their way to warn 'em either, fer fear they wud get found out. That's all I can tell ya, Hank, and if ya don't kill that beast today… well, somebody else is going to be serving you breakfast tomorrow. It won't be me, cuz when I don't show up, the reverend's going to know. But aahh am not goin' to the libarie, and Barry is seriously thinking about bringing his old Uzi Israel machine gun, just to stand with ya and even the odds a bit. He was a New Zealand Special Forces soldier in his day… Bet ya didn't know that, did ya?"

The old man's look of surprise caused Jamie to laugh. "You didn't think I could keep a secret, did ya?"

"Jamie, some questions are better left unanswered," the old man replied.

"Ha, you just answered it." And then, in a quiet whisper, "I'm so sorry, Hank. I was so wrong. We all thought the reverend was good until he wasn't. Some of us saw that. Others, not so much. Now we are all going to pay for it. Please forgive me."

Hank saw tears streaming down Jamie's cheeks, blurring her mascara and causing her makeup to run. He nodded and got up to pay his bill with Sarah tagging along quietly. She held his hand as he walked up to the counter. Barry met him halfway there. "On me today, mate, and I will be there when you need me. Don't count on the police though. Half of them are with the reverend, the other half not so much. Is there anything particular I can do?"

The old man thought about it a moment. His eyes widened as an idea occurred to him, and he leaned over to whisper in Barry's ear. It was a pretty long conversation with Barry saying, "Ai, yeah, sure… absolutely, I can. I will be there, waiting. Be careful though, be careful."

As they walked out, Sarah looked up and asked, "What was that all about?"

"Just taking care of some concerns, getting all my ducks in a row. You ready to go to story time?"

***

Nothing looked out of place as the old man's truck puttered into place. He parked in his usual spot, looked around to see how many other cars were there, and paid special note that most of the cars missing were those belonging to Reverend Long's members.

Only half of his little flock were gathered, and as Hank walked into the library, he wished they had all stayed home. The children were in the line of fire. If the dragon decided to attack while Hank was telling the story, the children would be slaughtered. The old man grieved over the idea of losing any more of his precious munchkins. Thomas's death had broken his heart. He did not want the children to be there, but if he had warned them all away, the dragon would have known he was exposed. If the old man had fled, these children would have been punished by the dragon anyway. He had to stand and fight with his children and family gathered around him. Nothing else terrified a warrior more than that vulnerability, and nothing else made him fight harder.

The old man's daughter met him at the door. She was distraught. "Dad, where have you been? Why didn't you answer your phone? I just got a call from one of the parents of the children telling me that Sarah was kidnapped, and you are the probable suspect! Dad, there is an arrest warrant out for you! What is going on?" Lizzy said, trembling in confusion.

After a quick glance back to the parking lot, the old man ushered his daughter and Sarah inside and secured the door behind them. Sarah, who had been holding the old man's hand, walked calmly up to his daughter, put her hands on her small hips, and said, "That's a lie! Whoever told you that is a follower of Reverend Laden Long. He is a Satanist hiding in sheep's clothing. He killed Thomas and he wants to take me away. My grandparents have been kidnapped and your father discovered all this and hid me to keep the reverend from doing the same thing to me as he did to his own grandson."

Lizzy stepped back in shock. "A Satanist?!" she voiced in a whispered shriek that turned the heads of the children toward her to see what had happened.

The old man gently took his daughter's hands in his own. "I am afraid so, honey. I wasn't sure until last night. I also wasn't aware of how extensive his influence was or how many followers he had till a few hours ago. Half the police force is behind him. I expect him to be here within minutes."

Lizzy gulped and then gestured toward the children. "Dad, what about these kids? What am I going to do to keep them safe? Why did you come here if you knew it would endanger the children!" she continued, starting to get angry.

The old man softly replied, "We didn't have a choice. Long knows we are scheduled to have story time today. He has Kenneth and Grace. He kidnapped them last night as a ransom for Sarah. He knows she will not run away if their lives are at stake.

"I stopped him from capturing Sarah last night after Kenneth warned us in a text, which the reverend and his followers were monitoring. In the text, I told him to meet us here, the place we were scheduled to meet, with breakfast and some clothes for Sarah.

"If Kenneth and Grace didn't show up," Hank explained, "Long would have known that *we knew* he had killed them and there would be no reason for us to come here. He intends to use them as a bargaining chip to leverage for Sarah. The arrest warrant just tells us Long has a judge in his pocket. Apparently, the good reverend has been planning this for a long time."

The old man's daughter stared at the floor, shaking her head in disbelief. Sarah reached up and touched her hand. "It's true, Miss Lizzy. The reverend is a very bad man. Please trust your daddy. He knows my family from a very long time ago. Don't let them take me, Miss Lizzy, please. Harry is the only one who can stop him. He's done it before. Please trust him."

"Harry? Who's Harry? Why did you call my dad Harry? I don't understand what is happening!"

Sarah looked at her and responded, "It is a very long and complicated story, and nobody has time to tell you now... you *have* to trust him."

Lizzy grimaced, uncertain. She didn't understand what was going on. She had no idea how her father, an elderly man who had been with her all her life, could have led a secret life she never knew about. How could he be mixed up with a Satanist, have a warrant out for his arrest, and be telling her a pastor in town was an evil kidnapper?

She took a deep breath, narrowed her eyes, and made a decision. "Dad, I don't know how you got into this." She stopped as a memory slid into the background of her mind. Her dad had teased her since she was a child that he was a legendary hero in another life, and a British secret service agent in this one. She had always laughed at his claim, but just now, she wondered if he had been telling the truth. Then, looking her father straight in the eyes with a withering stare, she finished, "But as soon as this is over, you have a lot of explaining to do!"

Harry looked back at the young woman he had spent his life raising, saw her as the baby girl that she would always be to him, and answered, "Lizzy, when this is over, you can read the diaries under my bed, beneath the floor, in an old army footlocker. We will dig them out, and you can read for yourself, but for now, I need you to get these kids to the basement. In the old coal locker, there is a false door that leads to a tunnel. Pretend you are playing a game or something, but get them out of here. Follow the tunnel to the city drains. When you come to the T where the library tunnel ends, turn right and keep walking about a block. The manhole cover should be open, and Barry, my old friend, should be waiting there. Get these kids to safety. You understand?"

"Daddy, I am not leaving you," she said adamantly.

He stared back and said, "Lizzy, if you don't leave, I die. If you get these kids to safety, I have a chance of surviving this. Please get out of here now!"

"Dad, what do you mean you die?" Lizzy asked, frightened.

"Hon, there is no time. I need you to get to the basement now!"

Lizzy took a deep breath and slowly nodded, realizing the time for explanations would have to wait. She called to the rug rats who had been restlessly gnawing on cookies and milk, heedless of the gathering storm clouds around them.

"Children, we are going to play the best game of hide-and-seek this morning. You have to be *real* quiet and come with me now, okay? Shush, shush!" she added as the typical loud questions started to arise like bees off a disturbed hive.

They gathered like the Pied Piper's factions, tittering and laughing in semi-hushed tones. They formed a very crooked line and then skipped down the steps into the dark basement. The last thing the old man heard before he looked away was, "Ewww, it's dawk down heah!"

"Whew! I am so glad they are going to be safe. That's a load off my heart," the old man said, looking at the 1,244-

year-old love of his life staring back from a six-year-old body. "Is there any way I can get you to go with them?"

"Not hardly, buster!" the ancient royalty replied. "I will not leave you! You can threaten me. You can tie me up and throw me into the basement, but if you do, I will chew the ropes off, crawl back up here, and bite you. You can even threaten to spank me, but this is my fight too."

The old man blushed at that remark, and Sarah laughed at him and continued her tirade. "And I promise you," she decreed in her best imitation of a grand princess from a former century, "if you spank this little girl, we will not be amused."

Harry dug in his heels. "If I die, and you're captured, everything we've fought for will have been in vain. Sarah, you can't help me here. You can only get in the way and distract me. You may be a 1,244-year-old princess, but you're working out of a six-year-old body, honey. So really, what good do you think you're gonna do?"

"I love you, Harry the Bold, son of Fergie. I will not leave you, and if you go down beneath the dragon's claws, I will leap on your body and fight the beast with all the fury of what little power I possess until he is forced to kill me as well. Whether in life or death… I will not leave you."

"Damn, woman!" the old man grumbled, both sad and fiercely proud at the same time. A knock on the library door brought him back to the moment.

The old man looked around the library to be sure all the children had gone. He checked in with the speaker. *Is the armor activated?*

"Yes… You are also ready. You are not an old man limping into the twilight of his life. You are a knight, a dragon rider. You have the resources of the King at your disposal. Now plunge me through the scaly hide of this beast! I am thirsty!"

The old man paused, took a deep breath, and opened the door. He was not surprised to see the smiling face of the Reverend Laden Long staring back at him. Neither said anything for a moment. Then Long began, "You know why I am here, but I am not sure you are aware that I have brought guests with me." He pointed out to the parking lot where Grandma Grace and the fire marshal stood, surrounded by several townspeople, each with a firearm pointed in the general direction of the elderly couple. Harry noticed Kenneth's and Grace's mouths were duct-taped and across each of their chests was strapped a bomb.

Harry looked at them, nodded, and then stared back at the counterfeit clergy.

"You're not going to say anything?"

Harry just shrugged, his face expressionless. "Nothing to say."

"Hmmmph," the reverend grunted. "Okay then, you have someone I want, and I have someone you want. Actually, two someones."

Before Harry could answer, Sarah cried out, "Yes! Yes! I will come with you, only let them go!"

The speaker whispered, *"He will not let them go. He intends to kill you all, take Sarah away, and turn her into a dragon."*

The old man thought back to his perpetual friend, *Yep, and that is why…* He knelt down to hold Sarah by the arms, looking into her eyes. "Sarah, you have to trust me on this."

"I know. I know. I can't bear this. It's all because of me. Just let me go, or he will kill them."

Harry bent low, placed his forehead on hers, and whispered, "He's not going to let them go. You know that."

She looked back at him, sobbing, and nodded. "Do what you have to do."

He whispered again, "Act like you're going with him. Distract him but do not get close enough for him to grab you."

Harry stood up and looked back at the demonized reverend. "We agree."

Sarah addressed the man. "You're not going to hurt me, are you?"

The reverend took his eyes off Harry and moved toward Sarah.

Then Harry struck, screaming, "FULGOR INCEDIUM MEA SATOR!" The invisible cloak over his armor that kept the dragon from seeing him also hid the brightly burning ancient sword. Harry struck without warning, slicing off the arm that reached for Sarah, and kicked the reverend through the door.

Harry kept up the attack and hacked at the surprised man, who, though bleeding profusely, was lightning quick, and moved back dodging the blows. Two things happened at once. The reverend signaled his followers to fire on Harry, Kenneth, and Grace. His followers hesitated, and the fire marshal jumped the guard, striking him with his bound hands, trying to push his wife out of the way. Harry glanced toward the struggle, his heart pounding. He raced toward them, slicing through the crowd like hot butter with his flaming sword. He was too late.

The couple was hammered by bullets under a burst of fire. Grace was shot in the head, Kenneth in the chest. The reverend's man, holding the detonator, was also bleeding, and confused. His eyes were wide and glazed as he stared at the detonator. Harry saw the look, raced toward him screaming, and slammed down with the sword, slicing the hand with the detonator from the rest of the arm. Harry looked down at his friends and cursed. They were lying in a heap, the fire marshal still trying to shield his wife.

Harry had no time for grief as bullets began to slam into his armor like sheets of hail. None penetrated the ancient metal, but the shock of their blows pushed him back. His sword sliced through the air, singing its violent metallic song as it hacked through flesh and gunmetal.

Suddenly a tremendous roar shook the earth behind him, shattering the library windows. Harry was glad he had moved the children to safety, or they would have been shredded. He turned to see a twisting, thrashing, changing shape, dancing in a crackling flame that baked the startled air. The atmosphere screamed and then popped like a cork freed from a champagne bottle as a whirlwind of flame curled around the wounded shape of Reverend Laden Long. The smoke cleared, sucked back into the reptilian lungs of a dragon that had been healed of wounds, and had razor-sharp claws ready to slice Harry's flesh to ribbons.

The dragon drew back its head and vomited a torrent of flame at Harry. Instantly, the armor's color changed from dark bronze to fiery gold. The visor fell over his eyes, and impenetrable glass shielded his vision. Harry braced like he was leaning into a fierce gale, lunged forward, and cut into the underbelly of the great worm. The beast shrieked as the glowing sword tore through muscle and nerve, disappearing deep into the insides of the dragon. An agonized roar of flame exploded from the dragon's mouth. It swung its claw and swept Harry across the concrete, streaming sparks as he slid across the parking lot. As he gripped the sword, it spoke to his heart, *"You hurt him, Harry! He knows you can hurt him. Keep swinging, old man. You're not out of this fight yet!"*

Harry picked himself up just in time to see the dragon charging like a raging bull. Harry felt the sting of a dozen bullets as the dragon's followers continued to shoot at him from behind parked cars. His armor held, but his strength ebbed. The spirit was more than willing, but his flesh was seventy years old. As he crouched to receive the dragon's charge, he was dismayed to see the wound he had ripped into its scaly belly was already half-healed.

The dragon's powers of regeneration were incredible. It lowered its head with the intent to gore Harry, break his armor, and crush him beneath its angry claws. Harry heard the speaker yell, *"Down on your back! Raise your sword and cut him from stem to stern!"* Harry ran and slid feet first toward the dragon, ducked beneath its great jaws, and thrust the sword upward into its long neck. The force of the dragon's charge carried it along the laser-sharp edge of the sword, whose hoarse voice screamed in Harry's mind, *"You got him!"*

The dragon braked on the sharp blade and cut itself open. Dark steaming blood spurted from the long wound of its underbelly, and the dragon's molten intestines squeezed through the seam. The smell of sulphur and rotten septic mixed with the metallic smell of blood poured out of the serpent. For a moment everything stood still. Harry, panting and wheezing, forced his bruised and bloody body to stand. His armor was coated in dark blood as he looked down on the still-breathing dragon. Smoke rose from its flared nostrils and formed small rings that floated into the morning air. Slowly the dragon moved. It held its belly wound with one hand, pushed itself up with the other, and then sluggishly pointed a crooked claw toward the end of the parking lot. Harry closed his eyes, took a slow breath, and turned in the direction the beast indicated.

The children who he thought he had placed out of harm's way were crowded together, along with his daughter. Several of the dragon's disciples, masked and armed, stood around them. One of the dragon's followers was yelling at the freckle-faced boy, who stared back at him with an unrepentant look.

His daughter's hands were tied behind her, and most of the children were cowed, leaning into his daughter. Many had been crying and their flushed faces were still struggling with sobs. Harry's face burned with anger, but he knew that he could never make it across the parking lot before the kidnappers fired on his daughter and the children.

The dragon gasped in pain, shook, and then laughed. "I am healing, old man. In a few minutes I will be as good as new, but you," it sneered, "are weak, and old, and fading. It's over. There is no way you can beat me. If I signal those men, the children die, and your daughter as well. But if you lay down your sword and surrender, I promise you, your death will be quick, and the children and your daughter will be spared." The dragon's eyes were riveted on Harry, who should have known better than to stare into a dragon's eyes. The beasts were famous for their ability to cast a spell with their gaze, and in his weakened condition, Harry was vulnerable.

"You know he is lying. I can smell the treachery on him. He reeks of deceit. Those children will be sacrificed just like Thomas. You know that, Harry," the sword whispered.

Harry's last wall of resistance was crumbling. He could hear his heart thumping against his chest, the rhythmic beat lulling him into submission. He rallied for a moment and yelled back in his thoughts, *What can I do? It's them or me...* and with that, Harry unbuttoned his helmet and fell on his knees before the hissing beast.

The dragon was suspicious that Harry had given in so easily. It had no context for love or self-sacrifice, for it loved no one, and sacrifice was what you did to the weak in order to feed the strong. The evil beast had expected Harry to fight unto death, with the dragon triumphant, Harry beneath its claws, being roasted by its flaming breath. This little recess was the dragon's attempt to buy time to heal. It had no intention of sparing those children. It planned to snack on them as soon as this ordeal was over. So, when Harry unbuckled his helmet and knelt, the dragon was wary and paused, waiting for a few more minutes of respite in which to complete its healing. *What stupid beings these humans are!* it thought. *What puny, worthless creatures!* With that, the dragon stood, its wounds almost healed, and pulled back a claw to grab hold of Harry so it could sink its fangs into the old man's weary frame. As it reared back its neck for a mighty spray of flame, a snarling dragon, the size of a small steam engine, suddenly flew in from the side and slammed it to the ground.

Chapter Nineteen

Harry was thrown free by the collision and watched, astonished, as another dragon, smaller but bellowing in anger, pounded the old serpent's head with its lacerating claws. In the heartbeat of that moment, Harry suddenly heard popping sounds like fireworks at a midnight New Year's celebration. He turned to move toward the children and his daughter, expecting them to be the target of the gunfire. He watched the scene like it was in slow motion, and to his surprise, the dragon's followers were mowed down in front of his eyes, each would-be executioner with a shiny new red orifice in his forehead.

At the sound of the rifle fire, his daughter screamed at the children to fall to the ground and, like obedient little dominoes, they embraced the earth. After the guns ceased their staccato fire, Harry heard, "Hands up," and turned to see the rest of the dragon's followers being forced to their knees by the members of the police force and fire department that had not been a part of the dragon's cult. Harry briefly scanned the crowd and saw Barry, who waved, bloody and beaten, leaning on Jamie, his wife. Harry nodded, then quickly turned his attention back to the ferocious battle of the dragons. In the back of his mind he thought the smaller dragon looked familiar, and then his eyes widened in shock as he realized what had happened.

Sarah had shifted. Somehow, she had changed into a dragon and then, without a moment's hesitation, charged, hurtling into Laden Long the dragon. Both dragons screamed and spewed flame, slapping at each other with their razor-like claws: ripping, shrieking, flame burning, and crushing everything and everyone in their path. Harry rushed in, slicing and striking the large, dark dragon, but was only able to hit it from behind, slashing its giant spiked tail. It was not enough, and even to his untrained eyes, he could see that the smaller dragon, Sarah, was losing the battle. She was bleeding from many wounds, one claw nearly severed, and she limped from multiple lacerations to her legs. The larger dragon was also bloodied, and the wound Harry had carved into its middle was torn in many places, but the dark dragon was larger, stronger, and, Harry realized, a great deal more experienced. As far as he knew, Sarah had only been a dragon for five minutes. Harry watched as the dark dragon would feint. When Sarah reacted to the false blow, it would hammer her in the chest, knocking the wind out of her and dropping her to her knees. After another blow, she fell completely to the ground, her head striking it with a thud.

Harry screamed, "Sarah!" and raced toward the dark dragon with his sword lifted high, but was hammered by the dragon's tail slamming him into the library wall.

***

The large, dark dragon sneered, cracked its neck, and then whispered to the smaller dragon, "It doesn't have to be this way. You can still be with me. It would even be easier now that you have finally given in and transformed."

Sarah blinked back, shaking her head weakly. "No. Never…"

The evil worm continued thinking, *If I can just get her to lock eyes with me, I can break her will and capture her.*

Sarah, unaware that a dragon could cast a spell with its eyes, did not resist challenging it with her stare. Harry looked on, trying to raise himself up in time to scream a warning, but it was too late. He saw Sarah's dragon form shudder and her face lock in a fixed gaze. He cried out in despair as he saw the dark dragon's evil, gloating grin.

The other dragon, however, failed to see a movement in the yard. The blackened body of the fire marshal shuddered, then staggered to rise. He was burned over most of his body, one eye seared away. He had been shot in the chest and possibly even the gut. But even in his mortally wounded state he had realized that the small dragon was Sarah, and she was in danger. With the same adrenalin that gives a mother the strength to push a car off her infant, he rallied in a defiant act of love. The bomb that the dragon's followers had strapped across his chest was still active. The fire marshal had managed to rip the detonator from the severed hand of the man who had held it. Without a moment's hesitation, Grandpa Kenneth roused and charged. He slammed into and held on to the bent neck of the dragon, and with his other hand, pushed the button on the detonator.

The blast tore through the dark dragon's neck, blowing the large head off its fleshly pedestal. Flames erupted upward. Harry, who had been running toward the dragon as soon as he realized what the fire marshal intended, was blown back through the white picket fence of the pretty landscaped library. Glass and debris flew like living shrapnel, slicing people a hundred feet away. Dark sickly blood, tar-like and putrid, covered everyone in the blast area. Sarah dragon was blown back, soot and burning blood speckling her green scales. In the shock of the blast, she slammed her head against the concrete and lay still.

The first person to move was Barry. He and Jamie hobbled through chunks of burning flesh to make sure the evil dragon was truly dead, and then moved toward the body of Harry, who, to them, still looked like he wore his street clothes. They could not understand how he had withstood the blows and flame of the dragon without his clothes being torn and burned to pieces.

They were about to rouse him when they heard a shuffle behind them. The smaller dragon was stirring, slowly pushing up until it stood on unsteady legs. It wobbled like a drunk, fell to the ground, picked its head up, stared at the broken bundle that had once been Grandma Grace, and crawled toward it. Barry watched, glued to the spectacle. Once the dragon reached the woman's body, it gently pulled her to its chest and wailed. Shrieking its grief into the lonesome sky, it softly stroked the body like it was some gruesome doll, then reluctantly placed her grandma's body gently on the ground. The beast looked around, searching the parking lot, when its gaze lit on Harry, who still lay unconscious. The dragon's regenerative qualities had kicked in, and its strength was quickly returning. Rising on all fours, it lumbered toward Harry.

Barry and Jamie were torn, not wanting to abandon their friend, but neither desiring to become a dragon's next meal. A few feet away from them, the beast stopped and spoke. Barry's eyes grew large, and Jamie squealed, "Sheeeeeittt!"

The dragon's human-like voice was feminine and polite. "May I see him, please?" it asked.

Barry was dumbfounded, but Jamie, who was never at a loss for words, recovered and asked, "Are you who I think you are?"

The dragon laughed sadly and answered, "Apparently, I am. This is as new to me as you. Please don't be afraid. I just want to check on Harry. Do you know... is he alive? How serious are his injuries?" Sarah reached out to touch Harry's still form, and in so doing, she brushed against the sword Harry still gripped in his hand.

"Sarah," she heard a voice in her mind say. It startled her and she quickly drew back, which also unnerved Barry and Jamie. *"It's okay, Sarah. It's me, Harry's invisible friend, the speaker sword. You can hear me because now you are linked to Harry, and so also to me. In your present form you are more sensitive to my voice than you would be in human form, so I can speak to you. By the way, Harry is in a healing sleep. His armor will repair the damage of his wounds, similar to the way your flesh can heal you, but he has to sleep, and this might be for a day or two. You need to move him to a safe place. In a few minutes the people here are going to start moving, giving orders, and looking around. You need to be gone by the time they do. I need you to pick Harry up and fly off with him. You understand?"*

Sarah spoke out loud, "Yes, sir, I do. But, where do I take him? Wait! I don't know how to fly!"

Jamie placed a gentle hand on Sarah's large claw. "Honey, I don't think that's goin' to be a problem. Seems to come natural to you folk, so just grab up the old man, spread your wings, and take a running start and jump. I bet you don't come stumbling back down. Keep flapping those big ol' wings, and you just see what happens from there. Looks to me like you ought to hurry though because there is a group of people starting to move this way, and they might not be able to tell the difference between a good dragon and a bad one. You know what I mean, hon?"

Dragon Sarah nodded her great head, then picked Harry up and held him to her chest like a mother would a sleeping child. Nodding toward Barry and Jamie, she took off running down the parking lot and leaped into the air. Just as Jamie had said, her instincts took over, and her wings moved naturally. She lifted up into the sky and was soon out of sight.

***

Harry awoke to the smell of cut grass and manure. He was extremely sore. When he moved, he hurt. When he lay still, he hurt. He tried opening his eyes a few times and finally realized his eyes *were* open, he just couldn't see. Then he remembered he still had his armor on, so slowly, aching with every inch, he reached his hand to his helmet and pushed back the visor. A blast of light jolted his sleepy eyes, causing him to cry out. He heard a large shuffle a few feet away and raised his head to find himself face to face with the huge jaws of a dragon. "Ah! Not again!" he cried as his head fell back into the hay. "Just eat me; get this over. I am too tired to care, and my body hurts too much to fight you."

He felt a claw touch his armor and braced himself for the pain he expected to follow. Nothing happened. The claw just shook him in a gentle attempt to nudge him awake. Coming from a fifteen-thousand-pound newbie dragon that was as clumsy as a toddler trying to learn to walk, the nudge felt like a bad roller coaster ride.

Harry's head jostled, and his armor banged against the back of the horse stable. "Ow! Dang it!" He reached for his sword and couldn't find it, but was so weak he collapsed again.

He was conscious enough to hear a familiar small voice coming from the large beast. It was crying, "Oh, oh. I'm sorry, sorry... oh. I hurt you again. I'm just a big, stupid, clumsy oaf." And then the words crumbled into sobs.

Harry opened his eyes, staring at the roughhewn timbered ceiling of the old barn. After a moment of thought, he whispered, "Sarah? Sarah? Is that you?" He forced himself to sit up, pushing against every stomach and back muscle that would listen to him. Once he sat up, he found himself staring at a great big seven-ton dragon that was curled into a ball like a German shepherd. A closer look revealed the eyes of a 1,244-year-old princess staring back at him, whimpering like a six-year-old child.

"Oooooh, Sarah," he sympathized. "Are you okay?"

She crawled toward him and was now just a couple of feet away. Her huge head lay in the hay at his feet. "No, I am not okay! I am a dragon and have been for four days! I have been worried sick about you, even though the speaker assures me you are fine and will just be sore until you start eating again. I have worried and worried, and when I wasn't worried about you, I was worried about me. I can't figure out how to turn back into a person. The sword has been trying to help me, but nothing is working. Then I got hungry, and I…"

She started sobbing again; great big, big dragon tears streamed down her face, pooling into large puddles that muddied up the barn floor. She continued, "I ate two of Grandpa's cows! And a couple of the stray cats! I didn't mean to, but they ran, and I raced after them, and before I knew what I was doing, I ate the cats! Oh!" She moaned, her tears streaming down her face again, soaking Harry's armor as they seeped through the seams. Their saltiness touched his scars and stung. He winced. Sarah saw it and bawled even louder.

"Sarah, Sarah, hush." He tried to soothe her, stroking her long muzzle. "Hey, we made it through the hard part. We're still alive, at least for the moment, unless you sneeze and wrap me around a post in here," he teased. She sniffled and sighed, which caused Harry to gag because it was rather pungent. He tried to smile through it, but it was like trying to say grace over roasted skunk, and his grimace gave it away.

She apologized again, "I'm sorry. I even have bad breath! I think I have a piece of meat stuck in my back tooth, and I can't get it out. I've been trying."

Harry, ever the caregiver, said, "Let me see. Open up."

Sarah opened her massive jaws, flashing a terrifying array of razor-sharp teeth that would have made a great white jealous. Just as Harry was about to reach in and pull out the piece of meat he saw stuck between two back teeth, he thought better of it and said, "Give me a minute." He walked to the back of the barn and picked up a pitchfork. "Now open."

Sarah complied but kept trying to give instructions, "Dooon stttttticc y toungne."

He laughed and answered, "It's not your tongue I am concerned about. It's my head. One small bite, and you're on your own. So, hold still!" Harry poked and yanked until finally the putrid flesh pried loose. Holding it up by what was left of a tail, he grimaced. "It's the cat." He pulled back the pitchfork with the bit of furry flesh, and Sarah swallowed, grateful. "See, that wasn't too bad. We can fix this. Just give me a moment, and we'll figure it out."

He plopped down on a stool in the barn and started taking off his armored boots. He stopped, paused, and looked at dragon Sarah, then asked, "Ah, we did kill the reverend and his followers, right? I realize after..." He paused again, remembering what caused the explosion. His face paled, and his heart ached as he remembered. "I hate crying," he whispered. "The pain I push back, just to be able to function, rips my heart apart and burns through my eyes."

Sarah began to weep again. Harry stood up, hugged her massive neck, and whispered, "He loved you, honey. He loved you so much he wouldn't die till he knew you were safe. I couldn't take out the dragon. You couldn't take him down, but your grandpa... your grandpa..." Harry began to sob and his defenses gave way. "He was... he was the fire marshal. A beast was trying to take his granddaughter, and he took it out. He blew that damn thing's head off!" And with that statement, they both laughed and wept again.

"Well, I'm glad to see you're up, and Sarah is feeling better," a familiar voice in Harry's head declared.

Harry went back to taking his boots off, stopped, sat down on the stool, and thought, *I was wondering when you were going to show back up. And hey, did Sarah just tell me you were speaking to her too?*

"Yes, sir, that is exactly what she said."

Huh… well, how does that work? And can she hear you right now?

Dragon Sarah scooted over to the stool where Harry sat in his bare feet talking to the sword in his head. She smiled at the scene and answered, "I sure can! And that is just fine with me. You two have had way too many conversations that I wasn't allowed to hear. The era of the woman has come!" she declared.

"Or not," the sword whispered to Harry. *"She can't hear me if I don't want her to. You and I have a blood bond. Her bond is filtered through you. But hey, I'm not telling her that, 'cause you know as well as I do, what she doesn't know…"*

Harry finished the sentence out loud, "…ain't going to hurt us!"

Dragon Sarah looked down her long nose and raised an imperial eyebrow. A shiver ran down Harry's spine. He gave Sarah a cautious glance and thought, *Maybe I'll keep this armor on for a little while longer.*

Sarah laughed and said, "You know I am a lean, mean, fire-breathing machine. You *do* see that, don't you?"

Harry looked back at her and said, "Nope, I don't. I see a little snaggle-toothed, ragamuffin, story time princess that I still need to rescue. So, Speaker, you were saying?"

"I was pointing out something that you have already realized: Sarah cannot shift back into a human." Harry sighed and Sarah

moaned, but the speaker continued, *"I know why. I have gone back over everything I have ever heard or read about this problem. You are not the first dragon and dragon rider to face it. From what I have read, there are ways around it."*

Sarah's natural feminine dragon curiosity aroused at the word *it*. "What is 'it'?"

Both Harry and dragon Sarah sensed the hesitation in the speaker's voice. Harry was first to address the "it." "Speaker, what's the problem? The only time I have ever sensed hesitation in you before was when you didn't want to tell me something and, most of the time, I found out anyway, or we were able to deal with it. So, out with it. What is 'it'?"

Had the sword had lungs, it would have sighed. *"It's the curse, Harry, the dragon's death curse from the time you rode it into the ground and killed it, or almost killed it: Your love will never leave you, but neither will you have it till it does."*

Sarah spit in disgust. The phlegm sizzled as it burned into the hay. Smoke quickly started to curl from the straw, and she stepped over to stomp it out. "You said an undeserved curse does not come to rest. You said there are ways to defeat it. I remember very clearly. If that is true, what is this?"

"You are right. An undeserved curse does not come to rest... and there are ways to defeat this. It just takes time, research, and to be honest, prayer."

Harry listened to the speaker and sensed he had not said all he knew. "And? And?"

Dragon Sarah tilted her head. "What are you holding back, Speaker?"

"I have been too close to you for too long, Harold Ferguson. You know me too well. If this keeps up, I will have no secrets."

"Out with it, you iron-pigmented piece of remelted horseshoe!" Sarah demanded.

"Okay already. Here's the thing. I think your predicament is purposeful. I believe, and that belief is growing stronger, especially now that I am processing it in front of you, that the reason Sarah cannot shift back is not solely because of any curse. It is because this story is not over. There, I said it."

"What!" Harry yelled. "What story are you talking about? You're talking about a stupid sequel? A larger picture? But I'm tired! I have rescued the princess twice now. Good people have died in the process, and you're telling me it's not over! Uh-uh! No, no! I am done. I am through!"

"I can understand how you feel, Harry, but your life is not your own anymore. You know that. And truth be told, you really… have just had one adventure, although a very, very long one. All I know is this: when a person's story is over, things reconcile. They work together for good, you might say, especially for dragon riders. And, well, obviously your story is not done. There is something else for you to do."

"Yeah, I got that. I have to teach a seven-and-a-half-ton dragon to shift back into a six-year-old girl, and then back into a 1,244-year-old princess."

Sarah added, "And a seventy-year-old man back into an eighteen-year-old handsome dragon rider."

Chapter Twenty

A knock at the barn door caused Harry to jump. Sarah panicked and tried to find a place to hide in the huge barn, but hiding places are limited when you are a seven-and-a-half-ton dragon. Harry finally realized there was nothing he could do but answer the door, while Sarah jostled through the large haystack, futilely trying to keep her long tail hidden. She might have succeeded, except for her need to breathe. When she exhaled, small smoke rings curled up and drifted into the upper sections of the barn, hovering like fog. Harry rolled his eyes, shrugged his shoulders, and walked toward the barn door. He pulled back the bolts that held it shut and cautiously slid the barn door back an inch, far enough to see who was knocking, but not far enough to give them access.

"Hey, Dad!" his daughter said in greeting. She stood at the door with both arms folded across her chest. She was trying to decide if she was madder than she was glad at that moment. Harry's bright smile decided the issue for her, and she grabbed him into a big hug. For a few minutes, they hugged and sighed and then hugged some more, but when the relief began to subside, Lizzy's ire began to rise. "Dad, you've been missing for four days!" Her head and neck stretched forward doing a poor imitation of Madea. "Why haven't you called me? Why have you been hiding? Are you hurt?" Her eyes looked past her father and scanned the barn, coming to rest on two huge eyes blinking through a pile of straw. "Dad!" she shrieked.

"It's okay. Lizzy, calm down! It's just Sarah, the new version, or maybe she is the old version, or the dragon version. I don't know, but she's not going to hurt anyone. Are you?" he asked, directing the question toward dragon Sarah and beckoning her to shuffle out from hiding. Harry, accustomed to seeing dragons, especially Sarah, forgot how a close-up first encounter might intimidate somebody else, especially somebody who was already distraught and worn out from stress and worry. Sarah lumbered out from her makeshift hiding spot, moving a huge pile of hay like a ship does water in its wake. Lizzy took one look and collapsed in Harry's arms.

"Oh my! Oh my!" he said as he held her and kept her from falling to the ground. Easing her down he thought, *Now what? Is she okay?* He gently slapped her face. "Lizzy, Lizzy! Hey, it's okay. You okay, honey?" After a few minutes, Lizzy groaned and came to. Sarah had stepped back into the shadows, trying to keep a low profile, which for a dragon person larger than an African bush elephant, was difficult.

"Dad, are you okay? There was a dragon in here. I saw a dragon!" she said in a near panic.

"You saw her at the library, Lizzy. She fought the evil dragon. Don't you remember?"

Lizzy was still groggy and struggling with all the trauma of the last few days. "Yes, I do… I just didn't see it up close. And then people began saying it wasn't a dragon but some drug-induced hallucination caused by the cultists. The media came from around the world, and the FBI showed up, and now, even those of us who were there aren't sure what happened. The city police are being hailed as heroes, as well as those local folks who were involved in the shootout. It has been quite an uproar. The mayor resigned and Barry Dinker, who was assistant mayor, has replaced him. While things are starting to simmer down a bit, people, of course, are asking questions." Lizzy sat up and brushed the hay from her pants. She looked around cautiously and fearfully. Her eyes stopped on Sarah. Lizzy gasped. Her eyes grew wide, and her face paled as white as chalk. Sarah, for lack of knowing what else to do, raised a claw and shyly waved at Lizzy. Lizzy, also for lack of knowing what to do, waved back.

Sarah cleared her throat, which probably wasn't the wisest thing to do, since it sounded like a cross between a sick lion and angry walrus, and Lizzy startled and stepped back.

Harry said, "It's okay. It's okay. She just has some phlegm in her throat. Happens when you eat a cat."

Lizzy stared back, disgusted at her dad, like she'd been asked to stick her finger in something the cat drug up and the dogs wouldn't touch. "She ate a cat?"

Sarah, embarrassed, squeaked in a voice extremely out of place for a fifteen-thousand-pound dragon, "I didn't mean to, Miss Lizzy. I really didn't. I'm not used to being a dragon, and I have urges and habits that I didn't know I had. The cat ran, and something in me had to chase it, and then I caught it, and before I knew it, I ate it like those animal crackers you bring to the library. Then your dad laughed at me and hurt my feelings."

Lizzy grew more sympathetic as Sarah spoke, and when Sarah mentioned that Harry had hurt her poor dragonish heart, well, mama bear came out and the scolding began. "Dad! I can't believe you. This poor girl," Lizzy said, pointing at the seven-and-a-half-ton dragon in the room, "has been traumatized out of her mind, kidnapped, and forced to fight off a deranged... deranged... whatever he was! She saved your life, has had to huddle in a barn for four days while you sleep off some type of... of... of...

hangover… and you mock her?" Lizzy's voice had risen in intensity as her lecture continued, barely avoiding scalding. Had she been a dragon herself, steam would have certainly shot out her nose.

Harry leaned back, knowing that most of what was discharging from Lizzy wasn't really intended for him as much as she simply needed to erupt, like a volcano, deadly but not intentional. Finally, Mount Lizzy sizzled to a slow grumble, looked at her father, and sighed, "Sorry, Dad, once it started, I couldn't stop."

The old man looked back at her and nodded knowingly. "Well, honey, it didn't bother me a bit, and seemed to do you a world of good."

Lizzy turned toward Sarah, raised an inviting eyebrow, and nodded toward her father. Then she bent down, grabbed an armful of hay, and threw it at him. Sarah followed suit, but slightly more forceful, causing a tsunami of hay to sweep over Lizzy and Harry as they tumbled out the barn door in a flood of mown pasture grass.

After everyone had picked the hay out of their hair, pants, armor, and from between the scales on their backside, and after both Lizzy and Sarah insisted Harry shower and change into some of Grandpa Kenneth's old clothes, they sat down for a talk. Lizzy moved some lawn chairs and a table into the barn so Sarah could easily contribute rather than having to look through a window of the house to participate in the conversation. Lizzy, unlike her father, liked things planned out, scheduled, and calendared. Harry kept telling her that he had been asleep the whole time he was missing, and since he just woke up, he had not had time to think too far ahead. Lizzy replied, "Well then, you should be rested now, and we have to discuss some things and make some plans."

"Obviously," Harry sighed.

While Harry had been scouring blood, barn dirt, dragon mucus, and smut off his body, Lizzy saw to Sarah's basic needs, like Cheetos, soda, and a few pounds of ground beef from Grandma Grace's kitchen. When Harry got back from his cleaning, the barn had been transformed. A plastic table from the hall closet now held a five-gallon bucket of soda and three large sacks of Cheetos, which had been poured into a crystal serving bowl and gracefully set on the table along with a notepad, pencils, and pens.

Harry sat down at the table and said, "Now what?"

"Well, Dad, Sarah and I have been talking..."

The sword, who had been unusually quiet, slipped in, *"You're in for it now, buddy!"*

To which dragon Sarah replied, "I heard that, Speaker! And Harry, you don't need to nod or think anything in response. Just sit there quietly and say yes ma'am in the appropriate places."

Harry thought before he could stop it, *The dragon killed and ate me. I died and arose in a barn... with two bossy women... dang!*

Sarah giggled. Harry thought she sounded more like a donkey braying but slammed those thoughts shut before they clothed themselves in words. Lizzy had not been introduced to the speaker, so she was at a loss as to what was going on.

"Why do I think I am the only one here who doesn't know what the joke is?" Lizzy asked, pulling her chair back and crossing her arms.

Harry sighed, "Well, Lizzy, how do I explain this?"

"Oh, Harry. It's simple. Don't complicate it," Sarah replied as she reared up and put her dragon hands on her dragon hips like a normal woman explaining a complicated thing to a simple man. "Miss Lizzy," Sarah began, only to be interrupted.

"Just call me Lizzy, Sarah, because I don't think you're just six anymore."

Sarah looked down on her and stopped in mid-sentence. "It is a little complicated, isn't it?"

"Hah!" Harry bellowed. "Now ya see, don't you, Miss Priss?"

And then they both began to talk at once about speaker swords, and age differences, and time streams, and nano futuristic armor, and Harry's boyhood, until an hour later, Lizzy, who had been trying to keep up, yelled, "Enough! Enough! Basically, as I understand what you're saying, is that you are the story you were telling. Right, Dad?"

"Exactly, honey. You got it."

"So, now what are you going to do?" Lizzy asked.

Sarah looked at the floor and settled down with her huge muzzle a few feet away from the table. Harry leaned back in his chair. Neither said a thing. Lizzy answered her own question. "You don't have any idea, do you?"

They both shook their heads no.

"Wow," Lizzy whispered. "Wow." Then a bright idea leaped into her heart and caused her eyes to sparkle. "You know, sometimes, when you just put aside your own problems and help others, your problems either become clearer, work out on their own, or go away. I think this is a time to set aside your troubles and help others with theirs."

The sword interjected a thought into both Sarah and Harry. *"Ahem... Ahem. I would be honored to make the acquaintance of Miss Lizzy. I think it would go a long way to expediting this conversation, as well as the many more that will follow."*

Harry beat Sarah by responding aloud for Lizzy's benefit, "How? How do we do that? I am bonded to you by blood. Sarah is a dragon bonded to me, so thereby, also to you. But Lizzy and I, although father and daughter, don't share the dragon to dragon rider bond. So, how do we introduce her to you?"

Lizzy looked at her dad a little surprised but also curious. She had been told about the speaker sword, and a briefly translated conversation had taken place between her and the sword, but due to the inconvenience of translating, and the out-of-sight, out-of-mind principle, she had not considered knowing the speaker sword an option, except through Sarah or her dad. She nodded quickly to her dad, listening intently to the conversation.

Her father acknowledged his daughter's nod and continued, "Lizzy wants to be introduced to you as well, Speaker. So, how does this happen?"

The speaker laughed, *"Harry, I can see the thoughts forming in your head before you can. Lizzy is your daughter and is used to your teasing, but you need to be sure, before you proceed with this little joke of yours, because she does have an advocate in Sarah now that she did not have before."*

Harry laughed and thought back to the sword, realizing that Sarah had been left out of this particular conversation. *"I don't know what you're talking abo…"* And then the thoughts formalized, and he grinned, but quickly changed it to a frown.

The speaker continued, *"Even so, it only takes a very small amount of blood, like a paper cut, to connect us. Now mind you, I am not responsible for the lie you are about to tell, just so we're clear. Have her gently pull a finger over my blade to draw the smallest amount of blood, and I will do the rest."*

Harry looked at his daughter and very solemnly asked, "Honey, are you sure you want to do this?"

"Absolutely, Dad. Good grief! Having access to an ancient artificial intelligence that can provide instantaneous information. I am a librarian! Of course I want to do this!" But she cocked an unsure eyebrow at her dad and frowned as doubt began to radiate off her like heat from a fireplace. "Why do you ask, *Father*? What is going on?" The only time Lizzy used the word *father* was when her dad was telling her some made-up story or something troubling. She instinctively slid into that frame of mind and asked again, "What is it?"

Sarah had been watching the whole exchange and was also growing cautious, wondering why the speaker had chosen to exclude her from the conversation, so she echoed Lizzy's question, "Yeah, Harry. What's going on?"

"Well, you both know that I originally bonded with the speaker by accident. I cut myself on the blade as I tried to place him back in his sheath. That blood became the basis for our bond, and, well, Speaker informs me that he can also bond with you, Lizzy, and be able to communicate directly, if you share some blood as well."

Lizzy gulped and then bravely nodded. "Okay, I can do that. So, what's the problem?"

Temptation got the best of Harry. "Well, you know it will hurt."

"So yeah, I get it. You have to get cut to bleed... so?"

"Well, ah... hmmm. Well." Harry hem-hawed teasingly, not yet ready to give away the trick.

Sarah's eyes narrowed, and she began to inhale involuntarily, the tension building.

Harry continued, holding his left hand up, stroking the end of its pinky. "I mean, I will do the surgery, Lizzy, and it will only take the last knuckle of..."

"*What*?!" Lizzy and Sarah both yelled. Lizzy continued, "The last knuckle! Just how much blood do you need?"

By then, Sarah, apparently apprised of Harry's teasing by the speaker sword, reached down and as gently as a mother cat lifts a kitten, placed her mouth around Harry's head and sealed him in with her lips. "Hey!" came the muffled protests.

"He is messing with you," she tried to say, but it came out more like "ee s essing ith ew."

Having lived with her father since she was a child, Lizzy understood perfectly and began to laugh and howl at her father's predicament.

Harry was also laughing, but Lizzy could tell it was tinged with an edge of nervousness. "Lizzy! I was just teasing!" Harry's voice echoed like he was in a cave. "It only takes like a paper cut. Okay? Sarah, you can let go now."

Lizzy looked up smiling and nodded courteously to her new best friend. "I suppose that will do. Thank you, my dear, for taking my side. He has teased me since I was a child, and I just think karma caught up with him."

Sarah opened her mouth and pulled away, leaving Harry covered in dragon slobber. A normal person would have been terrified or furious, but not Harry. He thought it was hilarious, and he fumed and fussed while wiping handfuls of dragon drool out of his hair.

Finally, after Lizzy had gotten a washcloth, towel, and extra shirt for him, Harry continued. Sarah was still snorting, which had the effect of blowing ever-expanding smoke rings around everyone. Harry looked at her, scowling, and said, "Now, let's get this over with so we can plan whatever you two have in mind." With that, he unsheathed the speaker sword, laying it carefully on the table, holding it gingerly on its edge. Then he directed Lizzy, "Lizzy, this is razor sharp. Rather *he* is razor sharp, so be extremely careful. You could slice off way more than you intend if you are not careful."

Lizzy nodded. She had grabbed a first aid kit from the corner of the barn and had a warm washcloth, a roll of bandages, Band-Aids, and triple-antibiotic ointment ready, just in case. Slowly, she reached forward with her right hand, her thumb pulled back about a half inch along her index finger and, like a nudist creeping around a fire ant hill, barely touched the tiniest piece of her finger, as gently as possible, on the edge of the blade.

Chapter Twenty-One

"Yee-ow!" Lizzy wailed as a needle-thin line of red oozed up from the end of her finger. "That hurt!" She looked at her father and grimaced, then suddenly her head began to sway, and she slumped back into her chair.

"She sure does faint a lot, Harry," Sarah asked. "Is she okay? Does she fatigue easily?"

"Not usually. Most of the time she runs herself ragged, then collapses. I think this is just a consequence of the last few days. It has taken its toll on all of us."

Then both Sarah and Harry heard, *"Something is not right. I have never seen this reaction before. She shouldn't have fainted, and I should already be able to speak to her. I should at least have access to her memories and thoughts, but I am shut out. Locked out would be a better word. I don't understand this."*

Sarah responded first, "You don't have any experience with this reaction? Have you a lot of experience with blood bonds? Perhaps you just haven't seen enough of them?"

The sword responded, *"I am not limited to my own experience. I have memories shared from every sword that has ever existed, and that means thousands of bonding experiences. Some are ancient and not all are immediately accessible. I need to meditate upon this. I have a vague impression, only one actually, but I am not ready to share it yet. Please be patient. I am going to need some time."*

"What are we supposed to do in the meantime?" Harry asked, worried. "This is my daughter here. Should I take her to the hospital, or what?"

"She is, isn't she…"

227

Something about the speaker's statement bothered Sarah, but she couldn't quite place it. Her focus quickly shifted, and the speaker stopped talking, his presence in her mind gone.

Harry wasn't thinking about the speaker's tone or his sudden disappearance. He was used to the sword being there and then suddenly not being there. He grabbed a piece of ice and gently began to move it back and forth across Lizzy's face. "Come on, Lizzy. Come on. Wake up. You have to stop this. If you keep fainting every time something…"

Lizzy's hand moved to push her dad's ice cube away. "Yuck, Dad. What is that? You're getting me wet." She blinked, frowned, and tried to sit up, fussing.

Harry was so relieved he didn't mind her complaining about her wet blouse or the water running down her neck.

Later, after Lizzy had gotten something to drink and toweled off from her dad's well-intended but sloppy attempt to resuscitate her, she looked up at Sarah and her father and said, "Did it work? I don't hear a voice in my head. Does it take a while, or what?"

Harry shrugged at Sarah with an are-you-going-to-answer-that-question-or-am-I look.

Sarah answered his unspoken question, "Hey, I may look like a dragon and sound like a 1,244-year-old medieval princess, but at heart, I am really just six. I have noticed my vocabulary has improved, but I am severely limited in my understanding, and especially in my experience with the sword, who, by the way, seems to have gone quiet."

"I don't know what to tell you either, Lizzy, except that there are more things we don't know than we do know, and blood bonds with mystical swords is one of the things we don't know much about. I am sorry, honey."

Lizzy sighed, then beat back the downcast look that wanted to own her face. "Well, we tried," she said woodenly, in a way she hoped would encourage her dad and Sarah. It didn't, but everyone understood the effort and danced to the tune a moment longer.

Harry scratched his chin. He hadn't shaved in a week and his face was starting to itch. He looked at his daughter, squinted, and said, "Lizzy, all of us are walking down paths few have ever walked. The few who have are not available to counsel us. I don't know why Speaker cannot, or will not, communicate with you, but I know this, this journey is not over. Like you were sharing before, we attempted to… to… heck, I don't know what you call what we were trying to do… but hey, it didn't work, or better, it hasn't worked yet. We don't know that it won't work. Speaker didn't say he couldn't make it work. He said it wasn't working, and he intended to find out why. He is a very formidable researcher, honey. So, like you said a little while ago, let's focus on helping someone else and push aside our own fears for the moment." Harry blew out a long breath and continued, "What did you have in mind?"

Lizzy nodded and pushed back her disappointment. "You're right, Dad. I need to practice what I preach. Soooo… here is what I believe needs to happen. Several people in this little community were involved in rescuing the kids in the library and taking down the cultists. Some of the children were probably earmarked for sacrifice, and they don't even know it. All they know is that their parents are dead or are in jail, and they are in a foster home."

Sarah moaned and another plume of steam shot out her nose. "My friends! They're all my friends." Harry slipped an arm out and laid his hand on her tear-stained muzzle.

Lizzy continued.

"Some of the police officers and first responders watched an old man, protected only by his street clothes, swing an ancient sword to fight a dragon, then saw two dragons fight, and watched Kenneth and Grace die beneath an onslaught of gunfire. Then, in stunned awe, they watched Grandpa Kenneth rise up, when he should have been dead, and single-handedly blow the fool neck of that awful beast."

"Yes, he did!" Harry yelled, slapping his fist into his hand. "Yes, he did!"

"Well, those people need, ought... deserve closure. They need to hear the rest of the story, Dad. They have been told by well-meaning—I think well-meaning—federal agents that the whole event had to be the product of drug-induced hallucinations. Most people were smart enough to tuck their heads and say yes ma'am and no sir in the appropriate fashion. They got bullied into signing forms saying they wouldn't sue anybody and made statements that nobody believed. It has been a week now. The federal agents have packed up and gone on to the next crisis. The funerals are over, and now people are settling into thinking or forgetting, whichever suits their nature. A few have contacted me, truthfully, more than a few. They want to know where you are and what happened to Sarah. I haven't said anything over the phone, and I'm not going to. But I am going to see some folks face to face and tell them that you're okay, and that if they want to see you, they can come here to find out what *really* happened. I'll make sure they know that nobody is going to laugh at them, or bully them, or threaten to arrest them, or put them away. So, are you and Sarah okay with that? With finishing this out?"

Lizzy, a born teacher, had begun to pace as she processed. She was waving her hands, emphasizing her points. Then she stopped, looked up at her dad, and asked, "Don't they deserve to know? Some may not want to know.

They would rather leave things as they are. I don't know how many people will show up, but I think we need to do this. I also think many of these people need to make restitution or repent for not speaking out when they had the chance. They were afraid, rightly so. Laden Long was a killer from a long line of killers."

Sarah puffed out a long roll of smoke and nodded. "Yes. Absolutely, yes. We need to do this."

Harry was less enthusiastic. "Lizzy, this is not my first experience with the government or some group's attempt to clamp down on information. I have even contributed to it myself in the past." Lizzy looked at him, puzzled. "It's all in the diaries under my bed, hon, and the problem is, people believe what they want to, see what they want to, and if they are forced to change their worldview too quickly or too drastically, they revolt. So, what you expect to happen may not. Who you expect to show up, and who *needs* to show up, they may not come. You need to realize that."

"Dad, I know what you are saying is true, at least I know it in my head, but my heart tells me we have to try. It's not like I am going to put up posters all around town or advertise in the paper or on the radio. Remember, half of these people were a part of that cult, and they know how to communicate secrets. Even the sheriff and deputies are aware. Nobody is talking. But everyone who knows wishes deep down that somebody who knew the truth will talk."

"Okay, honey, gather your tribe." He looked around the barn and said, "I think this barn is big enough, for the few that will show up."

Chapter Twenty-Two

Three days later

The morning of the event that Harry referred to as the secret meeting, he woke up restless. His head told him everything would be fine and all precautions had been taken, but his heart wasn't buying it and hadn't shared why. Harry had learned, through excruciating circumstances a lifetime ago, that the key to understanding his own motivations was to ask the right question, even if it required scathing honesty. He might not like the answer, but he knew that if his heart was right, his head would get there eventually. Although he said he didn't know what was making him uneasy, he had a pretty good idea. Finally, he admitted it to himself and went to find his seven-and-a-half-ton dragon. Sarah had begun flying off at night to prey on the wild hog population that had, up until recently, been a blight in the county. She usually came back long before dawn to hide in the barn the rest of the day. She had also started growing. Harry thought a pig or two a day would do that to a person but wasn't inclined to point it out to his lady-dragon friend. Harry searched the fire marshal's property for Sarah. He walked most of the large and wooded farm, until finally, after hiking out to the farthest, most isolated corner, he found her.

Sarah looked up and smiled when she saw Harry. At first, her dragon smiles sent shivers down Harry's spine, but he had become accustomed to her and walked right up and sat nose to muzzle.

"I have been expecting you," Sarah said softly.

Harry noticed her breath had improved remarkably since Lizzy had introduced her to the peppermint plants Grandma Grace had planted around the porch.

"Have you now?" Harry answered, trying not to stall but not doing a very good job of it.

"Yes."

"Why?" he dodged, not knowing how he should broach the subject.

"You know."

Harry started to say something and was interrupted by the sword, *"Sometimes words are not as powerful as thoughts. I might be able to help out. If you two are agreeable, I can increase your bond temporarily to the point that you can share your thoughts mentally. It might be easier than words, and a great deal more accurate."*

Before either could answer, the sword graciously bridged the gap and even provided a virtual image. Harry blinked and suddenly he was standing in a verdant pasture next to a noisy brook. He heard his name called and turned to look, and there she was walking toward him, not dragon Sarah, or six-year-old Sarah, but mature Princess Sarah. Harry looked at the princess and realized he had only seen her once in the light of day. Even then he hadn't taken a great deal of time to look at her. But now in the full radiance of the speaker's artificial day, he treated his eyes to something his spirit had known for ages.

Harry's heart nearly stopped at the sight of her. Sarah was beautiful. As she drew closer, he began to remember and now added to those memories.

Dressed in the ever-present Lincoln-green skirt that flowed gracefully around her feet, no longer torn or burnt, the dress simply sculptured her tall, slender body, accenting her softly rounded hips. As she drew ever nearer, he noticed her hair, black as a raven's breast, was cut short, gently covering her ears and teasing her neck. She had high cheekbones and creamy skin, speckled with a light spray of freckles that streamed across her nose, enhancing the youth that had been prematurely stolen from her.

When his brown eyes locked with her haunting green ones, his heartbeat returned with his breath.

As she looked up at him, he noticed how her long gorgeous lashes accented her high arching brows. But as he looked into those brilliant green eyes, he also saw pain like an emerald pool of ancient grief. Her eyes showed her soul and that soul had suffered for a very long time. His own eyes glistened, and tears formed when he saw something else. He saw love and knew it belonged to him.

"Wow," he gasped. "You're... you! You're finally you! I've tried to remember you a thousand times through the years. Finally, I began to lose the only memories I had, like a yellowed photograph crumbling beneath light. But now, I see you again, and I don't know what to say. I missed you, and yet I hardly knew you. Were you a figment of my aging imagination? Or were you real for a moment, then ripped away?"

Sarah laughed back and said, "You need to look in the mirror yourself, Harry!"

Harry stared down at his hands, which had been scarred and spotted with age. They were young again, the working hands of a young man of eighteen. "Wow! I could get used to this."

The sword interrupted, *"I hate to tell you this, but your time here is limited. It takes an awful lot of energy to create these avatars. I am sorry."*

Harry sighed sadly, "Well hell, Speaker, another two-edged sword: sweet and bitter intertwined with barbed heartbreak."

Sarah reached over and grabbed Harry's hand. "If there is not much time, use it wisely, Harry."

He stared back at her and his lips began to tremble. "Those people want to know how the story ends, but I don't want to tell them. It's over. It's done. And you... you have been restored in the most amazing fashion. You wouldn't be the most amazing and wonderful you that you are now if it weren't for the other. But I don't want to... to..."

"Expose me? Tell the truth about me. Make me look bad? Dishonor me?"

Harry tucked his head and held his face in his hands. "Yes, to all the above."

"How are you going to finish the story without telling the truth? I have had a lot of time to think about this. It is pretty much all I have thought about these last few days, thought and prayed about. Isn't that funny... a dragon praying? But it's true."

Harry laughed with her, then smirked and said, "And what have you concluded?"

"I had a picture come to mind of a woman doing laundry the old-fashioned way. My grandma Grace had an old washtub that had been her great-grandmother's. She showed me once how it had been used. Well, I saw that tub in my mind with laundry piled next to it that must have been a baby's because it was awful, if you know what I mean?" Sarah winced and curled her nose as she spoke. Harry got the idea. "In my vision, I saw all that filthy laundry, all those diapers as nasty as they were, and then I saw someone—I'm not sure who—taking them one by one and washing them in that tub. They went in nasty and came out so white they gleamed. I didn't know why I was seeing that picture until I thought about what I had been praying. It was then that I realized the laundry was *me*. That filth was *mine*. And now I, at least for the most part, am clean. Harry, if we don't tell them about the dirt, they won't hear about the tub or how to get clean. You know as well as I do some of the people who come to the barn tonight desperately need to hear that story."

Harry looked across the table from Princess Sarah and thought, *Wow! How did you ever get so wise?* Then he blinked and opened his eyes to see the big, scaly muzzle of a wonderful lady dragon. He bent over and kissed her gently on her nose. "I love you," he said.

"Of course you do, silly boy. You're still under my spell," she laughed back.

He kissed her again and whispered, "Always."

***

Cars began to arrive early for the "fellowship," as Harry had started calling it for lack of a better name. Most of the people invited knew what a fellowship was since they were mostly churchgoers. While some churches weren't as prone to worship demonized dragons as others, they all knew what a fellowship was. They also knew that if they wanted a good seat, they had better get there early. Many came nearly an hour early, yet there were still folks trickling in fifteen minutes after the scheduled starting time. Lizzy, the preeminent organizer, was not surprised that the early-birds and the later-comers were true to their nature and had planned accordingly. She had considered having music and ice cream, but Harry and Sarah both vetoed the idea. Harry complained the event was a closure event, much like a memorial service, and that they shouldn't turn it into a circus. Besides, he argued, weren't they trying to keep this huge event a secret meeting? Lizzy assured her dad that Jamie, the mouth of Moab, had a unique ability to screen people and dissuade them from attending. Harry wasn't convinced but had faith in Barry.

Sarah suggested security guards, but when they tried to decide who to ask, they realized no one would want to do it for fear of missing out on the story. Everyone who had been involved in the incident wanted closure. Some had come from fresh graves where tears of grief conflicted with tears of anger, even over the same graves. There were a lot of *whys* and *hows* gathering, but not a single *what*, for everyone invited was an eyewitness.

Harry wondered if Jamie had cast some sort of cultic spell on the property, and even went so far as to ask her, in his armor, of course. Her response was, "Hell no! Barry'd whip my ass if I tried that." Harry's respect for Barry's absolute courage, in the face of a maelstrom of fury, skyrocketed, as did his confidence that the closure event would be protected and secret.

Finally, everyone who was anyone connected with the event that had troubled and almost destroyed their town was gathered.

The old man's natural shyness had caught up with him. Lizzy, on the other hand, was born to please a crowd and so, quite naturally, started the meeting.

"I am glad you have come. As we all know, we have endured a great deal in these last few weeks. There is nothing I can say to comfort the loss of so many. We were seduced, deceived, and many paid a terrible price for that deception. Now we are like a broken person who has had the bleeding of a terrible wound stopped. But the injury needs to be closed. Most of you know some of what happened. Many of you know much, but only two know it all. My father is one of those who know all of it, and Sarah is the second person. I need to caution you here not to be afraid. Sarah, the little six-year-old, the adopted daughter of Kenneth and Grace Linscomb, well, Sarah has changed a little..."

The old man snorted and started coughing at Lizzy's "little." Lizzy looked at him with her "Dad!" look that had been honed sharp enough to make a razor blush. And he quieted. Lizzy continued. "Sarah was and is the dragon that you saw attack the evil dragon. How she became that dragon is a mystery to all of us, especially her. The truth is, Sarah is stuck in that form and cannot change back. We did not want to startle you, so consider yourself warned. *Please* remember not all dragons are evil. Sarah is still one of us. I am going to have Sarah fly in slowly to give you a chance to see her gradually, and then she is going to land right here.

Please, please do not be frightened. Remember, she is the one who saved us all."

Lizzy looked around the crowd, watching their faces intently. There was a little unease, but no one screamed or tried to run away... at least not yet. "If you will look toward the west, you can see what appears to be a large bird. That is Sarah. She is flying in from about a mile out."

At Lizzy's *mile out* remark, a few people gasped. They realized how big she must be if she looked like a large bird at that distance. The crowd watched, hands shielding their eyes, some pointing, murmurs and gasps continuing, but no outcries, no screams. Finally, Sarah lit on the ground. There was an awkward moment of silence and then someone started to clap. Immediately others joined in. People began to shout and yell. One of Sarah's little girlfriends recognized her friend, and with the courage only a child could have, ran toward the great dragon.

"*Maggie!*" her frightened mother cried.

Sarah, seeing the child running toward her, bowed to the ground with her head and nose resting on the grass. She did not reach for the child but stayed extremely still and smiled, trying not to show her great teeth. Maggie's mother was a heartbeat behind her daughter and grabbed her right as the little girl slid to a dusty stop in front of the lady dragon. Sarah crinkled her nose as Maggie screeched to a halt and was caught up in her mother's arms.

"Mom! It's just Sarah," Maggie said gently to her frightened mother. "It's just Sarah."

Sarah couldn't help herself. A large tear welled up in her eye and slowly trickled down her scaled face. She didn't want her friends to fear her but knew some did. At least her friends' parents did. Maggie's mom had known Sarah since Grandma Grace had brought her home. Sarah and Maggie had grown up together, had sleepovers, and played slippy slide in her backyard. Maggie's mom had tucked Sarah into bed many times and read her and Maggie bedtime stories. So, when she heard Maggie's gentle rebuke and saw the tears in Sarah's eyes, she fell to her knees around the great muzzle of the weeping dragon and hugged her. "Oh, Sarah... oh, baby girl. I am so sorry I couldn't see. I really couldn't."

"It's okay, Mrs. Loup. It's okay," Sarah whispered as she nuzzled into the embrace of Maggie's mom.

A half a second later, a deluge of shouting little urchins swarmed over the newbie dragon. Before Sarah could move, three little boys were on her back and two little girls were working their way up her long tail. One adventuresome child had even gone so far as to try and push up Sarah's lip in order to see her great teeth.

"Easton! Stop that!" A loud *whack* of a human hand collided with a small human bottom.

"Youch!"

"Leave Sarah alone, Easton! I am so sorry, Sarah."

"It's okay, Miss Katie. He's just being a boy."

"Mom, Mom! When I grow up, will I be a dragon? Can I, please? Can I, Mom?" Easton squealed.

"I don't know. Probably not. You need to ask your dad."

Lizzy realized that introductions were over and more time with Sarah would only lead to more problems, so she yelled over the shouts and laughter of the children, "Okay, okay! Everybody have a seat or there will be *no ice cream* at the end of this meeting."

Hank looked at Sarah, who shrugged guiltily. Lizzy had slipped the ice cream past him. Too late now, and he wasn't happy about it. He mumbled something about the *dignity of the event* and then got quiet.

"My dad is going to speak now... Okay, Dad, it's all yours."

The old man storyteller rose slowly, more from shyness rather than stiffness. He walked to the middle of the barn and looked around the room. Children had climbed up into the loft. People sat on bales of hay. Lizzy had tried to provide everyone chairs, but more people came than expected. Hank gulped and began.

"I think most of you have figured out that I am not just an old man who has lived among you for a long time. I wasn't born here. I guess the best way to explain it is to tell you and hope you believe me… and you probably will now that I have undeniable evidence seated in front of you." He pointed to Sarah and laughed. The crowd politely laughed with him. He was addressing adults now and had changed his approach. It was clear he wasn't near as comfortable with it as he had been telling the children a story.

He continued, "I am the young man of the story. The events of the story I have been telling all summer at the library are true. I lived them. I know you probably have a lot of questions. I may be able to answer most of those if you allow me to finally finish the story I began."

He didn't wait for permission but simply began where he had left off. "I am going to continue to refer to myself as Harry and tell the rest of this story in the third person. Now, where was I… oh yes…

"Harry felt the cave floor give way. His screams were cut off as he plunged beneath ice-cold water. He sank quickly, feet first, facing upward, the weight of his armor pulling him down. Finally, his feet touched the bottom of the dark lake, and he pushed upward when suddenly, steaming water erupted in dragon flames a few feet above him, forcing him back down. The ice-cold water instantly grew hot. The closer to the surface he swam, the hotter the water became. It was now hot enough to scald. Harry heard the sword screaming in his head, *'Put the helmet on, Harry! Put it on now!'*

"Harry lifted the helmet onto his head. Even in the confusion of the moment, he had not let go of the helmet. His hand had tightened around it, frozen in a finger-breaking hold.

"He was surprised to feel the helmet strap on and extend a covering over his entire face. A blast of cool air filled the helmet, and he could breathe. The visor opened, and he could see. A light shone out a short distance from the visor, and the bottom of the dark lake lit in a dim blue cast. Harry looked up and could see the flames of the dragon burning on the lake surface."

"He's got a diving mask on, doesn't he? My mom got me one last year at Walmart, but my sister sat on it and broke it."

"Shussh!" an angry flock of irritated little magpies croaked. "Be quiet!"

"Would you like to see the helmet?" the old man asked, now that the story had been interrupted. "I'm wearing it now."

"Really!? No, you aren't."

"I can't see it. Why can't I see it?"

"Are you sure?"

"Yes, of course!" The old man smiled, his eyes twinkling.

"Show us!" the eager children clamored curiously, and a few adults joined in, too.

Speaker, if you would, please, the old man thought to his invisible assistant.

The children, and the adults, and even a cute dragon were all staring at the old man when a bright haze, like a thousand lightning bugs on a July night, swirled around his head for a few seconds, and then just as quickly disappeared. When the swirling lights died away, the old man's head was covered with a bronze helmet that resembled concentric circles of a honeycomb. The visor projected from his head like a beak, and where his eyes should have been, small polished mirrors sat.

"Can you see us?" the little freckle-faced boy asked as he gingerly reached his hand forward to touch the beak.

"As good as ever," the old man responded. After a few minutes of show-and-tell, everyone settled back down. Harry thought, *Okay, Speaker, if you would, please, make the helmet go away now.*

The old man's whole body began to glow, and the lightning bugs were back, swirling in a bright cloud that brought a shower of "Ohs" and "Ahs" and a few isolated claps. The lights then quietly disappeared and left the old man clothed in the armor, minus the helmet. *That is not what I meant, and you know it, Speaker.*

"Yeah, but Harry, it adds mysticism to the whole story if you tell it while you are dressed in your armor."

Harry looked over at Sarah, who had children seated on her back and between her outstretched claws. She smiled a subdued but extremely toothy dragon smile back at him. With the speaker's help, Harry heard Sarah think, *"Harry, if I have to sit here as a dragon coupe, full of little munchkins hanging on me, you can sit there in your armor and tell the story."*

Harry whispered to himself, "Okay, fine.

"All right, all right!" he raised his voice. "Do you remember before show-and-tell that Harry was at the bottom of the cave-lake looking up at the evil dragon's flames that had scorched the top of the lake? Harry could see the dragon, but the dragon could not see him through the cold waters. Then, Harry heard the speaker, *'Harry, pick up the rest of the armor that you dropped on the bottom, then walk along the bottom until you come to a tunnel.'*

"Harry followed the sword's instructions and walked at least a mile before he finally managed to climb out of the huge underground lake and away from the evil dragon.

Harry looked back across the lake and was startled to see the cavern-lake was lit like a landscape on a rainy, lightning-filled night. The great beast still spewed flames and dove into the water, splashing around trying to find him. Quietly, Harry continued to follow the speaker's instructions until he came to a narrow tunnel, small enough to keep the dragon out and Harry securely tucked in.

"Harry sat down on a conveniently placed stone and thought, *Now what? Do I even want to know?* He placed his head against the side of the tunnel, exhausted, and closed his eyes. Soon, he felt the now familiar movement of his spirit down the dark corridors of the cave, racing toward the princess. As he approached her, he felt the need to move cautiously. He slowed down, stopping right before the entrance to the large fire-lit cavern that held her. For a few minutes he watched her, not knowing what to say. Finally, she turned toward him and spoke.

"'I sense you there, Harry. You can come out. The dragon is not here.'

"Harry slowly walked out of the tunnel and into the light. The princess looked at him. Her face was contorted, and scaly bitterness smoldered in her eyes. When she saw his face, her own feelings slipped behind a shielded wall, and she stepped back, staring at him. Her face again reflected her feelings, only this time, she was afraid of him. Her mouth opened slightly, as if to speak, but nothing came out.

"Harry stepped closer to her, alarmed. 'Are you all right, Sarah? What's wrong?'

"The princess looked at him, puzzled. 'Are you Harry? The brave boy who I've been talking to?'

"'Yes, of course I'm Harry,' he answered, a little taken aback. 'Who else would I be?'

"She continued to stare at him, her eyes squinting skeptically. Finally, she said, 'You have changed. You look older, much older. You seem larger, stronger, even taller. What happened to you?'

"Harry paused, thinking how to reply. The speaker whispered, *'Be very careful, Harry, because you are not the only one changing, and you don't know how far gone she is.'*

"Harry answered the speaker, *I am not good at lying.*

"The sword responded, *'Then tell her the truth. Just omit the part about the King and the hall.'*

"'I found some very special armor, Princess. It... it seems to be magical... you can't even see it, but it protects me, even now, even here.'

"She drew close to him and looked up at him. Her eyes were wild, tired, and confused. He stared back, locking eyes with her. Then he started to feel sleepy, then dizzy. He shook his head trying to throw off the heaviness. He felt like he did the time he snuck into his father's beer keg and gulped down several mouthfuls of the dark, foul-smelling brew. Later, Harry threw up and wouldn't touch the stuff for years afterward," the old man added for his audience's sake.

Several of the mothers seated and standing around the barn gave the old man a quick nod of approval or a deliberate, unabashed smile of thanks. Sarah even attempted a slight smile, but it slid away into old sadness as her memories continued to grieve her.

"Harry felt drugged and drained. Had he not been accompanied by the speaker and protected by the armor, even in the spiritual dream state, the dragon would have captured him, but he was protected. A bolt of light shot through his mind. He heard the speaker shout, and his armor began to glow. The last thing he heard, as his mind flew back down the tunnel, was the princess's infuriated shrieks, crying, 'No! Noooooo!'

"Harry woke with a start. He was still in the small tunnel of the dark cave, still covered in the ancient armor, with a powerful sword giving off a dim blue light from its sheath at his side. His breath was heavy, his heart hammered away in his chest, and his cheeks were covered in hot tears."

At this point the old man stopped his storytelling. The room was very quiet. Even the older children in the hayloft, who had scampered about throughout the story, had been caught in its spell and now slumped under the same weight of Sarah's betrayal. No one dared to look at the dragon in the room. They were afraid to. They knew the story had to have had a good outcome, or none of them would have been in that barn listening to the old man. Every eye in the room was riveted on the old man. His eyes were fixed on the lady dragon, whose eyes were locked on his. What the people watching couldn't hear was the conversation between the two, aided by the sword.

"I don't have to go on with this. It's old news, ancient history."

"Yes, you do, my love... we talked about this before you ever began. You know that. I didn't expect it to hurt this much, but I should have..."

"Now that you do, I can quit. I do not have to finish it. I don't have to expose you."

"And what about the people in this old barn who have walked that same path? Who know how it feels to betray an innocent soul? What about them? For the moment, they have been able to push those feelings aside, but we both know their guilt will not stay silent for long. It will raise its pointing finger, and if it does not find absolution, it will cause annihilation. Maybe slow self-destruction, but death, no matter what you call it. Yes, this story must be told, and you, Harry, are the only one who can tell it."

The old man stood up and the children who had gathered around his feet moved back. Some slipped back into their seats with their parents. He looked around the room, making eye contact with every soul there. Some looked back, others couldn't and bowed their heads. He knew what Sarah said was true. The people in this room needed hope. Some still wore the slitted eyes of the Reverend Laden Long. He knew he was the only one who could see them, but in that room, in that moment, no veils, no masks hid the mark of the beast they had worshipped. Harry also knew that as they pulled back from that evil, the mark would fade and their features return to true human. Many of these people had gathered not even knowing why they came. They were curious, yes, but they were also looking for something else. Release, absolution, restoration. They probably didn't phrase it that way, but they were looking all the same.

Harry stepped forward, no longer just telling a children's story. He began to speak, "I really don't know how to tell this next part. It was a very... difficult experience. But before I do, I want you to know that the dragon you see in this old barn is not the same person that..." He groped for the words.

Sarah gave it to him in her thoughts, *"Betrayed is the word you're looking for, Harry."*

"...who betrayed me in that dark place. I hate to recall that time because, even though it was one of the most miserable and painful experiences of my life, it is over, and the woman, the dragon-lady that sits here with us now, is the love of my life. I have been separated from her for a lifetime, chained by a death curse from the dark dragon you saw perish, thanks to the amazing bravery and self-sacrifice of your fire marshal, Kenneth Linscomb. He was also Sarah's grandfather," he said, pointing to Sarah dragon. "Kenneth gave his life for hers. Someone once told me the value of something is determined by what one is willing to pay for it. Kenneth and his wife, Grace, thought Sarah was priceless because they laid down their lives for her.

"That doesn't mean that what she did in another time, more than a thousand years ago, doesn't have consequences. It does, and Sarah would be the first one to admit that. But I will be the first to say that her actions have been wiped clean. They were absolved in fire and blood and ruin. I didn't understand how such stains could be wiped clean. I was raised to believe that evil people, or even people who did evil things, even though they might not be completely evil, could not change. I was also raised to believe that if you did something wrong, you are the one who had to pay for it and make it right. Then I realized some things could not be made right. They were too big for the person to lift the weight of their ruin, by themselves. The law of physics tells us this is true. It says that for every action there is an equal and opposite reaction, and that truth condemned me. It also condemned Sarah. I was too weak to remove the stain and the memories of that incident, and she was too weak to forgive herself and believe she could change. Then we met someone bigger than we were, larger than any stain any willful act of betrayal could leave. We met…"

"Harry, get down!" the speaker sword screamed. Harry immediately fell to the ground as a huge inferno of burning hay and pieces of barn wood ripped through the air.

Chapter Twenty-Three

Harry's armor reacted instantly, sensing the change in heat and pressure. The blast picked him up and threw him across the room. Others were not so protected. Children and their parents, engulfed in flames, screamed in helpless fear and pain.

The friendly hay in the loft, which had comforted and given the children a luxuriant playground, now reached for them with scorching tendrils and poisonous fumes. Coughing, screaming, moans, and the very present smell of blood, now starting to bubble in the pools forming from those killed in the initial explosion, created a gory background for those trying to drag people away or crawl away themselves.

People who had been in the back of the barn raced toward the huge doors only to find they had been bolted and chained shut from the outside. Sarah rose, impervious to the flames but not the flying pieces of wood, several of which had pierced her and stuck out like porcupine spines. She pushed through the debris and burning corpses to the entrance. As she got closer, her claws came out and she hammered the old wooden doors. They broke off their ancient hinges, and people raced out, some falling and others, in their panic, stumbling over or stepping on them. Over a hundred people had gathered in that barn, and they were all converging on the only exit to escape the flames.

Harry ran the other way. He saw people lying on the floor, wounded with pieces of debris sticking out of them.

Some were obviously beyond help, others were moving and crawling toward the exit, while the smoke from the explosion and the hungry flames raced toward them.

Harry picked up the bloody frame of one of his library children and grabbed the hands of a woman whose face was littered with splinters and blinded with blood. The exit had cleared, and some people were helping those who had been trampled get out. The barn had now become a smoke-filled pyre, and people were collapsing from the fumes, poisoned, with only seconds to get to the open air. The flames crackled as the wind, gusting, seemed to be drawn to it.

The screams of the wounded and the foul smell of the dead being devoured by the consuming blaze flooded Harry's senses. He wanted to run to safety, but his heart would not let him leave any who could be saved behind. He pulled several children and their parents out, his armor protecting him from the heat. Minutes passed, and the fire trucks came screaming into the place. Harry was about to move back from the crumbling old building when he heard a cry.

The beams of the old barn were charred and weakening, but when he turned to look through his armored visor, he saw a small boy moving, hidden under one of the hay bales. He had somehow survived, insulated by several feet of grass, but he couldn't hide any longer. Forced by the heat and fumes, he cried and tried to push free. When Harry saw him, he raced back into the flames. Sarah, who had been lying on her side, panting for breath while Jamie tried to staunch the streams of blood from a score of wounds, saw Harry run into the crumbling building and rushed after him.

Harry found the child and was futilely attempting to shield him from the flames. He looked up to see the barn ceiling start to give way. He hunched over the child to protect him with his body when a giant dragon wing spread, umbrella-like, over him. Then claws grasped him, tucking him and the boy to the great dragon body that now shielded them.

The ceiling collapsed, flames encircling them, and then the water came. Torrents of water splashed down on them through the gap in the burning roof. Harry had no time to be grateful. As the flames and water mixed into a hissing steam and the smoke curled around them, he felt his body start to tingle.

Then light covered him, and he realized he was underwater, surrounded by cool, soothing water. He looked up toward the light shining down through the surface and pushed up, swimming toward the top. His head broke through. He blinked and took a deep breath of cold air. Then he saw the shore within a few yards and swam toward it. As he did, he immediately noticed dragon Sarah was also pulling herself out of the water onto the beach.

Harry looked around for the child he had tried to save but couldn't find him. He was about to dive back into the stream when he heard the speaker. *"He is gone, Harry. You did your best, but you couldn't save him. He is safe though, and nothing will ever hurt him again."*

Harry, breathing heavily, collapsed on the beach. He heard the movement of a very large creature he knew was Sarah draw close to him. If he could have moved, he would have, but instead he simply lay on the bank of the stream, panting, trying to get his breath back.

"Are you okay, Harry?" he heard the soft, rasping voice of his favorite dragon whisper.

"You came after me."

"Of course I did, and do not start fussing at me. You would have done the same for me. You were doing the same for that child."

"It was the freckle-faced boy, the little rebel," Harry said, and then he began to weep. Heartbreak streamed out of him, scorching him with every tear. Finally, he stopped, not because he was finished grieving, but because he was asleep.

***

Harry awoke to the morning earthquake that had become lovingly familiar. Sarah was shaking him trying to get him to wake up. His eyes opened to tree branches shielding a morning sun and a gentle breeze skipping across his face. He yawned and sat up, stretching. He stood and realized he was filthy. He was covered in dried soot and ash, and with one look at the cool stream just a few feet away, he started stripping off his clothes. A giggle stopped him.

"Sarah?" He plopped down on the grass near the stream with one boot on, one off and his top armor sitting in the grass. Then he looked over his shoulder at the giant dragon that lay curled like a great wolf, her tail almost touching her face.

"Yeah…?" the smile slipping into her voice. "I thought I might ought to warn you before you plucked off all your feathers and trotted around naked."

Harry's face colored. "I appreciate that. Now, if you would just close your eyes, I am going to bathe in this delightful water."

"If I were you, I would wait a moment before I dove right in."

Harry and Sarah spoke together, "Why is that, Speaker?"

"Well, for one thing, you aren't healed up completely from that explosion in the barn, and for another, that is a time stream. It is good to drink from, but you need to be careful to only swim in the pools along the banks. Don't swim in the middle of it, or you might find yourself some time else. A few bends down, there are some heated pools, just so you know."

"A time stream?" Harry said out loud. "You mean *the* time stream, don't you? The same time stream Sarah drug me into on the night I rode the dark dragon? I thought this place looked familiar, but I couldn't place it because the last time I was here, I was burned and dying. I had just ridden a dragon into the ground and was broken, in both body and mind."

"Yep, that one, Harry, the very same."

"I wondered if that was where we had returned," Sarah said, "but I also thought we had died, and this was the gate to eternity."

"You're partially right, Sarah. You did not die, but this is a gate, just not to the afterlife. It is a gate to what was before, and even to what might be. I think one of your great seers, who nobody recognized as such, called it the woods-between-the-worlds. It is a portal to many places and times. It is the first place and the last place. You can stay here for a little while as the waters, and the leaves, and the fruit of the trees are good for healing, but then you will have to make a decision. But not now. Now you should bathe, and heal, and talk, and pray. Collect your memories and your questions and be ready."

Sarah interrupted, "Do I have to stay a dragon? Can you heal me from that now?"

"Oh, Sarah, no, you will not always be a dragon, but it is not something to heal from. It is part of your healing. For now, be content. You have a lot to learn and experience. I will return soon. Rest now."

The days flew by quickly. They slept a lot, and laughed a lot, and were careful to stay out of the middle of the river but drank deeply from the streams that flowed from it.

One day, after a short time in the woods-between-the-worlds, Sarah asked, "Harry, are you aware that you look younger? I mean *really* younger! It's like the years are shedding away. You could pass for thirty, easily."

"I wasn't sure, Sarah, but I had noticed my skin blotches clearing up, and that I felt wonderful and strong."

"Well, I couldn't help but notice, and well, you are a very handsome man."

"Thank you, my dear. Do you realize this is the longest time we have ever spent together when we *knew* who we were and while there was no threat of death hanging over us?"

"For a while anyway," the sword interrupted. *"Now I need to answer your questions. One of the first being, what happened in the barn? The second being, where do you go from here? Well, that kind of depends on what you think about the first answer. And the third and fourth intertwining questions are, will Sarah remain a dragon and can you two ever be together in a normal relationship?*

"First, who blew up the barn… the short answer is… well, you probably don't want to hear the short answer without first a little explanation… so here is the explanation: A witch did it. She is not happy with what you did to the Reverend Laden Long.

"Witches are also powerful manipulators. They can control the innocent minds of people, especially people of their own blood, like their children, specifically," the speaker's thoughts became slower and more deliberate, *"her daughter. Especially if that daughter also shared a bloodline with the witch's former lover. They don't call them black widows for nothing, Harry."*

Harry was clueless, and answered accordingly, "So, who was the bomber? The witch's daughter? Was she someone we knew?"

"Yes, she was someone you knew, Harry."

Sarah, who had the natural discernment and wisdom of both her sex and her species, gasped.

The speaker responded even quieter to their hearts, *"I'm sorry, Sarah."*

Harry was still slow. "Why? Who is it?"

Sarah, who had been hovering close to Harry, pulled back and stiffened.

"Sarah?" Harry asked, surprised at her reaction. "Sarah, what's wrong? Do you know who he is talking about?"

"Yes, I do," she said in a cold, stern voice. "And so do you."

"Who? For heaven's sake!"

The speaker answered solemnly, *"Lizzy, your daughter by the witch, Harry."*

Coming soon...

Dances with My Dragon

Chapter One

Belle knew a hundred ways to kill a man. That did not make her task easier. Neither did the rumor she had heard from one of her more intelligent pets stating Ernst Rohm had hired the kind of protection that could give witches trouble. Whether or not the report was true, it didn't hurt to be wary, to be crafty. She didn't take long to ponder it. She had already been planning for weeks. She walked over to her kitchen sink, carefully took out a cheese slicer, and cut her palm. She cried out as the blade quickly cut her flesh. Scars riddled her hands and legs, providing proof she had a lot of practice. The wounds healed quickly but the cuts burned and were sore for days afterwards. Clenching her fist, she held her hand over a silver chalice and watched as the blood dripped into the cup. It did not have to be full. Just a swallow or two was all that was necessary. Once the mark was reached, she covered her hand with a clean towel, then washed and bandaged it. Her pets would drink her offering and then be bound to her for whatever task she assigned them. Now to call them, feed them, and target them.

Not everybody prayed to the Most High God. Belle Rodum prayed to the cast-out angels who lied, declaring they were gods to foolish men. The old demons typically got away with it, till men caught on and bowed before the real one. Until then, however, Belle's prayers and conjuring paid for by her victim's blood got her what she wanted. With blood dripping from her bandage, Belle raised her hands above her head and chanted. Low murmurings in a tongue she'd never learned flowed from her. Hypnotic and rhythmic, she gradually increased in volume. A single word spoken over and over, then another added and another till finally a sentence formed repeated a hundred times, "*Čia kačiukas, čia kačiukas aš gydau*," louder and louder, till with a clap of her wounded hands she screamed. Then silence. A thick, wicked snowfall silence fell like a dark blanket covering and insulating. It was first warm then hotter and hotter, until a salty rain-like perspiration poured from every pore in her body, drenching her. She tore off her clothes, screaming as the rough cloth touched and blistered her skin. Then it stopped. Suddenly, the heat was gone. A light breeze blew across her burning skin in tingling caresses, making the hair on her neck stand in shivering salute.

The creature, a Jörmungandr, a demon from Norse legend, slowly flickered in front of Belle, fading in and out of view as though partly there and partly not. It was the descendent of a beast once labeled more crafty than all the beasts of the field. It was shrewd, beautiful. Its head was crowned like a cobra with a ribbed fan that sat behind its skull like an Indian headdress. When it spoke, cream-colored jaws and sparkling bright fangs glinted. Its forked tongue flitted through the air, sampling Belle's aroma like a lover does a bouquet. Its neck, bent just beneath the ceiling, towered over the small-framed witch. Unlike its earthly cousins, this serpent had hands, long, thin, and clawed with opposing thumbs so it could easily grasp and strangle its prey. As it stood before the witch, it moved back and forth swaying to the motion of an ancient song.

Finally, the Jörmungandr spoke in a chilling whisper, rasping broken words forged in sin's dark crevices. Piercing the silence like a heroin addict's needle breaks the flesh.

"You called, and I have come. What do you want from me?"

"Where is your brother? I called for both of you."

"You are not the only conjurer busy tonight, Belle Rodum. My brother is engaged elsewhere. Many are feasting. Tonight, much blood is crying out."

Belle nodded and realized that must surely be the case. Hitler had ordered the assassination of many, and given Himmler's involvement with witchcraft—he was the son of a witch after all—pets and familiars would be occupied.

"I repeat, time is short. What do you want?"

"You and I have a short journey; then you kill and feed. Simple as that."

The beast slowly nodded and replied, "Get on my back and show me the way."

Belle had ridden the Jörmungandr before. It was an adrenalin junkie's dream. Like the crocodile and the scorpion, the ride could end in both of their destructions. Other than that, so long as they both behaved themselves, it was an exhilarating ride for the witch. Moving with purpose, she quickly climbed on the back of the demon. Noticing the silky skin and knobby scales, she grabbed the harness and squeezed tight with her knees. The beast seemed to jump through the roof because of its ability to pass through material objects. As they burst into the night air, Belle Rodum gasped. The wind blew through her hair, and she pressed in close to the beast's neck. She whispered directions, and within a few minutes they reached their destination.

Ernst Rohm was a socialist who believed in the distribution of everyone's wealth but his own. As a good friend and the right hand of Hitler's paramilitary group, he had access to money and used it. The Jörmungandr settled easily into the huge backyard of the grand old house that had once belonged to a Jewish banker and now was occupied by Rohm. Immediately Belle Rodum sensed the guardians she had been told might protect Ernst Rohm. It was easy to spot them. They were wolf-like Shucks, fierce black dogs, twice the size of a normal animal, with glowing red eyes.

The three Shucks caught the scent of the Jörmungandr as soon as it settled on the ground. Their job was to alert the house when an uninvited guest arrived. The baying and growls drove all pretense of surprise away. Within seconds, they bit and struck at the Jörmungandr's feet and belly. As fast as the Shucks were, the Jörmungandr was faster. With a quick backhand, it broke the back of one of the huge beasts. The animal hit the ground with a yelp, then nothing. With its giant mouth, the Jörmungandr clamped down on the head of another of the wolf-like creatures. The Jörmungandr shook viciously, popping the big dog's head off its shoulders in a cloud of spurting blood and gore. The third Shuck, seeing what had happened to its companions, turned and ran but only managed a few feet before Belle Rodum's lance pierced its black pelt. Its cry wrecked the night and then everything grew quiet.

Well, the witch thought, *that didn't go as planned, but we are here, and there is work to do.*

The Jörmungandr climbed over the fresh corpses of the animals it had killed and slithered up to the back door of the house. It bent its head against the doorframe and pushed. The door groaned, and the brick-framed anchors broke. The demon crashed through the ruined doorframe and sniffed the house, flicking its tongue in every direction searching for Rohm. Its head swayed back and forth; then it caught the scent of the one it had come for. Belle Rodum watched the dark serpent hunt, her eyes wide, her face lit like a child's on Christmas morning. She turned to face the direction the Jörmungandr had gone and saw a stairway. She placed her foot on the first step and was thrown backward by the rapid fire of a Thompson submachine gun. She felt the bullets pierce her flesh, tearing through her. Blood spurted from her arterial wounds like water from a hydrant.

At the top of the stairs stood her prey, his famously scarred face obvious, leaving no doubt to his identity. Belle Rodum stood there. Rohm watched, fascinated, waiting for pain to mark her, her eyes to roll back, and her body to fall. None of that happened. She took a deep breath and sighed. Looking up the stairway toward Rohm, she laughed.

Under protective spells Belle Rodum's wounds closed and regenerated. Rohm's face paled as he raised his gun to fire again, but the Jörmungandr's lightning assault struck him square in the chest. Bones cracked, his lungs collapsed, and his eyes widened. The beast was about to press his mouth over the fallen man when the witch shouted, "No! The Führer wants proof, and if you eat him, somebody will have to sort through your droppings, and it won't be me!"

The Jörmungandr smirked and withdrew from the stairway, turning to look back at the witch. "My task is over. You are on your own. Good evening." With that, it stiffened like an antique photograph staring at her, growing fainter and fainter until, like smoke on a windy day, it was gone.

Belle Rodum slowly walked up the stairs and stared down on the broken body of Ernst Rohm. The dying man sensed someone was hovering over him. He opened his eyes and strained to focus. Disappointment crossed his face. Slowly he gasped out, "Why?"

She answered honestly, "Hitler's orders."

Rohm coughed, then laughed, "I knew it was coming… He will destroy you too…"

Belle Rodum leaned over the man and whispered, "The kisses of an enemy are deceitful."

Author Notes

Thank you for reading *The Princess Who Forgot She Was Beautiful*. If you liked it, please consider leaving me a **five-star review!**

Princess is the first book in a series of five. I hope you like twists and cliffhangers. But—spoiler alert—the heroes and heroines get together... well, sort of... well, maybe not... kinda...? Depends, actually. But the North Star doesn't lie.

Anyway, things you might like to know: I live in the little community where the adventures are set. There is a café where my characters eat breakfast and wait on patrons. People where I live actually talk like East Texans.

Other Books by William David Ellis

Dragons and Romans for sale at Amazon.

A Roman legion squares off against a dragon conjured by a demonized high priest of child-sacrificing Carthage. And that's what history actually records. What happens next is the action-packed tale.

If you like the supernatural, action, dragons, and alternate-history fantasy with a little cussing, and a little kissing, and some horror and gut-busting tension thrown in, you will love *Dragons and Romans,* winner of the BRAG Medallion.

Free!

Read my short stories at my website:
williamdavidellisauthor.wordpress.com

Books to Come

The Princess Who Forgot She Was Beautiful is the first in a series of five books. The next book, *Dances with My Dragon*, will be out as soon as my fingers quit tingling from typing, and I can get my editors to quit polishing and fixing, which means by mid-summer.

Next, *Kisses of My Enemy* will launch, hopefully, by Christmas 2019.

Then book number 4, currently entitled #4, and finally, the series will conclude with #5 soon after. Spoiler alert— the North Star didn't lie.

I would love to hear from you.

williamdavidellis@yahoo.com

ABOUT THE AUTHOR

William David Ellis is a storyteller. Whether it's weaving an old narrative into an entertaining and illuminating yarn or fashioning something brand new from wisps of legend, he can tell a story. Both oral communication and the written page bend to the will of this wordsmith. Other than that, he is the son of an English teacher, the husband of an English teacher, and the father of an English teacher. In spite of them, he occasionally punctuates and is prone to a lapse of consciousness where the Muse of inspiration grants him the heart of a skillful writer. His contributions to publication include columns in small and large newspapers across Texas, short stories, and novels, one which has been exhibited here, and the rest which are either shipwrecked on the shores of imagination or being gestated as we speak.

For more on William David Ellis, go to his website: https://williamdavidellisauthor.com/

Made in the USA
Middletown, DE
03 September 2024